HARD JOY

Susan Varga

Susan Varga was born in Hungary and came to Australia when she was five.

She has a MA in English Literature and a Bachelor of Laws. She worked in film, video and radio, and, briefly, as a lawyer, before becoming a writer.

Her first book, *Heddy and Me*, won the Christina Stead Award for non-fiction, and was followed by the award-winning novel, *Happy Families*. Then she published *Broometime*, co-authored with her partner Anne Coombs. Her most recent novel, *Headlong*, was short-listed for the Barbara Jefferies Award. Rupture, her first book of poetry, was published in 2016 and commended in the Ann Elder Award. It was nominated as one of ABR's Best Books of the Year. She has written many essays and reviews, mostly for Griffith Review and ABR.

Susan has been a periodic activist; with the women's refuge movement, around the Mabo decision, and was co-founder of Rural Australians for Refugees.

Susan Varga

HARD JOY

Life and writing

UPSWELL

First published in Australia in 2022
by Upswell Publishing
Perth, Western Australia
upswellpublishing.com

ISBN: 978-0-6452479-1-6

A catalogue record for this
book is available from the
National Library of Australia

Cover artwork: 'Portrait of the Artist's Wife' by Roland Wakelin.
   Oil on board. 1932.
Cover design by Chil3, Fremantle
Typeset in Foundry Origin by Lasertype

To my beloved,
to whom everything is owed.

Contents

Had I been blessed with an even limited access to my own mind there would be no reason to write.

Joan Didion

Prologue

Hungary has always exercised my imagination; a place of fear, shadows, danger. The place my family had to flee. I think all my deepest convictions, obsessions, the colour of my world, come from the first five years I spent there.

I wonder whether the moral and ethical life begins earlier than most people think. Mine is rooted in the highly wrought dilemmas of wartime and postwar life. At the time I was born my parents saw their life of middle-class solidity crumble before their eyes. From one day to the next my father ceased to be a prosperous citizen and became a prisoner in a labour camp. My mother, Heddy, was twenty-seven, left alone with my three-year-old sister and me, a newborn baby. The round-up of Jews in Budapest was beginning.

The bombing of Budapest began in April, when I was six months old. Our flat was expropriated and the feather business, too. Jewish houses were being set up all over the city – the first point of concentration. Heddy decided not to wait passively for her fate. She deployed her half-brothers, both still safe, protected by their Christian father, to find and buy illegal papers for her. She made a frantic decision to leave my sister Jutka with her brother and his Christian wife, believing her firstborn would be safer if passed off as Aryan. I was still on the breast and too small to be separated from her.

From then on, Heddy and I were on the run. First, to a hotel outside Budapest, where she holed up in a room with me. I developed an awful rash and shrieked and cried day and night. She tore up nappies and sewed them together again just to occupy herself, in order not to attack me in her frustration and fear.

When the hotel proved more dangerous than she thought, we fled again. Going through a checkpoint, Heddy hid her hands, rigid with fear, beneath my bundled form. I notice that I played a useful role, if passive, more than once.

She went to my father's village, where he had grown up. I drank my mother's milk in anxiety and fear. One day soon after, Heddy watched in terror as a seemingly endless parade of German soldiers marched through the village. That night her milk dried up.

As the Germans advanced she had to flee again and found a room to rent in a more remote village. No running water or bathroom, an outhouse at the back. A muddy track for a road. My grandmother, her daughter in law and her little son, three-year-old Robi, were holed up at the other end of the village, but it was too dangerous to make contact. Their differently forged passports would give them all away.

I became ill with dysentery and emitted a thin black fluid constantly for months. I barely clung to life. There was no doctor in the village and Heddy was afraid to travel on her false papers. I lost so much weight that I developed the signs of malnutrition – a wasting body and a big head. The months passed slowly and I continued to deteriorate. Of course I had no idea what was happening, yet my emotional world was already forming. I became apathetic, unnaturally quiet.

Then on 23 September 1944, the conquering Russians entered Hungary. Heddy decided to end her isolation and decamp to the other side of the long and straggling village, twenty minutes muddy walk away, to join her mother and the others, all in one room. It was there that a traumatised Jutka was returned to us – my mother could not bear the separation any longer. By then no-one could measure where was safe anymore.

A Hungarian army doctor was passing through Kisláng in retreat from the Russians. Mother appealed to him for help to get a message through to Budapest to procure some medicine for me. It only helped a little. She decided, despite the deep winter and the front zig-zagging between the Germans and the Russians, to leave the village and travel back across the country to liberated Hódmezővásárhely, my father's village, where there would be a decent water supply and medical help. There followed the nightmare crossing of the river at night in an overcrowded pontoon crammed with refugees and soldiers, aircraft strafing and bombing overhead. I cried weakly; Jutka cried in terror.

By the time she got to my father's hometown, Heddy's friends did not recognise her. I was very close to death. The doctor gave me vitamins and a special diet, saying I had only days left to live. In January 1945 I started to put on weight. In February I sat up for the first time. I was sixteen months old. I wonder now if the long illness was my unconscious way of keeping quiet, removing myself as much as possible from what was happening around me and to me.

Back in Budapest, Heddy learnt of my father's death in the Fertőrákos labour camp. There was not much time for grief. She resurrected the remains of his business and fought to get her home back. The flat had been taken over by Christians in the hope the Jewish owners had died.

She wanted to re-establish the old life as quickly as possible. By the time I turned three, we were, on the surface, ordinary middle-class kids. But, in fact, everything had changed irrevocably. I already knew that the ground could shift from moment to moment. I knew that other forces outside the tight circle of family protection could break in – evil, inexplicable forces.

Two dim memories come back, both postwar. In the clearest one, I might be three. We are restored to the bourgeois comforts. I am safe, clean, nourished. I stand on the balcony of our spacious fifth-floor flat. I see a slouching man with an empty bag. He is coming down the long street to get me. He is coming to take me away in the bag. I have done something wrong – I am not sure what but he is coming for me, even here. I am helpless against him.

The other memory is from 1948. Mother has put my sister and me into a kind of summer camp to get us out of the way as she makes the preparations to leave Hungary forever. The summer camp is actually a grim building, with a long driveway ending in big iron gates.

Mother and our stepfather come to visit us. After they leave, my older sister is panicked and scared. She is being left again, just as she was left in the war. I tell her that we can do nothing but wait. Surely they will come back.

These feelings of helplessness and bleakness would haunt me for the rest of my life, although it would take me a long time to realise their source. I was learning, in these glimpses, about the limits of personal control and the role of blind fate. And I was starting to realise that my own sense of justice and right was not universally shared. If you were on the wrong side of history and power, you could lose all your rights, and even your life.

From then on, I have always been on the side of the underdog. Or, to put it another way, my sense of social justice was being formed early.

I have no other conscious memories of the first five years. Mother used to say, 'Oh you were only a baby in the war. I saved your life and you began to thrive again.'

I bought that simple scenario for years and the guilt that went with it. Only Mother suffered during the Holocaust; I got off scot-free, a barely conscious child saved by a heroic mother.

It was only when I was writing my first book that I started to question this too cheery version. Towards the end of writing *Heddy and Me*, I was invited to a conference of child survivors of the Holocaust in Canada. At the time it was fairly new to acknowledge that children born in the war had been affected as much as the adults. I realised then that those first three years had been the most formative of my life.

* * *

In September 1946 Heddy meets a man called Gyula (or Gyuszi) Weiss. He has come back from Mauthausen concentration camp to learn that his sons, aged five and three, and his wife, not yet thirty, and most of his family have perished in Auschwitz.

He sits in a room in Pest alone for six months, in a torpor of grief. The only person he sees is his one surviving brother.

When he decides to live again, he is looking for someone to marry. Maybe someone widowed, like himself – maybe with children. A year later he sees Heddy, my sister and me at his friend's wedding and is impressed.

Mother decides she likes him. He has little money now but he will be a good provider and a good substitute father. There is little talk of love. Almost no-one marries for love in postwar Budapest. Love is not appropriate for survivors of the carnage.

Her mother thinks Heddy is marrying down, to a small-town Jew with not much education. She should wait and do better.

I sit on his knee the first time we meet.

'How old are you?'

'Thwee and a quarter,' I lisp.

My grandmother, Kato, soon changes her mind; this Gyuszi has charmed her despite his ordinary origins. Heddy marries him in the Dohány Street synagogue six months after they meet. No guests.

So one postwar family is re-formed.

In 1948 the Communists take over the country. Heddy is determined to leave. Gyuszi is more reluctant. 'I can work with the Communists somehow, and there will always be parcels from the West,' he says.

Heddy is adamant. 'I don't want to live in a country that tried to kill us. And I don't want to live the rest of my life relying on parcels.'

She wins. In December 1948, just weeks before the Iron Curtain comes down, we leave Budapest in secrecy. Even my beloved grandmother Kato is not allowed to come to the station to see us off. Our passports are stamped 'never to return'.

There are seven of us leaving: Gyuszi's brother, with his new wife and baby daughter, called Suzi, make up the contingent. Everyone is tense,

Heddy especially. We children are travelling under our stepfather's name. Will we remember our new names? Nothing is safe until we cross the border into Austria.

Near the border the guard, a tall heavy man with an important moustache, flips through our documents. I think I remember him – but is it Heddy's retelling, my imagination or my own storytelling in *Heddy and Me*? In any or all ways, he is real to me.

He looks at me severely. 'What is your name, Miss?'

I punch my fist and say, 'I know. I know it, I know! But I've forgotten.'

A heavy silence. The guard puffs up his cheeks and looks down his nose. Then he closes the carriage door, walks down the corridor and out of the train.

Silence in our compartment. A few miles further into Austria, we draw breath and dare to celebrate.

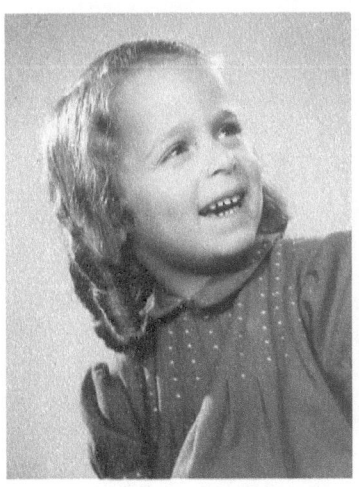

Part 1
BEARINGS

Our memory has a much stronger relationship to place than it does with the chronology of the clock. It is why we are often unsure about how long ago something happened but invariably know where it has happened.

Sue Stuart-Smith, *The Well Gardened Mind*

Seven arrive in Sydney

How to pin the myriad pieces of a life together in one's clumsy writing net? In the space of a book one has to make many choices, some conscious, some unconscious. In youth – let's say from birth till thirty – the influence of place is key in forming a personality. The houses, streets, suburbs of all the places you lived when young are what give you a sense of the world around you – how you start to make comparisons, see contrasts and ponder nuances.

In each new place I shed a skin and form a new one. Arriving in Sydney, a small Hungarian girl, *Suzsi*, has to turn into Susan, or Sue, and start to acquire a new language and a new culture. I become absorbed in my new country. Any memories of Budapest are forgotten or suppressed.

On the way to Sydney we stop in London to stay with a member of our complicated diaspora, Heddy's favourite cousin, who is married to an English Jew. The rest of her family ended up in Brazil.

From London we embark on a voyage to America on the *Queen Mary*. I have only one memory of the journey: a big rolling motion of the ship and I am in freefall from the top bunk. Oddly, no memory of fear, just the parabolic flying feeling.

In America we visit my father's surviving brother, who prudently fled Hungary in 1939 when the war began. Heddy picks up money she sent out to him for safekeeping as the noose tightened around Hungary's Jews. It will pay for a house in Australia.

When we arrive in Sydney the baby, Little Suzi, is one year old. I have turned five and my sister is approaching eight. The four adults range in age from thirty to forty-five.

Our only contact, a man Dad met on a Budapest street, has arranged our visas and booked us into a run-down George Street hotel. It has long dark corridors and stained carpets smelling of food, stale cigarette smoke and disappointed lives.

Sydney has no points of reference: the clothes are different, the smells different; faces closed, gestures minimal; even tea, served in bleak cafés, is coloured with milk! No lemon.

Heddy had been the main proponent of this move to this far continent. She fears an awful mistake, that the others will turn on her and say, 'What the hell have you got us into?'

After two weeks we move from the city to more genteel quarters in Elizabeth Bay, the first of many moves.

Elizabeth Bay
A fading boarding house. Two crammed rooms.
A sliver of sea. We heat the baby's milk
on a gas ring. Are asked, politely,
to leave.

Manly 1949
Tall sombre pines. An impossibly long
curve of beach. The unnerving, never-ending
sound of surf, the boom and rush of waves!

A line of liver-brick flats frown
down at the beach. We kids sleep
on a sagging sofa, Hungary
still in our dreams.

On a bench facing the ocean
mother writes to her mother;
'I don't think about now

but of the bright future ahead ...
Write down your recipes for me.'

Manly Infant School
First day of school
I walk into the boys' toilet.

Boys jeer yell point.
I have no language.

I run away.
Won't go back.

We buy a two-bathroom red-brick house big enough for two families
in Willoughby, 1949. The baggage of our old life arrives by ship. The
neighbours stare at the massive brass chandelier, the carved plush
couches jammed against the red-brick fireplace in the small lounge
room. The crystal chandelier remains in storage.

In the front garden, massed hydrangeas, struggling grass. At the back,
a fine mulberry tree for climbing. Soon there will be silkworms in
shoeboxes, with punched holes so they can breathe.

The Taits
Opposite live the gentle Taits
in their shady Federation bungalow.

Halting conversations by dictionary.
Hazel serves tomatoes on Saos –

salt and pepper, a sprig of parsley.
Mother serves her sour cherry slice.

The Neighbourhood
Every Sunday on our corner,
the 'Salvos'. Portly majors beat
the side drums, scrubbed girls
in black bonnets jangle tambourines.

Up the street, tow-haired scab-kneed Robert
shows off the family pianola – arcane marks
on slow-rolling parchment. Doilies light
dim spaces; drapes closed against the sun.

St Stephen's – the pinnacle of the street.
Girls in gloves and patent-leather shoes,
demure behind their parents. I watch behind
the pale tight hydrangeas as they pass.

'Casi yumbo siphora,' I say in my invented language, the only fragment
to come down through time.

At infants school I invent new phrases in my special language. I
escape from useless Hungarian which no-one understands, and stupid
English which I can't master. I will have my *own* language, an armour
behind which no-one can mock me.

Every day I arrive home with fantastical tales about my adventures between home and school. Mother half-believes them. Anything can happen in this upside-down country.

She ignores my chatter in my new language. So I chant my latest phrases to the silkworms as I feed them their mulberry leaves.

At infants school I wear an ugly brown-paper patch on one eye to stop it wandering. The teachers force me to write with my right hand to train me out of left-handedness.

I break my glasses accidentally and fear retribution. I blame an unknown boy in a higher class. That backfires. My embarrassed sister leads me through four classrooms so I can point out the culprit. I can't bring myself to accuse an innocent boy, so I confess.

The world doesn't come to an end. But my sister hates me even more.

I have no other memories of infants school.

Settling

First venture: a clothing factory
on Parramatta Road. Steep rickety stairs,
a tiny office on the landing – the brothers' domain.
Beyond, a vast room. Italians, Yugoslavs,
Aussie women in hairnets and slippers
tread the sewing machines. My aunt
at the cutting table.
The radio blares 2UE.

My grandmother, her second son in tow,
arrives on the SS *Volendam*.
The Taits hang coloured paper chains
on the gate spelling out
WELCOME.

Elocution

Mother has a little English.
She takes elocution lessons
from the very proper Miss Leary.

An invitation from Miss Leary
to afternoon tea
with Australian ladies!

Mother freezes at the door.
She is not wearing gloves.
Worse, no hat.

Primary School

One day English is THERE –
My magic passport, my New World.
I can tease, joke, make a friend.

In the dim grocery shop, I can buy –
now that the grocer understands me –
meat pies for lunch, musk sticks

and liquorice straps for the way home.
So new, exotic! Then on a magical,
unmarked day, normal.

In 1952 my uncle Joseph, his wife Clari and Little Suzi find a house in Strathfield. We move to a small white two-bedroom house in Lane Cove.

Grandmother sleeps in the room off the kitchen, doubling as the breakfast room. Granny, as we start to call her, loves us sternly and firmly. Lane Cove is not true suburbia – our small house faces a busy big road, and almost next door is the impressive and mysterious Masonic Temple.

Between our neat white house and the temple is our neighbour, Mrs Lawson, who lives in a rambling Federation house. She is a snobby, eccentric woman and a natural feminist. 'All men are fools,' she says, tartly and often.

Accordingly, Mr Lawson, a handsome Swede with a fine white moustache, lives in the back bedroom and seldom speaks. The rest of the household comprises a huge black cat perpetually prowling his territory, and a middle-aged son, Tom, who lives in a sleep-out on the veranda. Tom is treated with utter contempt by his mother; he is a 'failure'.

Mrs Lawson has strong opinions. The two I remember best: all Catholics, especially nuns, are to be abhorred and turned from one's door; David Jones, the department store in the city, is the only temple of good taste and should be visited once a week, always in gloves.

My sister Judy and I love to go over to her place. The house is divided strictly in halves: the prim living room, with its figurines of ballet dancers and toby jugs, is only to be viewed from the door, as is the main bedroom with its stately coverlet of pink satin and the ultra-shiny mahogany dressing table. In the other half of the house, things are more lively. In the winter there is always a fire in the dining–sitting room. We children are allowed to sprawl in front of it for hours and make up stories from flame-pictures we see, while Mrs Lawson reads and glances at us with wry amusement.

She has hopes for our futures. We might even reach the heights of *Esmé*, her adored daughter, who was a promising ballet dancer before she married a wealthy New Zealand grazier and became a member of parliament there. We hear endlessly about Esmé, always with the French spelling.

Mrs Lawson takes to us, even loves us. She thinks our migrant family is fine because we are not Catholics. Hearing that, my parents think we have found the right country. From now on, we should be safe.

There is bush nearby, not far from the house, where my sister and I play and are at peace for once. We find little gullies and creeks, and play for hours, unwatched. On Fridays we race each other to the shops to buy the weekly copy of *The Girls' Crystal*. I get my first dog and cry all night, as he does, when he is locked in the laundry.

The adults work long hours but a sense of purpose lightens the load. At school I gather up language, manners, gestures in great handfuls. We dare to become hopeful.

In fifth and sixth class I get into Artarmon Opportunity School and then worlds open up. We write 'novels' – bound and illustrated by ourselves, too. My first attempt is an Enid Blyton knock-off. My second is called *Seven Arrive*. A 'true story' of our escape from the wicked Communists for the land of freedom and democracy.

A writer's obsessions and themes begin early; I am already writing of the impinging traumas of world events on private lives, the upheaval of changing nationality and country. Of course, my little book is full of the prevailing myths of the fifties. No mention of the Holocaust; the wicked Commies are the enemy in our flight to freedom in safe Australia.

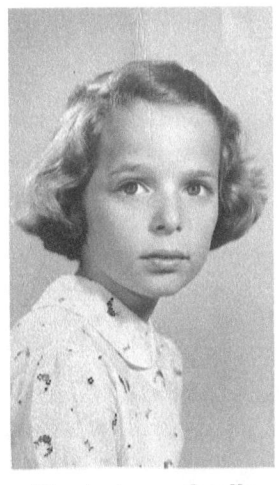

On the last page of *Seven Arrive*, Mr Lowry, my gifted, kind teacher writes: 'Susan, I hope to see more of your books in the years to come.' That was the seed for my writing life, the germ that grew, but was later buried in layers of shame as years passed and I still had not started writing. I was disappointing Mr Lowry, who was the first to see some promise in me.

At Artarmon, I meet a new friend or, rather, a life-long kindred spirit – Robert Jones, 'Jonesy' to my family. I remember the 'novel' he wrote then, a tale of derring-do with pirates and galleons on the high seas. I was jealous of his rolling handwriting in special blue ink and his deft illustrations. He already had panache. My novels were untidy with primitive drawings. But we also knew that we were the best writers in the class.

In 1956 Mum and Dad buy a battle-axe block where they build a modernist house. The new house in Killara, one of the classy suburbs on the North Shore, was seen as the acme of a migrant's achievement. The architect is another struggling Hungarian émigré. His wife, who teaches kids piano from home, had been a rising concert pianist in Hungary.

Judy and I reluctantly share a room with sleek built-in desks and matching butterfly chairs. On the beds, a modern print in oranges and yellows and bold angular shapes. Granny has her own small room with her antique clock from Hungary and her piano. She had been a successful opera singer before her second husband forbade her the stage.

In the last year of primary school and first year of high school, Granny is slowly dying. She had always been robust and strong, and smelled deliciously of her favourite cologne, 4711. Now as she declines, her muscles turned to paste, her arms hang down useless, her legs can no longer carry her. Her simple black silk dresses are replaced by hang-dog housecoats. Her eyes dulled, her skin pasty.

My mother and grandmother, two brave, strong women, battle the illness together every day. Mum gives up work. She cleans her, dresses her, brushes her hair and hauls her from bed to chair. I dread seeing her sitting listless on her big chair, staring out at the neighbour's pool. How her eyes flicker into life when I look in at the door; how I stay away for days, avoiding going in.

Occasionally, when there is a party at the Killara for the Hungarian diaspora, she will be wheeled into the living room in her best queenly black dress, her favourite brooch at her throat. For a couple of hours, the old charisma radiates from her. You can still imagine her on the stage of the Budapest Opera House, wooing her audience.

The only help Mum gets with caring for her iss from a cultured Viennese woman living nearby whose Jewish husband has recently died. She and her husband were old-school European intellectuals. I remember their house in Gordon clearly. It was the first house I had seen with bookshelves in every room and surfaces massed with books. With no money and an adolescent child to raise, Mrs Stadler needed work. She came twice a week to help mother wash Kato and deal with her terrible constipation. Mother used to say bitterly that the 'shit had to be dug out of her'. In the end there was no option. Kato made the decision to be taken to hospital.

I loved her dearly, yet I ran away from her as she was dying. I have never forgiven myself.

My improbable grandmother

My improbable grandmother
smells of fresh cologne, dresses
in white lace collars and black gowns.

She is large and handsome.
When angry, her swift hand leaves
a red-angry mark on a child's face.

Around the kitchen table she tells
and retells her glories, singing *Aida*
and *Carmen* on the Budapest stage.

She still sings in her small bedroom,
accompanying herself on piano until
her voice fades cracks
       gives out.

Muscular dystrophy invades her.
I watch her decay. The room smells of it.
I stop practising the piano there.

If she is afraid, I never see it.
She does not age into quietude.
'Don't cry,' she says to my mother

when the ambulance comes.
'It's better for all of us.
I won't be coming home.'

She dies as she has lived,
a strong wind gusting through.

Kato was not my first traumatic experience of death. It was my dog, Frisky. He was a much-wanted present for my eighth birthday. He was also a symbol of our family sending out roots in Australia; we felt secure enough to buy a dog.

I loved that little dog with a passion. My mother adored him almost as much as I did. I tried to hide him in the bedroom cupboard at night so I wouldn't be separated from him. He used to perch on Granny's capacious bosom. She wore him with indulgent pride.

Three years later, Frisky died. A car ran over him in front of our new house in Killara, just as I was about to leave for school. My mother ran towards me screaming, 'Don't come out! Don't come out!'

My grief was intense and long-lasting. I slept in my parents' bed for weeks, too frightened to sleep in my own. For months I wove a fantasy story that by some miracle Frisky was not really dead and would greet me with his usual enthusiasm when I came home from school.

So when a human death came not long after, my heart was already half frozen over.

Later that year, an influx of refugees arrived, fleeing the aftermath of the 1956 revolution in Hungary. First came Dad's sister, an ugly hard-natured woman with a beautiful stepdaughter. Both Gyuszi and Joseph detested her but did their duty by her. She and the beautiful stepdaughter stayed for several weeks.

Next, on Mum's side, came her cousin with her family. Again, we shared the house with them until they found their first lodgings. I was not very gracious or kind to my new relatives, even the two girls who were a similar age. They seemed alien, so Hungarian, to my brand-new Australian self.

Then came Faith, the child of the Viennese woman who had come to help with Kato. Mrs Stadler died suddenly and Faith was basically homeless. Mum took her in. My sister moved into Granny's old room; I reluctantly shared the bedroom with Faith, a strong personality, with a bad case of acne and with problems galore, the chief of which was being orphaned aged fifteen. I did not behave very well.

I was struggling to be the 'good girl' I once had been but that person had fled for good. I was now an adolescent and suddenly my parents were not god-like creatures. I was thrown out of the paradise of my progressive primary school and into a huge high school of a thousand girls. I felt marooned in the cold snobby suburbs of the mid-North Shore.

To top it all, sex came to stay in my innocent body. What was I going to do with it? It seemed as if one day I was still sitting in my mother's lap, which I used to do after dinner until I was almost twelve, then the next day I was a surly adolescent with large breasts and puppy fat who hated both school and home.

* * *

Killara was very quiet. Tall gum trees mingled with ordered gardens. I walked home from Gordon station after school, the long limbs of gums above my head, splashes of violet jacaranda and the smell of burning leaves in neat piles.

Killara was upper middle class, or so it thought of itself. We only played with two younger girls, our neighbours at the back. They invited us to Sunday lunch and we tasted roast lamb for the first time. Everyone else ignored us: this was private school land and we went to Hornsby Girls High School. A selective school but still a state school.

I hated Killara almost as much as I hated Hornsby Girls High, at the end of the long railway line. The school tried to imitate the snooty private schools that surrounded it. It stood for the worst things of the 1950s: repression and blandness, good manners, manufactured school spirit, Queen and country.

In fourth year the headmistress was set to expel me. My little group of outsiders had started an alternative magazine to the boring school magazine. The headmistress banned it, innocuous as it was, because we printed an article about sex (the sex lives of frogs) and about religion and politics, all no-noes in polite conversation and certainly unacceptable topics for high school girls.

We went to see Professor Stout at the Sydney University School of Philosophy and pleaded our case for freedom of speech. We also went to the *Sunday Mirror*, which put us on the front page, the article titled 'Three Little Maids from School'. That was the last straw for the school hierarchy.

My mother was so anxious that my high school career would go bung that she pleaded with the newspaper to have my face on the photo blanked out; all her work to make a new, unblemished life for us would be ruined. She succeeded.

She also begged with the headmistress to let me stay on and I limped through the last year. The only honours I got were for English. The headmistress felt vindicated. I was a bad apple.

I no longer cared. I was desperate to escape from the niceness and the emptiness of the North Shore and the loving but cloying clutch of my parents. We should have been happy – we had arrived, we were doing well, but somehow we were not happy. The pace of our transformation left us bewildered. In the background was the Holocaust, rarely mentioned but threatening to engulf us.

I was saved only by a group of girls who were in different ways outsiders like myself. An Israeli girl with Polish-Jewish origins, Masha, who was reading Nietzsche at fourteen; Inge, who had émigré Communist parents from Germany, in whose home I first heard Bach. There was shy Alison, with a keen intelligence and Left-leaning parents, a rarity on the North Shore; and Elma (now Liz), a tennis and language prodigy whose family struggled with poverty. That was also rare on the mid-North Shore. And Meryl, who I first met at Artarmon, where she was devouring Austen and Scott and Thackeray at ten. She was a loner, an only child of devout Methodists. At fifteen she discovered boys and acquired a cute 'steady' boyfriend – the first in our group to do so, thus the object of envy.

They were the core group; a few other interesting misfits clung to our frail boat. For me they were a lifeline, my education, my emotional support. We also had a lot of fun.

My university of friends
My university of friends began in high school,
on the wilder reaches of the North Shore.
I met a ruthless mind and a personality
that fitted it. Another who embraced the starry
universe of books and found endless
treasure and consolation.

I met another, shy, gentle, lost.
Brilliant and beautiful although
she did not know it.

From them all I learned books,
music, argument.
The joy of meeting other minds,
the treacherous depths of affection,
                              the plumb of true feeling.

* * *

It began with breasts. They started growing alarmingly when I
was still at primary school. They grew and grew. I hated them. In
retrospect they weren't gross – let's say Renoir-esque. But I longed for
the polite little mounds fitting neatly into B-cups like most Anglo girls.
By thirteen I had to go to David Jones in the city for special fittings,
where the saleswomen would tactfully bring ugly harnesses. 'Oh, you
might need a D fitting, dear ...' My breasts were heavy on my light-
boned frame, and hot and sweaty in summer. It never occurred to me
that they might be objects of lust.

The first period came as a total surprise, before I turned twelve. I
rushed to Mother with bloodied pants, thinking I had had an awful
accident. Her face became solemn and she led me into a quiet room
and said a few vague things about 'becoming a woman'. I emerged
from that conversation no wiser but resolved never to discuss physical
or sexual matters with her again. She was useless.

Sex was not a grand unfolding into the adult world, more like a series
of semi-comic stumbling blocks. Also a constant source of confusion,
fear, shame. My body remained a mystery and burden. My friends
were mostly as taciturn and confused as I was. Then one, Meryl,
seemingly overnight, acquired a splendid body – small rounded
breasts, a tiny waist tightly cinched, long tanned legs. This bookish,
aloof girl suddenly had a weapon and started flaunting it. Another,

Inge, the most 'free thinking' and least inhibited, was next and, without doubt or fear, started 'fucking', as she called it casually.

The rest of us were dispirited. Without going to the beach or to Fellowship on weekends (both were out, for different reasons), how would we ever find a boyfriend? How to deal with surging sexual feelings?

I learnt to masturbate while reading the sexy bits of popular novels my parents might be reading. This was fraught, too. I had no idea whether anyone else did it. I was also terrified that the way I did 'it' was also somehow perverse – rubbing my legs together instead of direct contact with the clitoris. I did not know what the clitoris was. An addictive new pleasure 'down there'.

I was approaching seventeen, when most girls had already some sort of boyfriend, and I started to feel desperate. Then I met K at a Workers' Educational Association course in Morpeth. A truly nerdy way to meet a boy. I mainly remember group singing of Australian folk songs in the evenings and the thrill of mixing with grown-ups.

K was a year older than me, a child migrant from England brought up in the Barnardo's boys home and foster homes. He was brash, intelligent and wrote poetry. He also looked like a bodgie from the western suburbs. He was smallish in height, lean, with brushed-back blond hair, bold blue eyes and a cocky kind of confidence which crashed through my shyness. I was interested, especially because he came from a 'deprived' background totally different from mine.

Rebellion through the choice of boyfriend was to become a pattern. I had already determined that I would never go out with a future doctor or lawyer, especially if he was Jewish. I wanted a more expansive life, more cosmopolitan than what the North Shore in the fifties offered, and very different from what my parents expected.

My mother reacted with horror when she met K. That never abated. We fought over K all the time. One morning when I came into the kitchen for breakfast I heard her hissing at my sister, 'She has a love bite on her neck!' The disgust in her voice made my soul wither in shame. My loyalty to K grew in proportion. My mother and I were on the way to a long and bitter battle about how to live.

K and I went on 'dates'. He even took me to a nightclub or two. He thought that was a way to impress me. The two of us played at being grown-ups: drinking cocktails and eating something flambéed by the waiter at our table.

* * *

After I turned eighteen, I made a decision to stop being a virgin. I thought it would be too, too bourgeois of me to hang on to my virginity. Losing it would be a portal towards independence. With that kind of mad resolve, the actual deflowering was sure to be lame. I was passive and scared. It happened on the pink brocade sofa in the room with the big plate glass windows, and the Venetian lace curtains brought all the way from Budapest. K and I were both tense about making a mess and being discovered. Not the best entrée to adulthood.

Another awful 'first' was the St Paul's College formal. K, a first-year University of Sydney scholarship student, invited me. I'd evaded my own school formal – anything to cock a snook at my hated school. My mother still nursed fantasies of bringing up two perfect young women. She loved to dress us up and I submitted to a frothy black lace knee-length number, my hair stiff from the hairdresser. I look startled (or trapped) in the photo. I hated being surrounded by boozy

rugger-buggers and snooty private school students who seemed to own the world.

K and I broke up a few weeks after I started uni. I was relieved, yet incensed and jealous when, not much later, he took up with Inge from school. It was obvious in their body language that she was giving him 'real sex', in which I had patently failed.

My next boyfriend was a total contrast. I began volunteering backstage at the Independent Theatre, being intrigued by the theatre world, and was assigned to help the lighting man. The Independent was an old-fashioned theatre in North Sydney, semi-professional in that they paid the actors but not anyone else. It was tightly run for many years by the formidable Doris Fitton. She treated volunteers as acolytes, privileged to serve her.

B was in his early forties; I was eighteen. He had the face of an aesthete or mediaeval thinker: lined olive skin, hooded eyes, a strong aquiline nose. A face I never tired of looking at. His long tapering hands were beautiful. He was a gentle, kind, reserved man. People liked him.

We worked together comfortably on the small platform above the stage. I pulled a lever or adjusted a light at his instruction. Stage lighting was his passion, a creative release from his unhappy home life and a dull day job. Underneath us on the stage, a Pinter play with two brilliant young actors. I loved seeing the play over and over, looking down from our perch above the stage and feeling B's calm presence.

During the week he worked at the new AMP building near the Quay. As the friendship developed, we met during his lunch hour and took a ferry together, sharing his homemade sandwiches, and he would give me a letter or two, written since we last met, in his small neat handwriting on closely folded notepaper. They were full of his wonderment at falling in love, tender and innocent. We held hands, occasionally kissed. I remember going to bed with him only once. He was full of awe, treating me as a sacramental object.

He was married (not happily) and had kids, so there was much Catholic guilt. After a few lovely months, I ended it. I think he was grieved but deep down relieved. I kept him at a big distance from my parents, so they were not as panicked about B but were happy to see it come to an end.

Once I started at Sydney University in 1962, I had an escape plan for leaving home. When my parents were about to make their first big overseas trip since their arrival, I said I wanted to experience life on my own until they came back. I found a landlady in Kirribilli that they could approve of. Secretly I knew that I was never going back.

I met my first poet on the ferry from Kirribilli to the Quay. He was neat and dapper, with an English air, but was actually from New Zealand. His name was William Hart-Smith, or Bill to his friends. No histrionics as I would have expected from a 'poet', just an intensity in the eyes and a curiosity and quickness. I was nearly nineteen; he would have been nearing fifty. We started to talk: books, what I wanted to do with my life ... He gave me two of his poetry books. I was impressed by their jaunty directness and the breadth of his subject matter. We were each a little in love with the other – he with my freshness, I with his kindness and talent. He took me out to dinner a couple of times and never made a pass. I knew he was married.

A Small Spell of Enchantment
    A small walk from my lodgings
to a small jetty.
A small friendly ferry.
A small journey in the shadow
of the dwarfing Bridge
every object
              smaller still.

In memory the water is always sparkling,
the clouds always fluffy
the ferry never crowded.
The poet and I sit, talk.
The delicate air protects us,
the breezes sigh
in sympathy.

1962
An innocent time.
Girls wore girdles and suspenders
and had secret ambitions.
Boys respected 'nice' girls.
Men opened doors.

My older poet was kind.
He listened.
Our shy words wove
the lightest of bonds.
No scars.

Around the corner
a new era
lying in wait.

I had no aspirations to be a poet then and was repressing any desire to
be a writer, believing I would never be good enough. But, in retrospect,
I learnt a few things, unconsciously, from Bill Hart-Smith: the virtues
of directness, the power of story in verse, and the enlargement of a
theme beyond oneself.

Here are the first lines of his *Poems of Discovery*, a verse narrative on
the famous voyage of Vasco Di Gama to find America.

Prologue

Said Bishop Cosmas,
The world is flat
and that's that!
The Holy Word is explicit
that Christ will come and visit it
again, when all mankind shall be
illumined by the Light will shine
from His Countenance Divine;
and if the Light touch on a ball,
the heathen will not see at all!
That is not so,
said Augustine,
the world is round,
for I have seen
from my tower above the sea
the ocean of infinity,
and watched the far horizon sweep
in one great arc from deep to deep.
And Christ His Word has this great merit:
the things of spirit are seen by spirit!

(From *Poems of Discovery*, W Hart-Smith, 1959, Angus & Robertson)

The Sydney Push and its princes

I was still at school when I started to go to Jim Thorburn's bookshop in a little bohemian lane that no longer exists, behind King Street in the city. Rowe Street was a mecca for bohemians and arty types, and the simply curious like me. It was demolished for high-rise buildings and is still mourned by those who remember it as an oasis of civilisation in hard-scrabble Sydney. It had a continental café, an art gallery and the Pocket Bookshop, stocked with Penguins and Pelicans. It was run by the gentle-mannered, soft-voiced Scot, Jim Thorburn, a committed socialist. My schoolfriend Masha and I paid many visits there and to Edols, the record shop nearby which had the best of classical records.

Jim was not intimidating, being quite avuncular with young women, but his assistant was. George Molnar was a woolly-haired intellectual from Sydney University who worked there part time. He was the real deal – he could expound on virtually every subject with vehemence and depth. He had fair springy hair and pale blue eyes, a waxy pale European skin, a loud, weirdly accented voice. He was hugely voluble, opinionated and knowledgeable.

It was through George that I met the Sydney Push. I was only a few months out of school when he took me to the public bar at the Royal George Hotel, where the Push drank. 'The George' was made notorious by the afternoon tabloids, the *Sun* and *Daily Mirror*, as a place where free sex was available and the 'beatniks' hung out.

In the crowded noisy bar, a drunken bloke next to me pissed on my leg. I looked down – it was true. His grizzled face was stuck in his schooner; he was too pissed to care. I tried not to react and didn't mention it to anyone. That would have exposed me as a lily-livered bourgeois, not fit to be a candidate for the Push. I was already under the spell of Push ideology.

It was 1962. Drinking in the public bar was in itself a brave and transgressive act back then. Women were barred from drinking with men. Men got their wives or girlfriends a shandy or a sherry as they sat in the Ladies Lounge. But in the Push pub *du jour*, women mixed with men. Push leaders always made a deal with the publican that women could drink in the public bar. The pub's fortunes skyrocketed from then on because the Push were regular and hard drinkers.

Women's Liberation was more than a decade away. I was a young, inchoate rebel, and the people in the Push seemed to me the ultimate rebels. As I stood in the public bar, piss pooling into my polite sandals, drying on my calves, I was horrified yet excited. Maybe this was my mob. These people rejected conventional politics. They wanted to live outside state power. They were anarchists, they advocated free sex and had a life centred around pubs, parties and vigorous discussions of society.

For me, the Sydney Push was another country. Although it occupied a miniscule part of Sydney, it had its own signposts, language, hierarchy and mores, its own holy books, favoured pastimes and ways of relating. And like any country, if you stayed there more than a few months, its influence was lifelong. I was a part of the Push scene, on and off, for many years; sometimes intensely, more often loosely.

In the 1940s John Anderson, an abrasive, brilliant Scottish academic, came to town. He became Professor of Philosophy at Sydney University and his ideas influenced generations of philosophy students who became known as Andersonians or Libertarians.

The Push was an inner-city movement with two strands: one based in the Philosophy Department of Sydney University, the other in the chosen pub in the city. It spawned outposts: the Balmain Push, the Bayview Push, the Baby Push and so on. All the strands mingled on Friday and Saturday nights at the pub when EVERYONE came to rub shoulders, talk endlessly, look for sexual partners and find where the party was that night.

In Australia in the fifties and sixties, the only other such movement was the Drift in Melbourne, a looser collection of bohemians, artists, students and others. But the Drift did not have the intellectual rigour that the Push liked to think it had. The two names said it all. A few Melbourne-ites drifted to Sydney and were immediately absorbed into the Push. Germaine Greer was the most famous. Germaine had been confused and unhappy in the Drift but when she arrived in Sydney she liked the brashness and self-confidence of the scene. And she'd already fallen in love with one of the princes of the Push, Roelof Smilde.

Later, in 1972, came Sasha Soldatow – young, openly gay, gossipy, rebellious and soon to become a talented writer. He took to the Push instantly. Until Sasha there had been only one token gay, who went by the nickname Della. Sasha was curious and hardly shy, disarming the Push quickly.

While the Push lasted until the late 1970s (and there are many remnants today), its most potent and influential years were the fifties and sixties. Although it remained under the radar of the general population, its radical ideas and somewhat louche reputation spread widely. In its heyday there might have been a thousand people affiliated with it. But the inner circle was always small – about thirty, rising to maybe fifty people at its height.

But what was the Push, in essence? I don't think anyone has quite put their finger on it. It remains an elusive beast but for those interested in the era, the definitive and fascinating book *Sex and Anarchy* by Anne Coombs comes very close. I introduced Anne to the Push at a party for Andre Frankovits's fiftieth birthday. Surveying the scene, she said to me, 'This is interesting. I might write a book on this.' I was delighted as some people in the Push had often talked about writing THE BOOK but never did, being too much on the inside.

The Push valued straight talk, no bullshit, no sentimentality and the need to be clear-eyed about illusions, to see the narrow strictures of society. They believed you should free yourself from the bonds of family, religion and conventional work (where possible). This manifested as a virtual taboo on talking about your background: no conventional chat about jobs, study or family outside the Push. It also meant no proper introductions. To this day I have only a hazy idea of people's backgrounds.

Talking about your fears and hopes, your inner self, was also a big taboo. The goal was to free yourself, especially in your choice of sexual partners and how often you changed them, too. Jealousy was a constraint on freedom and was seen as a weakness to be suppressed.

In the sixties the 'princes' of the Push, Darcy Waters and Roelof Smilde, were at the apex of their power. Both had good looks, charisma and strong personalities. George Molnar was also at the apex; not a glamourous figure like the other two but still a prince because he had such intellectual heft.

Alongside this triumvirate was a kind of fourth leg, the academic philosopher Jim Baker. A bit older than the others, a strong Andersonian, he had a stable life outside the Push, with a wife and kids. When I knew him, his hold of the Andersonian dogma had somewhat waned but he seemed to sublimate his loss of power in other ways. I always thought that Jim was not a player in the sexual life of the Push so much as a purveyor or 'pimp' to the stars – Darcy, Roelof and George. He would chat up new young women and assess their viability and introduce them around. This was never explicit or even deliberate but was a subtle modus operandi.

My most important relationship within the Push was with George Molnar. (Not to be confused with the *Sydney Morning Herald*'s cartoonist of the same name. In August 2003 I wrote an article in the *SMH* about the confusion of the two men and the contrasts and parallels between them.) I gathered he was Hungarian, although the accent was a strange hybrid peculiar to George, and I sensed he was Jewish. In visits to the bookshop I concentrated on not allowing George to guess the depths of my ignorance. Not that he would have cared about the state of my intellect; George was totally unreconstructed and he saw only a young attractive woman with big tits whom he could lecture, entertain and train. He knew I was Hungarian and possibly Jewish. Yet these common traits were never discussed between us until many years later.

My next memory of George is when he was already a big cheese at Sydney University. An intellectual. A strong Libertarian, a follower of John Anderson. Yet his style was so utterly different from the others. Not a laid-back larrikin like Darcy, not a suave charmer like Roelof, but a man with an impassioned, over-articulate and utterly *European* brain. For all his passionate style, all he ever displayed was his highly functioning cerebral cortex. He led me to believe – mistakenly – that the brain's logical exercise, its extended reasoning power, was all that mattered. That everything else, especially emotion, was to be subordinated to it.

At the time he was with Val. They made an impressive couple, she dark and tousled with wonderful kohl-rimmed blue eyes. She looked sexy and wild, a little threatening. (I believe she ended up a respectable mum on the North Shore.) He was in cords, a messy handkerchief always at the ready for his constant rhinitis, and a lava flow of talk and argument.

I can't remember exactly how our affair began. I was almost nineteen, he was approaching thirty – a huge difference in our levels of sophistication. When I sensed he was interested in me, I was torn between terror and feeling flattered. The fact that I felt little sexual attraction to him hardly came into it. I fell in love with his persona, with the possibilities of learning from him, with the whole deliciousness of being nineteen and the most intelligent man on campus saying he was in love with me.

Were such words actually used? Probably not, but in the code of the day I was henceforth to be his woman. While no vows of fidelity were made, I thought that George would not mess around for the sake of it.

A period of great unhappiness began. My intense emotional needs and intense idealism clashed with George's ruthless determination to suppress his own emotional needs and idealism. Yet we did display some affection towards each other. He was fond in a generalised patting kind of way, as if I were a young foal or trainable dog. He'd ask me often if I was all right, to which there was no real answer. I tried, by silence and withdrawal, to tell him I was unhappy, unfulfilled, but he either ignored it or talked over, or at, me.

That formed a pattern. For years I believed that men who talked at me and over me must nevertheless be teaching me something. The reality was that as soon as they started talking, I would shut down. The talk actually became a barrier to communication. I did not learn much in those years of listening to intelligent, logical men.

George had lodgings in a small room in Arundel Street, right opposite the university. It was on the first floor, not much more than a single bed and an overflowing desk, its single window looking out on a narrow Glebe backyard. Our first unsatisfactory couplings took place on that single bed. I thought I might get better at sex in time. I doubted George would. He treated sex as a merely functional thing. I didn't mind that, particularly; it was how we could express our 'love' that worried me constantly. How to encourage George to be a more relaxed, intimate person, how to make myself more interesting, dynamic, a more equal partner?

It didn't help that George was brilliant in his already chosen field, philosophy, while I was struggling to pass Philosophy One. I could manage Ethics but was totally flummoxed by Logic. I was certain to fail it. He offered to coach me. He'd take me through the simplest of syllogisms patiently, sucking on his pipe, throwing me a quizzical look now and again as if to say, 'you must be pretending not to understand', but never was cruel or angry. Such endearing character traits kept me encouraged – glimpses of a kind, quite simple fellow, an affectionate child inside the carapace.

Deep down I knew that we would never have an adult, equal interchange, emotional or intellectual. Emotionally I would remain alternately his pet and a sex object; intellectually he would always be my teacher and I his unconsciously resistant pupil. One day I took all my courage in my hands and called it quits.

He was hurt, much more hurt that I had anticipated. We were apart for a few months. I was confused. I missed him. Finally, I approached George and said I wanted him back. He gave me that sideways half-sly, half-timid glance of his – one of his few signals of emotional involvement – jiggled his leg, and said, 'I don't know. You know the saying, "Once bitten, twice shy".'

The maxim sounded odd in his hybrid accent. It was his only comment on the separation and a few days later we were back 'on' again. Nothing changed; he was even more removed and I just as inept at engaging him.

Then a body blow. He told me he was interested in someone else. Part of me was relieved – it was clearly hopeless – but my usurper! A perfectly turned-out doll-like beauty, the immaculate and recently elected Miss University. In those pre-feminist days, she was quite a trophy for George. But could he possibly love such a sleekly synthetic version of female beauty? Someone mindless enough to enter a Miss University contest? (She wasn't dumb but in those times when female rivalry was unselfconscious and deadly, I had no trouble in traducing her.)

At some other level I felt protective of him. George evoked a complex and often cruel reaction in many people, a mixture of derision and envy, scorn and reluctant admiration. He was too loud, too European, too aggressive, too weird and, although no-one would have said it, too Jewish. He was an outsider even in the professionally outsider Push.

And now he was squiring Miss University. While I was angry and jealous, I also feared that people would ridicule him behind his back.

In the end I had no choice but to retire gracefully from the field. For months afterwards, each time I saw him with Miss University – the Beauty and the Beast as some called them – my stomach heaved with jealousy and humiliation.

* * *

Darcy Waters was tall, with longish blond hair and a natural grace, even when leaning against a bar with a beer, his habitual posture. He was a bright kid from Casino, an early dropout from university, and he was, as all the core Push people were, heavily influenced by John Anderson. Darcy made a living on the wharves, sometimes as a cabbie, and would gamble on the horses regularly. He was naturally lazy but not a big drinker. Cars and traffic were a serious obsession for him long before other people understood the urban chaos that they wrought. His published intellectual output was one famous paper, entitled 'The Motor Car Has to Go'.

Women were attracted to Darcy and he did not bat them away. The years I remember best were when he was with his long-term girlfriend, Gill.

The Norse Gods
They looked like gods from a Nordic saga.
He, long, loose, easy, she almost as tall as he –
long ash-blond hair, often dressed in white,
cool blue eyes, alabaster skin.
He loquacious, she silent.
A rare queenly smile.

Lonely on her pinnacle, I now think,
her twin beside her but not with her.

He died early – of poverty and long
illness, his legend a little tarnished.

She freed herself, found Women's Lib,
made a film, took other lovers,

married, had kids, a mortgage.

Sometimes you can see the glint

of the old grandeur in her eyes
and a hint of triumph –

'I have survived.'

In this early period, Darcy saw me only as George's young girlfriend
and treated me with an airy benevolence and charm. Later, I found
out that his impersonal goodwill was not universal. He could be
callous with his women. With Gill, as much as I thought he loved her,
he sometimes would bring other women home and fuck them in the
next room, within her hearing. All this was acceptable in the codes
of Push behaviour.

When Darcy was still quite young but already a seasoned punter,
his girlfriend at the time, Lois Haydon, a slight, wispy young beauty,
would follow him around the racecourse, crying out, 'Darc! Darc! Save
the rent!' Darcy would go to the races with ten dollars in his pocket. He
won every single race that day and the ten dollars turned into several
hundred. On the very last race he lost the lot. Asked afterwards how
the day went, he would say laconically, 'I lost a tenner.'

Darcy had a light, warm singing voice. His rendition of 'Joe Hill', a
beautiful union song, would still the room.

Even as Darcy surfed through time as the archetypal handsome
larrikin, he could also change when needed. In the seventies, when

he fell in love with Wendy Bacon and she became the famous face of *Thor* and *Thorunka*, the student papers which printed obscene images and articles in defiance of censorship, he backed her to the hilt. He became a backroom helper, spending long hours organising the paper, mixing well with much younger students.

When charged, Wendy appeared in court wearing a nun's habit. On the habit were emblazoned the words: 'I've been fucked by God's steel prick'. The furore that followed in the tabloids! Darcy delighted in all this. He was proud of Wendy. As for me, this period left me somewhat alienated. I liked the daring of it but the aesthetics of the paper – crude, without much wit or beauty – made me slightly sick, and I wondered when we could move on.

Roelof was the other major figure in the Push. While Darcy was the quintessential Oz larrikin with a good brain, Roelof was a true ideologue who wrote serious papers and articles on Libertarian themes. He and Darcy were both friends and intense rivals, especially in the sexual field. Several women ping-ponged between them over a long period, myself included.

Roelof was of Dutch origin and had a touch of European class. As a boy he excelled academically and in sport and became the school captain of North Sydney Boys High. Despite dropping out spectacularly from university and becoming a professional gambler and renowned bridge player, there was always a faint air of the school captain and an intense moral seriousness about him.

He developed a double life: a life inside the Push and one outside it. Punting linked these two worlds but he had become a far more serious punter than most. The game of bridge took over more and more as he went to international tournaments, often winning. That was a very different world again, with a new set of friendships and rewards.

I always liked Roelof. Despite the rigidity of his Libertarian views, he had an innate courtesy. Roelof could listen as well as talk. He was generous, especially when he was flush after the races; he gave

Roelof Smilde
1930-2017

personally and to causes and to projects, without fuss.

With women he gave no quarter: no concessions to the 'weaker' sex. He saw the sexual arena as a level playing field. There was a line of dazzling women from Marion Manton to Germaine Greer, Liz Fell, the feminist writer Lynne Segal, Wendy Bacon and others, all of them rigorously schooled in non-jealous behaviour. Thank heavens I was about thirty when I had my on-and-off affair with him. I had enough self-protection by then to expect nothing. Yet our short time together proved to be a basis for a lifelong, if intermittent, friendship.

Darcy's main nickname was 'The Horse' from his addiction to the races, and even better, 'The Noble Horse'. He enjoyed a huge circle of friends and admirers and he was always up for a conversation. No-one questioned his style of life; if they did, he would brush them off. He became ill with emphysema and related complaints. I would see him at parties with an oxygen mask on, his face ravaged and lined but still handsome. His messy abodes, littered with oxygen tanks, masks and medicines, took on a nightmarish aspect.

It was a sad comedown for The Noble Horse. With Darcy's decline, Sasha Soldatow collected money to support him. Years later Sasha himself needed collections to stay alive. This was the Push way: the hat went around for abortions, illnesses and other misfortunes. The Push was an alternative and enduring family which embraced you after you had fled your own. To this day I see Andre Frankovits, pushing eighty, acting as a backbone for or, more accurately, a caretaker for elderly Push people. He is a caretaker in the best possible sense: keeping in touch with people, visiting the ailing, and literally cleaning up after their death.

Roelof, despite drinking and smoking to excess, had the common sense to acquire better survival skills. He finally gave up smoking and had a long battle with drinking where he wouldn't drink for months then would start again. He tried to keep himself physically fit. He lived till eighty-seven, loved and admired. Among his many nicknames were 'Roo', 'Lofty' and 'Uncle Dutch'. At one of his wakes, my poem, in my absence, was read by his two daughters.

I use this poem here, written after he died, because it gives a glimpse of his complex character and life.

Roelof the Brave
All his monikers:
School captain
      Prince of the Push
Successful gambler
      Champion bridge player ...
Ladies man.　Puritan.
      Accomplished flirt, gentle tease.

Fair to a fault, if a bit haughty.
      Oz Egalitarian, old-world European.
Anarchist.　Ideologue.
      Supple mind, unbending will.
Troubled son, thoughtful father.
      Always generous friend.
Pacifist.　Activist.
      Lone loved man in a house of women.
Hidden man, full of warmth.
      Upright man, uptight man.
Looser, milder, as he grew older.

To the end, clear-eyed, strong.
Roelof the Brave – a true Humanist.

What was it like for me in the early Push days? I don't remember coming to the pub with George much. Sometimes he would be there, nursing a single drink among the band of heavy drinkers. Mostly I would wonder, as Friday night or Saturday grew closer, whether I would have the courage to go, hesitating at the door as I inhaled the roar of talk, massed bodies, smoke and the sour smell of beer. I looked for a lifeline, someone I could be easy with. Sometimes I would spot Andre or Ian Bedford or my old schoolfriend Alison and the always-cheerful Bulgarian, Jack the Anarchist. I would head to their safe proximity. The more established women ignored me or treated me with disdain. I was new, younger and competition. A drink or two and I would start to blend in. The talk flowed, I was part of it.

Closing time was six o'clock in the early days. By magic, the lifts for the party and other arrangements came together. I bought my flask of brandy and, thus armed, carried by the throng, was transported to a messy front room or a tangled backyard in the inner city. The party surged around me, raucous and raw, jazz or blues in the background. The liaisons forming and changing as the night went on.

Some parties fizzed. More sparked with the energy of alcohol and people living on the edge, freeing their minds and bodies after a more humdrum week. The best parties were in the backyard of Ken Buckley's house. Buckley was known for his work in civil liberties. The garden was thick and mysterious, good for hiding a cache of drink in brown paper bags. You could not trust anyone with grog left exposed.

I remember a luminous night when we were happy, in a flight of spirits. We seemed golden and fabulously intelligent in our own eyes. The pick of partners for the early hours were full of sexy promise, even romance.

This was also the famous night bringing on the New Year of 1963. Geoffrey Chandler was there with his girlfriend. His estranged wife, Margaret Chandler, was on the other side of the Harbour Bridge with her new lover, Gilbert Bogle. They were wandering around the Lane Cove National Park looking for a place to make love and were soon to meet their agonising deaths. The papers headlined their mystery deaths for months. Our golden party was tainted by it; somehow we felt complicit, soiled. The case was never officially solved.

* * *

At the time I more or less accepted sexism in the Push. It was the way things were. Later it dawned on me that its social hierarchy affected my whole subsequent life.

Some remnants of the Push will argue even today that it was not a patriarchal society; that would be anathema to all their theoretical beliefs. But, in reality, that's how it worked. Although the women were meant to be equal, it was truly male-centred.

A handful of women had no trouble being as sexually predatory as the men, so fitted in well. Another handful of women who could argue theory with the men were also respected. If you could do both – fuck and talk well – you became a Push heroine. A few could find their own way and build some status of their own – Germaine Greer, Lynne Segal and Liz Fell come to mind, and some others from an older generation, the contemporaries of the men, who grew up alongside them, like the redoubtable Margaret Fink and her friend Judy Smith.

But many young women were left floundering, a sex object to be handed around from one powerful Push male to the other. They might have the glamour of interesting boyfriends and a free-wheeling lifestyle, but their status was almost entirely dependent on sex. There was no deliberate cruelty – free love was meant to be equal – but in practice it was the most sexist society I have ever encountered. I made almost no friendships among the women; we were too busy competing for men.

When Women's Liberation finally made a mark, there was a huge rethink from some of the men, but many of them could never change their ways or admit their lack of empathy or understanding for women. As Anne Coombs wrote in *Sex and Anarchy*, 'The Push had seemed like a magical place, where as a young woman you could spread your wings and fly. Now it was beginning to look like a Venus flytrap with no way out.'

My feelings for the Push were ambivalent at best. Much of it was a nightmare of loneliness and confusion. Even with friends from high school, Alison and Inge, also caught in the net at different times, we would not admit weakness to each other. Indeed, Inge was one of the few young women who thrived – she had both the sexual pizzazz and the intellectual agility needed.

I did make a couple of male friends, such as Andre Frankovits and the gentle Ian Bedford. My weekly lunch with Andre at the 'Greeks' – the Push favoured three Greek restaurants over the years – saved my life. I could talk to Andre naturally, about almost everything. While he was already a Push stalwart, and has remained so all his life, he retained a quality of lightness and humanity, and he could detach himself from Push conformities. He was never an alpha male laying down the law.

Years later I began to assess the damaging effect of the Push on me. It put me into a straightjacket and strangled my emerging personality. I supported the basic tenets; for many years I abstained from voting and kept a distance from politics. I was happy to live outside the strictures of society, to a point. Yes, everyone should be able to fuck who they wanted, but I did not fuck many people. Yes, jealousy was not a good emotion, but I could see that the awful lengths people went to suppress it were even more harmful.

The years I spent around the Push distorted and delayed my own development as an adult. I regret the role it played in my fear of striking out and finding my own path. Certainly any idea of being a writer was pushed to the farthest reaches of my mind.

Yet a lot of things I value about myself come from that time. A certain directness, no bullshit attitude, and an ability to sniff out pretence. I don't regret being part of the Push, its many amazing people, the quality of the talk, the parties. It was vital, organic, special. How could one regret that?

Above all else, it was a wonderful grab bag of people: dubious drifters, students, uni dropouts, rogue academics, a scattering of petty criminals. A wide range of people from various fields, and from the Left and the Right: the fiery barrister Jimmy Staples; the transport mogul Gordon Barton; Eva Cox, the feminist and activist (who is still seen at Push gatherings even though she's decried their no-interventionist stance for many years); filmmakers like Michael Thornhill and his friend and collaborator, the writer Frank Moorhouse; the poet and short story writer Vicki Viidikas; and eccentrics galore, among them Adrian Hebe, brilliant but often unstable, and Jack the Anarchist, a small bearded Bulgarian who was an anarchist long before he met the Push.

Above all, I valued the deep humanism of many Push people. Despite their brusque matter-of-factness there was a deep humanism and a strong moral sense. These were traits in both Roelof and George, and more hidden in Darcy. Andre and Ian Bedford also had a luminous perception combined with kindness. That's what kept me in the Push and loyal to it for many years.

Holland

I met the Dutchman at a university party on Sydney's lower North Shore in 1964. I was twenty-one, he was approaching twenty-four.

He was very tall, white skinned, blond hair already falling out. He was awkward, not given to talking too much, but there was a kind of quiet superiority about him. I thought, this is a man who thinks about things. He came from a family of Dutch farmers and was studying Veterinary Science.

Anton started to write to me while away on holidays. My interest quickened. The letters were wry, full of left-field observations. Strangely, he presumed an intimacy of mind between us. If he had designs on my body, he kept that quiet.

I loved the room he rented in a three-storied house in Forest Lodge (almost opposite the university), almost as much as I loved him. It was a biggish sparse attic: some books, in English and Dutch, a desk, a washstand in which we pissed sometimes when the three flights of stairs to the outside loo in the dark were too much for us. The landlady, who had lived there all her life, was a silent ghostly presence, occasionally seen flitting about in a worn shawl.

I thought that my Dutchman was brave, making a life for himself alone, his family on the other side of the world. He played university soccer at a time when soccer was still a strange un-Australian game played only by 'wogs' and other oddballs. With his big spare frame, he was the goalie. He became friendly with the activist Charlie Perkins, also on the team. As well as a family in Victoria where he worked one holiday, the team became his surrogate family. Otherwise he was a loner.

There was a deeply serious side to him which rather scared the other veterinary students and engineering hearties with whom he drank. But they liked him, too, partly because he could drink most of them under the table. Drinking was no problem back then – everyone drank. But it became a problem later.

We had other things we liked to do. We hitchhiked and took trains around the back blocks of Queensland and slept in the bush. We would wake up sweaty from our sleeping bags by a wide riverbank, no-one else there, make a fire for tea then walk into town to eat a greasy fried breakfast in a fly-blown café before hitching a ride with a local farmer between towns. Some of the men who picked us up were expansive yarners, some never said a word. The dust-smeared gums along the rutted roads flashed by. We took everything in, hugged it to us. In a sense, Anton introduced me to my own country.

Later, he also gave me my first glimpse of Holland on a flying visit home to his family farm. Years later I wrote the first of these poems, called Dutch Landscapes.

Mother and (Youngest) Son
Ten years
in another country

and Anton is at
her door

bulky in the cold
Christmas air.

I hold back,
the stranger

from Australia –
the wife to be?

'Welcome,' she says
her voice high.

He bends his balding
head, towards her,

shakes her hand, steps
over her threshold, home.

Funeral
Church in a winter field
coats sombre by the door
preacher in black
snow-grey sky.

Old man in open coffin
pyjamas buttoned tight
on his dead neck.
Mourners file by, dry eyed.

I never knew him
but sob, suddenly,
for his homely pyjamas,
the death rattle grin.

The relatives trudge silent
in falling snow to the gravesite.
Afterwards, they partake of tea
in the spare widow's house.

Mother Tongue

Long level land.
Frozen earth, furrows
for fences. Cattle's breath
hangs in the high barn.

Inside, in the lamplight
his mother greets me
seats me
gives me tea.

The men stamp out
to the cattle.

We sit silent in
warm air until
she speaks.

She tells her life
in a language
I don't understand.

I listen. I look
into her face.

Hours pass.

Later, language learned,
we hardly need to speak.

In 1969 Anton and I got married in Sydney. Neither of us believed in marriage, that ridiculous bourgeois institution, or in religion (his Protestant, mine Jewish). Our rationale was that, as we were going hitchhiking around the deeply Catholic continent of South America, it would be safer to be married. In hindsight we were really shoring up our difficulties with each other because we did not want to part.

After six months, we flew straight to Holland. We spent the first few months with his parents, in the Northeast Polder, not long reclaimed from the sea. Its capital was a new neat town called Emmerlood.

The Family
I like them all –

the rigid upright father with his periods
of mania dreaded by his family.

The quiet contained mother,
the spine of the family.

The solid firstborn son
who will inherit the farm.

The second son, the brilliant one,
now locked in an asylum.

The feisty married daughter
in Friesland, the very tip of Holland.

And the youngest son, my beloved,
who brings me to live amongst them,

as the new wife – curious, uncertain
in this place where people are

like frozen volcanoes.
I come from a vast warm land;

my family erupts
all the time, spectacularly.

Here I watch for underground signs,
stumbling about in a new language,
                    groping for new ways to live.

Sunday Lunch
the father
at the head
of the table
folds his hands
in prayer.

        Silence except
for the
clack clack
of his false teeth.
        The soup's
getting cold.

        His wife
and children
hate him.

Clock ticks
teeth clack
air tense
for the
last clack
that says
        Eat.

The Asylum Garden
The second son
in a leafless garden,
hair lank,
scarf correctly folded,
gloved hands
        loose.

Behind his pale eye,
quick intelligence
        grown cold.

It's Sunday –
Visiting Day.

An hour still
till he's free
to go
        inside.

Weekend Visit

Through a long weekend
of silent meals
they sit
father and second son
jaws working

Each on edge
for the other's madness

while she serves them
breakfast
morning tea
(with sweet biscuits)
lunch
afternoon tea
dinner
supper
(coffee
with cake)

She dreams secret violent dreams –
breaking each window, slamming
strong doors, hitching a ride
with the vagrant wind,
and never, ever, coming back

and feeds them
breakfast
morning tea
(with cake)
lunch
afternoon tea
dinner
coffee

supper
(coffee
with sweet biscuits)

Sanity
Their madness her prison.
Sanity her straightjacket.
She will not live
to a great age.

The Eldest Son
inherits the farm.
The madhouse claims
father and brother.

The married sister
goes to live by the sea.
The youngest brother
flees far to Australia.

Once the eldest son got away,
too, to Canada
but the low waters
and flat fields
pulled him home.

Three children
a worthy wife

a good life

His wistful dreams
of adventure, freedom
        divined only
by his quiet mother

Water
A farm by a winter sea
a wall to keep water out
winter fields, white bridge
to a welcoming house.

Who lives here across
the lonely water?
The married daughter.

The only daughter, big
hands like her father.

She grasps sanity with
these large hands, shaking
it hard by the hair.

Each week she takes
the children, crosses
the bridge, walks the two miles
to the pub on the promontory,

drinks lemonade, buys the kids
sweets, walks home, water
between her and the world.

When the Curtains Are Drawn
In this country of
quiet suicides
and display windows
I have walked past
row after
row after
row
of identical houses,
watching the same
TV show winking
down the street.

The uncurtained windows
say no madness here
no death here.
Try next door.

Next door too
lights ablaze
actors arranged
in armchairs

eyes fixed
to a blind blue
screen.

Upstairs
misery seeps
under curtains
through window sills
onto the streets
into clean gutters.

In the bar
refugees drink.
They drink
and drink
and drink
until all the lights
go out
all the TV sets
are stilled
and all the curtains
(finally) closed.

Anton got a job in Utrecht, in the veterinary faculty of the university. I was writing my MA on Dickens. At times I was working for a Dutch documentary filmmaker, making a film about fishermen working off the rough coast.

We found rental places, first in a satellite town near Utrecht where I played Dutch housewife, shopping every day in a heavy coat, mittens and woolly caps.

Next we found a run-down but magical cottage at the edge of a large lake, frozen over in winter.

Holland in Winter

We live in a house
by the lake.
From early to late
     on winter evenings
     I watch the skaters
          lean and stroke lean and stroke
          the rough ice.

Hiss and swish of skates.
     Hiss. Swish.
Lanterns slice the dark.

In a nearby pub
an expat Yank
     makes fancy cocktails
          in a chilly bar.

It was an isolated spot, and as Anton went off to work I was left alone with Dickens. He was pretty good company. But to go anywhere, I had to learn to ride a bike. This being Holland, where everyone including Queen Juliana gets around on a bike, the local kids did not believe that an adult could not ride. As they watched me wobbling to the butcher a mile down the road, they laughed at me openly, but with such good nature that I did not mind.

Once I got used to the bike, I loved the long flat road, pines on either side, the whistle of the wind, my cheeks red with cold, the triumph of returning with a kilo of sausages and cold meat.

* * *

1972. We found a flat in Utrecht. I liked being in the city and spent hours in the old junk and antique shops by the river. I did an intensive course in Dutch and finally understood that I had been using a dialect from his parents' village rather than High Dutch.

We made a few friends. My Dutch was learning to cope with more complex conversations. But the marriage was in trouble. Anton was drinking a lot in the late-night bars of Utrecht. Sometimes I drank along with him. It was better than being lonely at home. I was almost falling from my stool by midnight but he would drink on till three in the morning. I sat trapped and miserable with him. If I nagged, he drank more.

In the mornings I was struggled to wake him. Arriving at eleven or twelve for work was a common occcurrence. The university was very patient.

Conscientiously, we tried an open marriage, in the hope it would bring some air into our relationship. There was an attractive couple living in a beat-up but charming houseboat, both young doctors. Many spirited late-night conversations with them and increasingly more flirting. But nothing much happened.

Then there was H, a young cousin of Anton's. I liked her a lot. She was energetic, idealistic and a bit earnest in the way the Dutch could be. But loveable. She said she loved and respected both of us. We spent a lot of time with her, talking about Life. Then, would I be OK if she and Anton ...? It was the seventies. What could I say but yes, it would be OK.

The three of us agreed to be open; there was to be no hiding. I tried to hide my jealousy. I upped my flirtation with the doctor. But I liked his wife too much. In fact, in hindsight I might have preferred her to him. Dimly, I remember one fuck. That was it. He loved his wife too much and I understood why.

Our marriage ambled along in this uneasy way. There was desperation creeping into the fabric of things. I felt lost, the MA was going slowly and I had only a hazy idea of what to do next. We were both in limbo, in a country we liked but could not find a place in.

Then a stupendous event in Australia: Gough Whitlam came to power! The first Labor leader in almost thirty years. I was on a plane soon after. Anton followed later, overland.

Branching out: London, Paris, Bendigo

When you look back on your life, with its peaks and valleys and hidden places, you alight on a mountain for a while, glimpse some hidden half-remembered cove, but mostly you skim through vast stretches of your life-landscape hardly giving them much attention.

So it is as I write; whole years dismissed or swallowed up in a paragraph or page. Others not mentioned at all. This is the freedom which memoir gives. It frees you from the metronome discipline of autobiography. It better allows for the vagaries of memory, the disjunctions formed by the unconscious without any discernible sense. What you remember, and don't remember, is not under your control.

Another troubling conundrum is whether you actually remember correctly or through a veil of assumptions, self-protection or self-promotion. Or through many repetitions of a story which change the memory over time. Allowing for a degree of artistic licence – what would any writer do without that? – I try to tell the truth.

I have already done much swooping over time and place. In my twenties, the Push and my time in Holland caught my inner attention – personal mountains I wanted to write about. Now for a skim through some plains and valleys.

* * *

My three years as an undergraduate studying for an arts degree is a mist of hazy impressions and constant disappointments. I had found school such a straightjacket that I was raring to get to university. But even in school I had misgivings. I saw some copies of the university newspaper, *Honi Soit*, and was so disappointed that I wrote a letter to the editors, asking where was the serious thought and debate instead of the adolescent jousting that I was reading in *Honi*'s pages? They printed the letter and headed it 'Brickbats from an Alien'.

From the beginning I was disillusioned, alienated, bored. The Libertarian meetings in the Philosophy Room, next to the famed jacaranda tree, were the highlights of my week. The atmosphere in that room was the closest I could find to my dreams of Sartre, de Beauvoir and Camus in Paris.

Opting to study for a BA is what bright girls did if they had no aptitude for science or medicine. Few girls then were thinking about a career as a lawyer or engineer. An arts degree was better than going to teacher's college but after that things got very vague. Still lurking was the idea that you might get married and settle down after some 'interesting' job.

I went to lectures on and off, I drank coffee in the foyer of the theatre where the arty and theatrical types hung around. The very young Peter Carroll sat at my feet, perched on his suitcase in innocent admiration; a boy from the suburbs if ever there was one but transformed into brilliance when acting.

I was in the audience when Germaine Greer played Brecht's Mother Courage with ferocious dignity. I was a spear thrower in the bloodiest of Shakespeare plays, *Coriolanus*, in which the young John Bell electrified audiences. Opposite him, a young John Gaden played a convincing old man. (As Gaden said to me recently, 'I grew into my face as I got older.') That was their first play together; they are still acting in plays together, fifty-plus years later.

But of them all, it was Arthur Dignam who broke my heart each time I saw him on stage. He had a special vulnerability, a rare ability to portray human nuance. I knew that these student actors were talented but realised only later where that potential would lead them.

I could choose from some of these people when I proposed a production of Chekhov's *Three Sisters*, with myself directing. Peter Carroll was keen, as was the redoubtable Marie Darcy. I think Arthur was interested in a part. The whole venture was ridiculously ambitious; I had no experience and this was probably Chekhov's most difficult play. The idea collapsed after the second read-through. I scuttled away.

In these circles I met Bobbie Gledhill, with her bare feet and skimpy hippy dresses, trailing a guitar and gobbling up philosophy with her agile bowerbird mind. Sexy, waif-like, talented and an unapologetic show-off, Bobbie stood out, which was her aim. We became close. She could drop her flamboyant public persona with me. We held each other up as we drifted through various worlds – in the Philosophy Room, in a play with the university's drama society or singing Victorianas in the music hall tradition, often held at the redneck colleges like Paul's or Andrew's.

Bobbie was brilliant in the Victoriana setting but she also had strong competition from pianist Will Scarlett, the versatile and endearing Alan Walker and the slyly brilliant Paul Thom. Thom was having an affair with Germaine Greer around the time she was playing Mother Courage. A compact man, he came up to the top of her shoulder. They looked a little incongruous but he was one of the few people who matched her erudition, capacious mind and wit. He never matched her talent for attracting attention.

I drifted through the three years at university, occasionally excelling, mostly disengaged. Just passing exams. Even English, my old standby, hardly roused me; I was bored by Chaucer's Middle English, irritated by the Romantics. Only John Donne and the Metaphysical poets woke me up, and the poetry of nineteenth-century eccentric priest Gerard Manley Hopkins.

I recall only two memorable lecturers – I am ashamed to say that I don't remember their names. One, a dynamic English lecturer, awakened me to the genius of Dickens; the other, an elegant man who taught Ancient History, brought the Greeks and Egyptians to life for me. For them I tried to write brilliant essays. For the rest: hours in the stacks, taking copious notes I wouldn't read again, even before writing the essay; many more hours spent hanging around the foyer, drinking bad coffee, hoping that someone interesting might come through the door.

In the last year I became involved with some vet students and met Anton. The vets and the occasional engineer were refreshing in their uncomplicated energy, compared to the effete arts mob and the brash cynicism of the Push.

* * *

After he graduated, Anton moved to Bendigo in Victoria, posted there to repay the government for his university fees.

I took off to England. I had a BA and a year of coursework for an MA in English Literature. I could put off writing a thesis for a year or two. I still nursed a vague ambition to become a theatre director despite my dud attempt at the *Three Sisters*. I applied to drama schools in London. I did not get into the top school, the Royal Academy of Dramatic Art, but did get a place at the London Academy of Music and Dramatic Art, another respected establishment.

Much to my dismay I hated LAMDA and London. I also missed my Dutchman and Oz. I found London bleak and mean, its people closed, eerily polite. In a fit of snobbish pique, I would not go to see the guards at Buckingham Palace, or the Tower or other icons. I did trail through a couple of art galleries and saw too many eighteenth-century and Victorian pictures, which bored the shit out of me.

Call me stupid and immature, whatever. It was a bad time. My nine months at LAMDA are a great black hole in my memory. I remember not a single face of a student or teacher. I have no idea what I did there each day. I tried to fit into the place which I privately thought was both conventional and mediocre. And very English in the worst possible way: mindlessly traditional, and didactic without substance. My Australian accent broadened in defiance, as did my anti-authoritarian streak. I had a few clashes with the people in charge. They thought me a bolshy upstart from the colonies.

A revelation during my unhappy time in England was a short visit to France. My English relatives, part of our extended diaspora, had booked me into a hotel on the Right Bank, all bourgeois stuffiness. Huge maroon drapes cut out all available light. It wasn't a good start. But the next morning, when for the first time I sat in a Parisian café and observed the street life around me, it hit me: 'Aah! I'm a European!'

This kind of city stirred my pre-memory. Even though I was steeped in the novels and poetry of England, I was sensing that my real roots lay elsewhere. It was a clap of thunder, although it did not mature into anything meaningful until much later.

I went back to England to my bedsit, where I had all my clothes heaped on the bed on bitterly cold nights and the bathroom was two flights down, with its coin-operated water heater. The redeeming feature of my large but cheerless room was the two tall windows overlooking a heath-like common garden. It was an unexpectedly wild patch in the middle of the suburbs, which I found strangely consoling.

There were probably a thousand miserable girls like me in London. But there were more thousands making a good life and having fun. I did not deign to go to Earls Court, nicknamed Kangaroo Court, where I could meet hundreds of other Australians. I wanted the 'authentic' English experience.

In my room I cooked little messes on the gas ring, the recipes gleaned from a yellow-covered paperback called *Cooking in a Bedsitter*. It was a must for Australians living in England in the sixties and early seventies. My ingredients were stacked on a single shelf. I ate at a table where I could look out on the common garden. I never saw anyone walking in it.

The only contact I had with other residents were shifty glances as we passed each other on the way to the bathroom or loo. I often met an Australian woman on the stairs; she was maybe forty-five. It seemed a great age to me, in my early twenties. We would murmur a greeting and look away, both embarrassed. She was always dressed in a faded pink chenille dressing gown, clutching a yellowing wash-bag. She was a secretary in a big firm and had never got around to going home. She smelled of failure to me. Maybe she saw me as a younger version of herself who still had possibilities in life.

One incident tells of my fragile state of mind as the months wore on. There are heavy blanks on either side of this memory: I have no idea why I was having a drink in a London pub in the early afternoon on my own. Usually I drank only at night and have no recollection of having drinking buddies in London at all. But there I was with a scotch in front of me. A man came up and wanted to buy me another drink. He was pleasant looking, about ten years older than me, and not a bad conversationalist. We had a couple more drinks. No food. He offered to drive me home. Once in the car, he asked me to come back to his place.

OK, I said.

He had some sort of job in sales. His flat was ordinary; slightly untidy. We had another drink. Then he was pulling me towards the bed. Suddenly I woke up from my trance. I did not want this.

No! No! I said. NO! I have to go home!

He took no notice. He forced me down to the bed. He pinned my arms. I struggled. He was stronger.

Come on! Come on! Why did you come here? Relax!

He strengthened his grip. I started to cry. I beat my fists against his chest. He took no notice.

After it was over, he was apologetic. I'll drive you home, he said.

I'm sorry, he said repeatedly in the car. Can I make it up to you by taking you out again?

I did not speak and scrunched myself up against the door.

Back in my bedsit I was shaken but knew that I'd behaved foolishly. I tried to forget it. I had a couple of bruises; the violence had been minimal. He was really sorry.

What happened later was more curious. I began to think of him again a few days later. I could not get him out of my mind. I went back to the pub at the same kind of time, hoping to see him. I went back again twice more but never saw him.

Then I realised I was doing something mad, and stopped. I did not understand myself and never talked to anyone about it. I was ashamed, not so much of the rape but of my own inexplicable behaviour. Maybe it's simple enough; I was unhappy in London, marooned, inactive, lonely. So I whitewashed my rapist. He had roughed me up a bit and left me with a lifelong puzzlement at the workings of my own psycho-sexual being. Why did I try to seek him out again? Was it like a child who seeks comfort from the very father who has abused her?

It was the time before the seventies version of feminism. I thought myself a progressive, enlightened young woman. I had been close to such situations before and managed to get out of them, but I had walked into this one like a zombie.

It never occurred to me to report him to the police. Even now, I'm not sure what I would do. Maybe I was influenced by my time with the Push, its laissez-faire attitudes to sex. I did not think he was a habitual rapist or a dangerous man. But I also thought the law couldn't deal with the wide spectrum of sexual behaviour. The law doesn't allow for nuance.

* * *

About eight months into my time in London, a male acquaintance, almost friend, said to me, 'You don't have to stay the course, you know. You are so unhappy. Just go home.'

I nearly kissed him. It had not occurred to me to leave; it seemed too much like defeat. Now it seemed like common sense.

A few weeks later I was flying home to Anton. He met me at Melbourne airport and we drove straight to Bendigo, only stopping for a delicious hamburger with purple beetroot dripping down my chin. An Australian hamburger! Beetroot!

I was in bliss.

* * *

Bendigo was a sprawling country town with an impressive main street of grandiose Victorian buildings and many pubs left over from the goldrush era. We found lodgings in a motel-like place with a disused gold-digging rig out the back, and played husband and wife, awkwardly. Later we moved to a flat fashioned from a lovely old house, closer to the centre. Bay windows, a fireplace, creaking floorboards. We nested there more happily. New-found friends began to drop in.

Anton was busy with a brucellosis outbreak in Gippsland. I got a job at the local technical college, teaching night classes to young men who had already left school. 'Social Studies' in the mid-sixties in Bendigo meant whatever the teacher wanted it to mean. I wanted to challenge the kids and myself, so one term we read through *Hamlet*, treating it as a kind of whodunnit. Another term I decided to teach the basics of Marxism. I hardly knew more than they did but we stumbled through the two hours without getting bored. I might have converted one or two to see socialism in a better light, but my real claim to fame among these young men was in my nickname. They called me 'Tits Varga' or 'TV' for short. I heard later that they used to hang out the second-floor windows to get a better view of TV going past.

Night Café. Bendigo, 1963

Winter
The café near the evening college
closes at 8pm. Often
I am the only customer.

Grey roast lamb
grey-mottled gravy
grey-green beans.

He hovers near the door,
a tall skinny old man,
long flapping greatcoat.

As I leave, he unfurls
his coat like a flag,
waving his long skinny

penis at me – once, twice,
three times. Later he grows
bolder, stands at the window
waggling his thing
as I eat my lamb.

If the café owner sees him,
he never says.

Spring
Brings a menu change: Lamb Salad.
Bright beetroot stains yellow
lamb-fat. One pineapple ring,
two chunks of greenish tomato,
one ragged lettuce leaf.

He's at his usual post, waiting.
I've got used to him,
silly skinny old man.

Once he scuttles away,
I compose myself to teach
my young men: 'Turn to page 50,'

I say, 'What do you think Hamlet
means when he said to Laertes ...'

Summer
The nights grow longer,
the main street busier,
the lettuce fresher.

He stops coming.
I almost miss him,
my silly lonely old man.

I wonder now whether
the young men remember me
when the word 'Hamlet' washes up
on the shores of their later lives.

The locals viewed Anton and I with some suspicion: we were blow-ins. We found a few other misfits in town and spent long nights at Diamond Lil's, the only bar with any sophistication, serving cocktails mixed by the eponymous Lil. It stayed open until the witching hour of midnight (this was the mid-sixties) but if Lil was in a good mood, till 3am.

Diamond Lil

By day, she ran her empire,
'The Grand' – grand for its size,
longevity, its born to rule air –
with an invisible hand.

In the vestibule the red carpet
worn plush. In the room where
the Premier stayed, mahogany
gleamed, curtains red-gold.

No-one saw Lil during the day.
Only the night made her visible.
In her bar, open at 9pm, liquors in
fancy bottles, unknown wines.

At midnight Lil came to life.
Silver hair piled high, glitter through
her raiments – a squat pagan
goddess, lofty, in command.

In the small hours, after
the punters had drifted off,
Lil kicked off her heels, made
her cocktails with a freer hand.

The stayers, once bar flies
in Buenos Aires, Paris, Nairobi,
swapped heady tales of faraway.
Anton was at home, at ease

and Lil mixed her special drink
for me, Crème de Menthe on ice
with a swirl of fresh cream,
kept in a jug below the bar.

After Bendigo, we set up in Sydney in a rented one-storey terrace in Annandale. It was a temporary house before our journey to South America.

The house in Annandale had a lovely front room which we used as a mutual study, but vacated it for my friend Bobbie when she had her weekly tryst with the amiable and handsome Bill Bonney, a philosophy lecturer who was also in the Push. The affair had to be kept secret as Bill was married with two kids.

It was the time when Anton and I got married, in a strange affair that combined traditional wedding dress (for my mother) with an ex-minister spouting Bertrand Russell rather than God. Later that night, a big party in Dad's clothing factory where Push people mingled with my relatives.

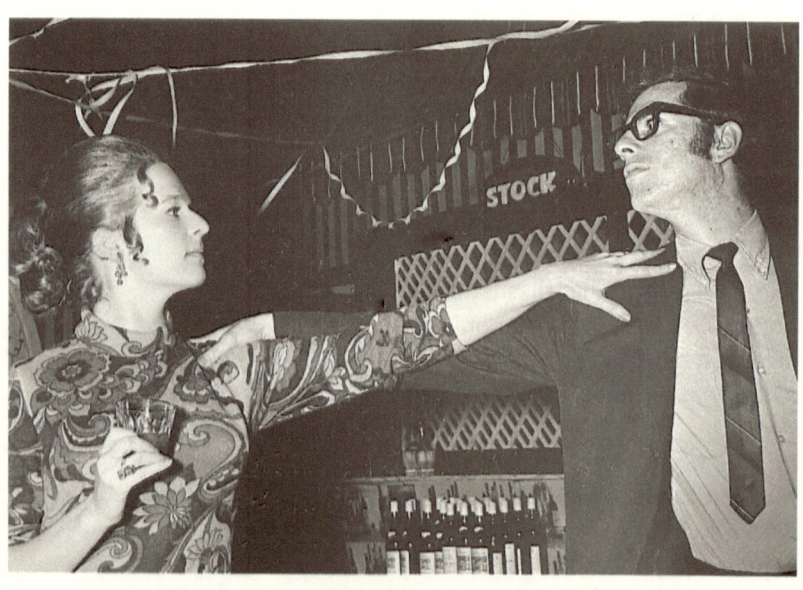

It was also a time when we both reconnected with the Push. Anton had a wary, if intrigued, relationship with the Push, too. He liked the anarchic elements and the heavy drinking but was put off by some pretensions and the exclusiveness. Roelof and he eyed each other off, knowing their mutual Dutch backgrounds but not wanting to acknowledge them.

Down the street in Annandale was George with his latest girlfriend. Noelle met him when she was still in school. He had a long-established taste for young and pretty women, and she was probably the youngest and prettiest of them all. She was seventeen, he would have been thirty-five. No-one thought anything of it in our circles but I identified with her and felt enormously protective of her.

I was twenty-four when she came to live with George in a red-brick flat. I thought she handled him better than I had but, still, she was unhappy. And very asthmatic. George often had to rush her to hospital. I wondered if the asthma had as much to do with the stress of living with George as anything else.

As far as I knew, Noelle was the only girlfriend George let near his mother. Maybe she insisted, which I never had the courage to do, but he introduced her to Rose and they sort of fell in love with each other. Noelle enjoyed Rose's fierce love and heated intimacies and endless food that poured out of her. Rose couldn't believe that this beautiful girl was so kind to her. Noelle was not Hungarian or Jewish but she was smart, kind and pretty and Rose still hoped, hopelessly, for a daughter in law.

Noelle became a sort of go-between for George and Rose. She encouraged him to be more patient but had only minor and temporary successes. Long after she and George split up, she remained close to Rose, listening to her endless complaints about George, looking at George's baby pictures, and hearing again Rose's tales of her lost life in Hungary.

When Rose died, George was intent on throttling his grief. Noelle argued with him about throwing out his mother's photos. When he insisted, she kept some of the photos herself. She honoured the old woman's memory as her son turned his back on her.

* * *

I spent time in France during my stint in London in 1963–64, and again while we were living in Holland in 1971–72. The first time, I took a job for a couple of weeks minding the amiable child of some Americans in a flat very close to the Tuileries Garden. We adults tried and failed to speak only French to each other. It was a benign, easy job. Every morning I tripped down five flights of stairs to fetch the croissants, a chore I never begrudged. But the stinking dark toilet of a bourgeois French apartment was a horrible by-product of the ancient French plumbing system.

My next job was with a French couple with two boys aged six and eight. The younger was called Hervé – I remember his name because he was so obstreperous. That job was a true immersion into French life; not a word of English passed this family's lips. I slept in a tiny room on a landing between stairs. Mornings I spent in French classes. I'd pass working-class cafés where older men, unshaven, untalkative, would down a couple of glasses of strong spirits before work. Afternoons I'd pick up the boys from school to play in one of those prim, over-trimmed parks the French love.

The boys were arrogant little shits. I didn't exist for them except as someone to whine and wheedle at to get their own way. Evenings I sat with the family in a cramped room off the kitchen and watched the daily baguette doled out. The boys sipped watered-down wine, while the parents and I downed a bottle of red.

They were formal and cold with me for the first six weeks. Then the wife's sister started to visit often. She was a more sophisticated woman, who worked in Dubai and spoke English. She liked me, and the *froideur* lifted a little. Then a bombshell: the sister was pregnant. She was over thirty with no stable relationship. It was a true family drama. From one day to the next I was transformed from an outsider to a family confidante. All the formality vanished. They were vivid, warm, alive. Even the little shits became more affectionate.

My three-month stay came to an end. They wanted me to stay on but for some reason I couldn't do it. Yet with another couple of months, my French would have stuck forever and my French employers would have been friends for life. I made the wrong choice, one of the handful I regret.

My next visit was also to mind a child for a month in the French countryside. During my year in Holland, I visited Paul Thom, then living in Paris with the remarkable and talented Sue Falk, who was studying singing. She was friendly with a family of Hungarian Jews who had lived in France since World War II. I was to mind their nine-month-old grandson so his mother and father could have a holiday. Their summer house was a dilapidated but charming old house outside the village. There were lovely lunches in the back garden. The old people were kind. It was the hazy golden summer that only France can produce. Languorous bees breaking the silence, a walk to the village to buy cherries or still-warm baguettes.

It was delicious, except that the child had constant diarrhoea. Having never minded a baby on my own, and never having changed a nappy, it was beyond horrible. I seemed to spend hours in a hot attic room changing and wiping, before starting all over again.

Still, as the weeks went past and the little boy got better, he started to coo at me. He was a happy, playful child and before I knew it he was holding up his arms to me and saying 'Maman'. I knew his parents were coming home and when it actually came to pass, he turned away from me and crowed with joy to see his real mother as she walked into the room. I will never forget the knife in my guts at that moment – the jealousy! The pain of impending separation. I had bonded to him in less than a month.

After that experience I thought, 'I will never become a mother'. It was a lesson to me how easily that bond could take over your life entirely. In my rational self I knew his mother was coming home but my body and my emotions were going in a totally different direction, as if he had become my child.

It seems to me now that those jobs were a try-out in the battle with myself as to whether I should have children or not. This question had been with me a long time already. As an adolescent I began to wonder about who I would be as an adult. Would I marry and have kids? Probably. Would I have some sort of career? Of course. I had some intelligence and possibly some talent, and I would make some contribution. Maybe as a writer, maybe as ... it was a bit blank after that.

It was also clear that putting marriage, motherhood and serious work together was going to be hard. I needed to forge more strength and new capabilities to pull it off. As a child of migrant parents anxious to secure my future, I felt the burden of their expectations, but I rebelled against them. I would not fit in with my predestined spot and marry a Jewish doctor or lawyer, treading water as a social worker or teacher before dropping out to have kids.

I never dreamed of having my own kids as some girls did. Kids were OK, but there was no nascent maternal pull. I also feared that I might turn out like my mother: fiercely protective, anxious, but a mother who could not truly enter a child's world. I would probably love them to death, smother them, and distort my own identity.

At the same time, I was growing warier of my own mother. She had endless love for her children – in theory. But in everyday life, she was moralistic, impatient and insensitive to our individual personalities. Even though we were the front and centre of her life, she was not a 'natural' mother. In another age she would have pursued a career.

My thoughts on motherhood roles were influenced by the other mothers who I experienced in smaller doses. My aunt Clara was the opposite in all ways from Mum. Quiet, introverted. She understood our separateness and left us alone. She chose to stay in the background of a child's life and pull strings invisibly. On weekends at her house, we were given more freedom; she seemed interested in our thoughts. She had patience. My sister Judy, especially in adolescence, fled my mother for Aunt Clara. It caused enormous tension in our family.

Edit was another mother figure, so different from mine. She was one of a handful of Christian women who had married Jewish men in Hungarian émigré circles. She was childless and felt the lack badly. When she was minding us, it was a blessing to both parties. She had an open, smiling face, hair braided around the crown of her head. She smelled delicious. She was plump and an enveloping lap was always available. Afternoons at her place in Strathfield were magical. Rum balls in the fridge, made just for us. We ran around almost naked under the sprinkler with a hot blue sky above and felt loved and wanted, a relaxation we never felt at home.

These different experiences of motherhood were swirling around in my mind. I hoped the conundrum would be resolved in time, once I was free from the constraints of North Shore life and had found the 'right' man for me. But at university, my confusion was complicated by contact with the Sydney Push. For them it was a badge of honour to not believe in romantic love and not plan for a stable future based on monogamy. Men and women were 'equal', but in those days just before the Pill took hold, it was the woman's responsibility to get rid of unwanted children. Mostly the men helped financially but there was no acknowledgement of any emotional aftermath. I was lucky at the beginning. The minute the Pill was available George took me to the Push doctor, Rocky Myers, who didn't ask questions. I was on the Pill at age nineteen.

In the years after, I don't remember exactly when, I had an abortion. Was I off contraception for a while? Again, I was lucky; I had only one abortion. Several Push women had serial abortions. I have almost suppressed the whole episode. A vague memory of the building, a hazy impression of the room, a counselling session lasting five minutes in which neither party was engaged. I wasn't even certain who the father was. I only knew that I was not ready to have a child. The rest is blanked out. It was a necessary duty done. Yet, if it wasn't traumatic, why do I hardly remember it?

I was at the tail-end of a generation of women for whom having an abortion was something to be faced quietly, with courage and common sense. A couple of days after the event you got on with your life as if it hadn't happened. Abortion was still illegal then and women often died in backyard operations.

Strangely, it was not talked about with others who'd had the same experience. It was a hangover from the time when it was a deep secret, veiled with shame. Most Push women only began to share their feelings in the women-only meetings in the aftermath of Women's Liberation.

Even as my thoughts about not having children became firmer, I never quite made up my mind. The question haunted me well into my late thirties, and only started to fade as it became too late biologically. Only then, and not coincidentally, did I begin to write.

Part 2
TUMULT

I do not think that the remembrance of things past can be done any longer with Marcel Proust's power and candidness. The society that he was describing was still stable, a nineteenth-century society. Proust's memory causes the past to reappear in all its detail, like a tableau vivant. Today, I get the sense that memory is much less sure of itself ... we can only pick up fragments of the past, disconnected traces, fleeting and almost ungraspable human destinies.

Patrick Modiano's Nobel Prize speech, 2014

I wondered if there was a word that coupled joy and sorrow.

John Hughes, *The Dogs*

Plunging in

Sometimes the confluence of the larger world and the individual self propels you forwards despite yourself. Gough Whitlam's ascension to power was a political and personal junction for me. Early in 1973 I was back in Sydney from Holland, after a three-year absence. When I got off the plane the very air seemed different. I felt as if a wand had been waved – let a new world begin.

I plunged in. There was so much going on: the Green Bans in Victoria Street; the Women's Movement; women's health centres; women's refuges; a new wave of feminist filmmaking.

In its first year alone the Whitlam government passed 203 bills, more legislation than any other federal government had passed in a year. Gough Whitlam reformed not only Australia's laws and institutions but the way the country saw itself.

I had given myself a long apprenticeship for life; I had been in no hurry to make major decisions, to take up 'a career' or 'settle down', and I had a few more years to decide whether I wanted a child or not. But now, approaching thirty, I knew I did not want to stand on the sidelines anymore. I wanted to act, to be instrumental in changing my society for the better.

Anton was returning, too, but by land, travelling through Asia for some months. Our future together was uncertain. I had the vague sense that my marriage might be over.

A few days after landing, I ran into a friend from Push circles, Jean Buckley. She told me that a Women's Movement meeting was scheduled the next day in the city. The organisers wanted to ban all men from attending, even as observers. As good Push girls, we both thought this was censorship and narrow thinking. Would I help her? Of course I would. We teamed up immediately to compose a leaflet voicing our views. Then we spoke passionately at the meeting. A few men, mostly gay, huddled in the back of the room. I don't think we won the argument. The separatists in the movement held a very strict line.

* * *

If I count the six months spent backpacking in South America, I had been away close on four years. Maybe those years had a strengthening effect on my character. I think I was more self-assembled; more parts of the jigsaw puzzle were falling into place. I surmise this from the swimming pool party I threw within weeks of coming back. I was still staying with my parents. I invited all sorts of people: several Push mates, my old schoolfriends Masha and Alison, my sister with whom I've always had a troubled relationship, and my mother and father. They were all there.

It was the kind of warm bright day that only Sydney can produce. My clashing worlds were mingling amiably beside my parents'

pool. There is a photo of Paddy McGuinness, at that stage still a Trotskyite, schmoozing with my father, talking about the economy, politics ... who knows? Sasha Soldatow was snapped lying by the pool looking positively Grecian. It seemed a propitious start but that momentary integration soon fell apart, burdened by events and personal downfalls in that era of change.

Within weeks of being back, I was installed in a Push house in Nimrod Street with Darcy Waters, and sometimes with Wendy Bacon when she was not with Roelof Smilde. On the top floor was the stylish and debonair Lyn Gain, who made a point of keeping up with the men by way of frequently changing her sexual partner. We lived in a rented terrace on a short sloping street, around the corner from the Stables Theatre. The house had a grotty kitchen, an almost acceptable though not clean bathroom. No living area that I can remember. I took a big room on the first floor. On the landing was a small room where Darcy lived, surrounded by a row of piss bottles which he used when he was too lazy to go down the stairs to the loo. They were the only decoration, apart from piles of clothing on the floor and general detritus. Lyn lived upstairs in her eyrie. Her principal lover at the time was a young man called Lance. He was pretty and almost as dashing as Lyn herself, but not destined to live a long life.

(Ah, I have just solved the mystery of the missing living room in that house, having just read a lively account of Lyn's Push life. Mervin Rutherford, the ex-cop turned playwright, lived there. Not that Merv was forgettable. I chatted with him at the pub. It's just an example of the vagaries and pitfalls of memory. In that sense a memoir is a random collection of memory, a bit like a bird nest, scraps and twigs collected from obscure places of the psyche. And a further correction; it was not Lance inhabiting Lyn's eyrie back then but Blake. Both men were beautiful, blond, tall, young and wild. To me, who hardly knew them, they were interchangeable. Blake turned into a life-long friend of Lyn's, whereas my memory of Lance is sadly true. He died young and not in good circumstances.)

Suddenly I was in the thick of the fight to save nearby Victoria Street in Kings Cross, a gracious street with mature plane trees and crumbling mansions and terraces. One evening in March, Arthur King came to the house on Nimrod Street. Like me, Arthur had been hanging around the Push for a long while and was a casual friend who had recently been a boyfriend of my schoolfriend Alison. He had lived in a flat in Victoria Street for years and became a leader in the fight against a huge development that would engulf the street. He wanted help from us, and maybe from the Push in general.

Behind the handsome old facades in Victoria Street, there was a warren of flats cascading down the hill to Woolloomooloo, inhabited by hundreds of low-rent tenants who had lived there for many years. It was one of the few remaining enclaves for poorer people, some on protected tenancies, in the inner city. There were eccentric and arty types, families, long-term bachelors and the simply poor who wanted to hang on to a tiny one-room flat. Most of them could not imagine a life in the outer western suburbs, where the developer wanted them to go. Many had already given in to the offers to move but a hardy group remained to fight it out.

The Green Bans originated from a small group of women in Hunters Hill who were determined to save a local park from unsympathetic development. To the amazement of all, the NSW Builders Labourers Federation, led by Jack Mundy, involved themselves in that fight. Arthur contacted the leadership. For us, having the BLF on board – a union with brain, muscle and money – was a huge boost to the stakes. Their involvement made the battle for Victoria Street winnable.

The residents of Victoria Street had a couple of other strong leaders. At the regular meetings, strategies were planned and dreams for public housing were voiced. The National Trust classified the street. The Push was attracted to the scenario. The issues were plain: keeping low-rent accommodation in the inner city, putting the brakes on greedy developers, preserving a beautiful street. Working-class people were being pushed out to make way for middle-class housing. It was clearly unjust.

The Push had held back from 'causes' but now was energised by the bold leadership of the Green Ban movement and by a younger female generation of the Push, women like Wendy, who were more attracted to activism. They dropped their previous stance of sitting on the sidelines, commenting only. Roelof Smilde threw himself into the fight, having held himself back for a long time. No-one was surprised when he became a level-headed and courageous leader. He was totally committed.

The leaders of both groups melded rather well. On the Push side, Roelof and Darcy, George and some younger Push, headed by Wendy; on the other side, Jack Mundy, Joe Owens, Bob Pringle and some of their fellow unionists. Both sides were forthright, politically educated and had a clear agenda. They were surprised by how much they liked each other.

There were other repercussions in this new political alliance. Some of the leading unionists embarked on affairs with Push women. These new pairings were just part of the heady mix. But the long-suffering BLF wives remained in the background; there was no mutual exchange in that way!

At the time both Roelof and Darcy were in love with Wendy. She was young and the first female 'star' in the Push since Germaine. She was torn between the two men. She would spend a couple of months with one and then the other. I was also part of this equation for a while – sometimes with Darcy, sometimes with Roelof.

It sounds strange but at the time no-one gave it a thought. All of us were embroiled in a savage fight for the street and our private lives were a mere backdrop to dramatic events. I saw Roelof more often than Darcy and developed a relationship with him but both of us knew it was temporary and provisional. Still, some long-term liking and respect grew between us, which we both drew on later.

It was clear that the developer Frank Theeman was going to play dirty from the start. He opened an office in the street and employed professional bouncers and thugs. He had underworld connections; Abe Saffron, an infamous underworld figure, was a friend.

Quite early in the piece something truly horrible happened. Arthur King, who first involved us and was prominent in the fight, disappeared on the night of 13 April 1973. We knew that Theeman's thugs had taken him – he left barefoot and in disarray. The next day Wendy and I went to the cops; in the evening we officially reported Arthur missing. It went against our anarchist grain to cooperate with state power, but a friend's life was in danger. The police building in Surry Hills was grim and our interviews were also grim.

Eventually Arthur was dumped from a car boot where he had lain trussed with no food or water for three days. Back at his flat and thoroughly terrified, he would only trust his best friend, Andre Frankovits, who didn't reveal anything to the rest of us or to the cops. This caused a rift in the Push and a reassessment of our strategies. The kidnapping was meant to frighten us off but all it did was steel our resolve. We tightened our own security; we went in twos everywhere.

With Arthur's disappearance we realised that the 'enemy' would stop at nothing. But who was the real enemy: the state, which had given the go-ahead to the redevelopment of the street, or the developer? Frank Theeman was no distant stranger to some of us. Roelof knew him from the world of first-class bridge; my dad (also an excellent bridge player) occasionally played with Theeman at the Double Bay bridge club. I used to know his daughter, a pretty, rounded, amiable girl. They lived in Bellevue Hill, not far from my parents.

Danger accelerated as the stakes grew higher. The squats in Victoria Street started after most of the tenants had left. The idea was to protect the few that remained and to stop Theeman's lieutenants, led by Joe Meissner, who was a body builder and Kings Cross 'identity', from trashing and setting fire to the buildings. An Aboriginal woman living on her own in one of the buildings died in a fire, adding to our sense of threat.

Wendy and Sasha Soldatow established a squat in one of the houses. Some younger members of the Push from the University of NSW, including Val Hodgson, squatted in the derelict buildings for months. Others, like me, were on a roster, squatting by night to support the residents when the developers' thugs roamed the street with batons and bars.

Eventually, the only remaining tenant who refused to move was a feisty seaman called Mick Fowler, who lived in a one-bed but spacious flat in the most beautiful building in the street. All the meetings now centred in his living room. He became the rough but charismatic emblem of the movement, a legend. His portrait is now on a prominent wall in Woolloomooloo.

These were times of real tension with six to twelve of us squatting on the floor in sleeping bags. A time of camaraderie, discomfort, grog, cigarettes and pot, but not too much of anything as we had to be aware and awake.

Victoria Street
Night falls on the street.
On the railings the clicking
of the goons' sticks
in a sinister rhythm.

They tread up and down the street,
a trail of hamburger and onion
a bass note of their journey.

Joe Meissner, their chief –
a menacing jollity towards us,
his goons in silent phalanx behind.

We start the night jolly too.
A joint, a shared bottle,
last night's skirmish made
less nasty in the retelling.

The hours wear down.
The quiet of a street dying,
its people fled.

The next crescendo of clicks
on metal fade to diminuendo
a tiny triangle
barely heard.

A high laugh
stops.

The old house groans,
whimpers,
impatient for its end.

Towards the end of this saga, something else happened beyond any-one's imagination. A woman called Juanita Nielsen, flamboyant with a lot of mascara and towering beehive hair, had lived in the street for a long time, publishing a local newspaper. She became involved in the fight, her paper advocating for the Green Bans. She was an unlikely ally but an effective one. She had a lot of contacts and plenty of chutzpah. Along with Mick, she goes down in Sydney's colourful history. One night she disappeared and was never found again, presumed murdered. No-one was ever charged. At the inquest Arthur finally told the story of his three days in the boot of a car and his violent kidnapping. The known criminal Fred Krahe was the main suspect, but he went to ground in England.

The nasty fight ended as a loss, but not a complete loss. The squatters were evicted by the police. In January 1974, the federal boss of the BLF, Norm Gallagher, the sworn enemy of the NSW branch, lifted the ban on the street. But the developer had to trim his new flats to two-thirds their original height and the street facade was mostly preserved.

Another good by-product: the Push women began to see that their bravery and initiative was equal to that of the men. That was a big step on the long road to enlightenment.

To this day I can't walk down that street without a shiver down my back.

In the meantime, I found myself a job, although I have no memory of how I got it, as a production assistant at the Commonwealth Film Unit, later named Film Australia. It was housed in a red-brick building and a couple of demountables, at the end of a long street in suburban Lindfield, amid a few acres of straggly bush.

It was an unlikely spot for creative filmmaking. It was staffed with an odd mixture of public servants left over from the 1950s, secretaries and administrative time-servers, along with several promising young filmmakers who would eventually make big careers for themselves: Tony Buckley became a well-known producer, Chris Noonan went on to make the film *Babe*. I ended up working for the most famous one, the young director Peter Weir.

In the first few months I seemed to spend most of my time roaming the corridors trying to cadge cigarettes and trailing, bemused, into the tearoom at 10.30 each morning, where everyone gathered, filmmakers and secretaries, to gossip and munch free biscuits. I was assigned to odd jobs, watched a lot of films and picked up a little knowledge. Then, out of the blue, I was assigned to Peter Weir as his assistant director for a documentary he was making called *Whatever Happened to Green Valley?* Green Valley was a 'model' housing estate on the outer edge of Sydney, beyond Liverpool. There had been a lot of stories in the media about its dysfunction, poverty and lack of infrastructure. The film tried to turn the sensationalist takes on the suburb inside out. Weir chose an unusual method. The first ten minutes was a mockumentary in which Peter himself played a portentous presenter à la Channel 9. Then it turned into an experimental film. The rest of the footage was handed over to five residents who lived in Green Valley – two kids and three adults. Rather than being talked about and commented on by outsiders, the concept was to give the residents themselves agency. Armed with a video camera and minimal training, each one made a ten-minute film about their own lives.

It was an exhilarating project to work on; we knew we were breaking new ground. I grew close to two of the local filmmakers, Frank and Joan. Frank was a widower, an extrovert, articulate, a single father with six kids crammed into a small Housing Commission house. It was the messiest house I had ever seen. Frank cooked and his eldest daughter did her best to run things. Despite the chaos, it was a happy household. The kids adored Frank and vice versa. He had a certain charisma and a cheery drive to keep the show on the road. He was also very interested in politics and the world around him.

Joan was a widow in a house a few streets away, with another brood of kids, more grown up than Frank's. Joan was prim, conventional, a strong Catholic and shrewd. Nothing defeated her. They made an unlikely pair but the bond between them was strong. Of the others involved in the project, young Scott, then about ten, soaked up the technology and the ideas avidly and later in life became a TV producer. My role was to help find the people and organise the production details.

I was totally unsuited to the production side of the job, having not a practical bone in my body. But it proved to be the first prolonged experience of finding a more confident or 'higher' self who took over from the everyday messy self. I organised time and equipment schedules, transport and so on. This unknown person, who could function well, came into my body. Unfortunately, she disappeared as soon as the job was over.

Living on the edge

After a few months in Kings Cross I was persuaded to buy a house. I still didn't have any resources of my own; as always, I had the backing of my parents. My younger cousin, Suzi, was deputised by the family to find me something. She was already married and settled. I was the black sheep.

We found a rather lovely old sandstone and brick house on a corner in Birchgrove, a small suburb adjoining Balmain. It had two attic rooms upstairs, one overlooking the semi-industrial harbour around Balmain, a couple of small rooms downstairs, and a large but basic kitchen.

There was a long nineteenth-century Australian cedar table in the kitchen. I begged the house's owner to sell it to me. In truth I was in love with the table, worn and patched, telling a thousand stories, more than the house itself.

I bought the house and the table. There wasn't much other furniture. A small TV perched on the end of the table. When Reggie (my first Push tenant) and I weren't watching it morosely over dinner, we were at our various pubs or, in my case, listening to Joni Mitchell or Leadbelly, Linda Ronstadt or Bonnie Raitt. The great blues singer Bessie Smith was my idol and still is. At a drunken Push party at 3am I stole a double album of hers. I never felt properly guilty. I believe it was my first and last theft. Apologies to the hosts from long ago.

In the Birchgrove house I was the landlady in name only. It was a kind of cooperative. We put ourselves on a makeshift roster for cooking and cleaning, and saved the house from actual filth. But my poor mother came one day, surveyed the household and the state of the kitchen, and left quickly, believing I had finally gone to the dogs.

It was not a genteel house; nothing elaborate. The fireplaces were simple, no fancy ceilings. Maybe a ship captain's house. In the front room there were canary-yellow curtains with a brown broad stripe around the edges, left by the former owners. No-one went in there, unless putting on a record. Everyone ate, talked, drank and quarrelled, around the long, battered cedar table in the centre of the house before weaving off to their lairs.

The best bedroom was upstairs. A view of the cove, rusty ships and small craft in the distance. I slept there for a few months. I remember the bed, the low window. There must have been a cupboard ... After my first lodger, Reggie, left, I took the two small rooms downstairs, nearer the bathroom, and fitted them out with narrow cupboards on either side of the fireplace.

In the other back room upstairs there was an array of tenants: Inez Baranay of the fresh complexion and bright curly hair who was to become a writer; Ross the nascent academic, impossibly handsome. When he moved out, he left behind a very pretty casserole dish that I still have. (Possibly the only reason I remember that he was there.) Later, a couple with a new baby; then Penny Tweedie, a well-known photographer, and her partner, Clive, who made video programs with Indigenous people in the Central Desert.

Sometimes Anton would arrive, usually drunk. By then we were semi-officially separated. We were friends still but quarrelled, too – both at sea, our futures unclear. Sometimes he passed out at my place and by 11 or 12 o'clock the next day I would try to wake him up, despairing at the foul hangover breath. We were still bound by countless threads.

But he was having an affair with a woman who was married and I was free floating, deliberately, for the first time in my life. 'Free floating' is a polite description … I was bobbing rudderless in a rough sea.

I arrive home from Green Valley.
A hot night. Change into a
long semi-transparent white shift.
Arrive at the local pub wearing it.

What the fuck am I doing?

A one-night stand with a man
I recognise from primary school
(cute and smart even then)
A week later, drunk, at 2am

I blunder into his house.
I find him in bed
with his wife.
I blunder out

What the fuck am I doing?

A decaying waterfront mansion.
A paunchy red-haired ex-soldier,
as lost as I am. A mattress with
unwashed sheets, nothing else.

What the fuck am I doing?

More one-night stands.
A shadowy charmer,
half his teeth missing.
Then a wild hard drinker

who fucks
to the verge of violence.
For a couple of weeks,
I imagine myself 'in love'.

What the fuck am I doing?

This unhinged marooned period went on for a few months. I imagined myself to be finally sexually free. In the mornings I'd wake up with a hangover and drive one and a half hours from Balmain to Green Valley in the far west, with a strained neck hurting like hell, and begin the day. At night I'd drive back and often land at the pub again.

Anton was leading the same kind of life, but jobless, usually in different pubs and drinking far more, more dangerously, than I was. One night he came to Birchgrove more than usually inebriated. We quarrelled badly. For the first time ever, he hit me, a single blow. He was a strong tall man. The blow knocked me over and I fell and gashed my head. He apologised immediately and drove me to Balmain Hospital.

I was not angry, nor scared. But during that drive to the hospital, I knew we had come to the end of our relationship. It was as simple as that. I think he knew it, too. We had driven each other too far. Better to break apart before the long downwards spiral.

* * *

For a while, there was an older lover, an ex-Communist, considerate, kind, devoted. He lasted only a few months. I took his taste in décor and clothes as a sign that we had no future together.

This shifting population came and went. Jean Buckley, whom I ran into just after I flew back from Holland, lived there briefly, too. Jean was gifted and beautiful, and drifted in and out of sanity. She was the daughter of Ken Buckley, academic and civil liberties crusader and owner of the Balmain back garden famous for its parties. Jean was one of the few children to follow a parent into the Push milieu. When she came to stay at my house, she was going through a period of mental instability. The household and other friends stayed with her in shifts to keep her from being admitted to an institution. That was the time in the seventies when we were all influenced by the books of Scottish psychiatrist R.G. Laing. Mental institutions were absolutely the last resort. We thought it was our social obligation to keep her in the community.

Jean was petite, graceful, almost sloe-eyed with olive skin inherited from her Greek mother. She never slept. She flitted from room to room at night, trailing diaphanous scarves, sometimes talking, mostly to herself, but mostly dancing. After a few weeks of staying up all night, with Jean's mania no better, it got too much for us. Her father came to take her away. She ended up back in hospital.

Jean got better and resumed her life. When well, she was brilliant and spirited. For years our lives crossed paths, sometimes close then not. She met and married a good, patient man and had a child. For a while life was good. But the marriage broke up. There were big custody battles. Her life was going steeply downhill. We were on the phone a lot.

A week before her death in 1994, Jean sent this letter to Anne Coombs, who was then researching her book on the Push. It gives a flavour of her intelligence and bravado.

> The Push gave me a 'tribe', and lifted the notion of 'family' to a plateau which was always accessible. The reality is always imperfect, but the sense of 'tribalism' (an inadequate word perhaps) endures. For that I will always be grateful – and proud ... As Frank Moorhouse once put it, 'Where the Fuckahoi!' He was drunk at the time. I was barely sixteen. We were all but fucking in the back of someone else's car, in a very long night which I thought (and hoped) would never end. And, in a very real sense, that night (and the journey it sent me out on) has never ended. For that much I owe my father.

We were on holiday in Greece when I heard the news of Jean's suicide.
In shock and grief, I wrote these poems.

Jean
Jean
  beauteous
  gifted
  flawed.
      Dead.

  You said to me
      'It's too hard
  a woman of fifty

a father rejecting
  a child taken
  a woman of fifty
      alone

Too hard'
                    you said

'Keep going
stay in life
    you'll win yet'
                    I said
lying in my teeth
wishing the agony
    over

knowing I couldn't
    wouldn't save you

I rang your friends
'She's always at it'
          they said

'always
    threatening'

You got up again
'I'll beat the odds yet'
        you said
    'Somehow, maybe
    if the job
    the money
    the lover
    something
    falls my way
      maybe
        life will turn its head
          towards me
     one last
time.'

'I've failed again'
     said the message
on the answering machine

I didn't call back.
    No failure
    this time Jean.

A triumph of courage
and grace.

This time a quick
    clean
decisive
    death by hanging.

The Funeral

A beautiful funeral
                    they said
for Jean

No-one lied
about how awful
she was
how wonderful
how unbearable.

'Is it possible'
Jean asked
'to recover from this?'
'this' her ruinous ruined life
Suddenly free of rage
          of spite
          or fear

answered herself
some days later
made a decision
made a hanging
made an end to protest
and to passion

hung herself
on a Sunday morning
for her mother to
come home to.

Revenge extracted
some say

I don't think so.

At the funeral
They read her poem,
then her daughter's,
played the right
music.

I wasn't there, Jean
I heard on the telephone
in another country
smelled across continents
that absolute darkness
knew why you fled
our guilts and impatience
our small helpings
and larger withdrawals
our shrugging shoulders
here she goes again
what can you do
       for Jean

took yourself away
left us clean, empty
relieved

with a picture
of you
hanging forever
in the inner room
of our house.

Six Weeks
it's got to be
six weeks at least?
since I thought of you
Jean

I thought of you
on a Greek island
after making love
seeing a red sun
on a calm sea
a white moon
after

strolling to
the restless town
to drink retsina
in the taverna
and then thinking
of you

Six weeks at least
It's getting longer
Jean

Sometimes your voice
rasps under the sea
or sputters in the wind

but not much else

Just give it
another six weeks
        on
six weeks
        on
six weeks

                on
six weeks
on

Enough of them
and
                you'll be gone

Eight Months On
Your image no longer
haloed in horror
eyes bulged
tongue splayed.

Grief and relief
receding
your death digested
filed.

Speedily greedily
we forget accept
dispatch you
to the land of legend
because, after all
Jean
suicide fits you
        like a glove

Perfect Afternoon
Months now, Jean
without you, and then
on a perfect afternoon
(always on the best days)
you ride my shoulder
rile me with the knowledge

that you left all this
deliberately
and with forethought

always on the best days
when I dare to be happy

The clematis hangs
from the bower
the smoke rises grey
from the valley
the light softens
moment by moment
into evening

It wasn't enough for you
such wonder
the promise of a moment
broken off from all others

How awesome, Jean, turning
your back on the temptations
            of tomorrow

Did you hope though
even as you hung that someone
might come
that there'd be
a crack in the door
an alarmed cry of love
and a tomorrow after all?

Falling off the cliff

After the Green Valley film was over, Peter Weir left Film Australia to make his first feature, *The Cars that Ate Paris*. He offered me a job, wanting me to be assistant director. It was going to be filmed in the country and for various reasons I said no. I was plotting with Frank and Joan for another initiative for Green Valley and was deep in the life of that community. But the main (pathetic) reason was that I didn't want to leave my boyfriend.

That was the era of another Peter, Peter the wharfie, the married Communist who used to tap at my window after his evening shift had finished at the Balmain wharves. Peter was a political player in the wharfies union. I met his older mentors and drinking partners, who were sweet to me but a little bemused by me as well. A boyish innocence clung around Peter. We peeked into each other's worlds and played with love for a while.

I knew Peter Weir was talented but had no idea that he would become an international name. It is one of those decisions you wonder about later – could your life have been quite different?

Even though it might have been foolish to not quit Sydney for this interesting job offer, staying in the city opened up something totally different. At the time, a Canadian documentary film series called 'Challenge for Change' was using film and video as a tool for social change. The Whitlam government was open to these ideas and made money available to set up four video centres, three in the western suburbs, in Blacktown, Fairfield and Parramatta, and one in the inner city, in Paddington. Additional funding was given by a new department called the Department of Urban and Regional Development, or DURD.

Green Valley wasn't included in the planned centres but it seemed to me and Frank that it should be, as we had already made video films and local interest was high. I threw myself into the campaign, assisted on the ground by Frank and Joan. We were in Whitlam's electorate, which was a huge help, and I knew the centre was winnable. We lobbied successfully in Canberra.

Whatever Happened to Green Valley? premiered at the Green Valley High School, and Gough was to 'cut the ribbon'. We had organised for him to announce the new video centre at the end of the film, but the announcement didn't come. I was furious – all those weeks of work to set it up! I stormed up to Whitlam after the ceremony, entirely forgetting that he was the Prime Minister, and demanded: 'Why didn't you announce the new video centre? It was all planned!'

Gough, flustered and contrite, said, 'I'm sorry, I didn't know I was meant to.'

This little scene highlights the excitement and euphoria of the times. With the first progressive government in Australia after so many years of conservative rule, suddenly people like me and Frank could access politicians in power. We felt we were part of the action, not just powerless bystanders. Margaret Whitlam was also a huge asset, a great supporter of the centre and totally approachable.

Not long after, the extra video centre was approved. I was the director, Joan was my assistant and we opened the Valley Video in the new community centre, in a big room facing the street.

Eventually I found a small room in the community centre where I could stay two nights a week. At night the centre was deserted apart from me. After a quick meal in the lone milk bar, I locked myself in. It was a long spooky night, like jail with no-one in it.

The centre had a few regulars, mostly boys in their teens, and a few housewives dabbling in this new medium. But the video centre never really took off. After a year we moved into Liverpool. I found premises near the railway station and as soon as we moved the centre there, it became much more active and lively. In Liverpool we could work with other projects and more easily access people in government. Frank, whose passion was community radio, set up the first community radio station in the Liverpool area from a booth he created in the centre.

The centre's main achievement in Liverpool was in bringing the Liverpool Women's Health Centre and a women's refuge into being. In Green Valley a few women had begun to meet at the centre to talk about a need for something similar. We met with activists from the city, notably the feminist Betty Pybus, who became involved. International Women's Year was coming up and the idea was to make a video which would be integral to the submission for funding. In the video, local women talked about how a health centre and a refuge would improve their lives immensely.

We modelled the women's health centre on the first one, in the inner suburb of Annandale. It was unheard of to ask for the same in the outer western suburbs. As to the refuge, it was inspired by 'Elsie', the first women's refuge in the inner city. It had been set up despite huge controversy but was proving successful from the start.

I had a good contact in the Housing Commission. She was a big supporter of the video centre and an old-style feminist before Women's Lib was born. Through her influence a house was seconded to us even before the funding came through. The house was in Bonnyrigg, so we called the refuge Bonny, later changed to Bonnie's.

A few years ago, when I was in my early seventies, I got a phone call from Moya Sawyer-Jones, who was researching the origins of Bonnie's for its fortieth anniversary. It was still in existence, the only women's refuge that had survived funding cuts and changes in ideologies.

'Oh! You are still alive!' she said, happy to have tracked me down.

'Only just,' I said.

I gave her the phone numbers of two other people involved in the early days, Christine Sykes and Dianne Powell. We were invited to the anniversary celebration and hailed as the 'founders' of Bonnie's.

Refuge

                    1

1975.
International Women's Year.
Whitlam's comet in brief trajectory.
A Government was listening!
We were young, or youngish.
We marched in the streets one day,
wrote submissions the next.

Hoped for funding,
found a house
and opened anyway.

We slept on the floor
and waited
for the first desperate women
to fall in the door, trailing kids.

A cup of tea.
A life story.

In the morning the kids played
in the dusty backyard, safe –
for now,

People gave blankets, sheets, chairs.
A sofa appeared.

2

Forty years later
Bonnie's is still here.
A bigger better house.
Other houses. Offices!
Paid staff.

This sole survivor
of the movement
                still needed –

In dark truth,
needed more than ever,
as men pickled
in resentment,
brined in hatred
continue to kill.

3

Today, a birthday bash.
Yellow balloons in the courtyard.
Yellow and black posters proclaiming
'You are NOT powerless!'

Swings and slides for the kids.
A row of suited men,
respectfully silent
in a sea of elated women,

On leaflets, brochures, lips,
an old phrase to gladden my heart –
'By Women, For Women'

4

I wonder
what really mattered then
– or now –
words or actions?

I always thought words –
they enshrine action,
pinning the butterfly
to the page, trapping action
beyond its brief life.

But looking back
across oceans of words,
expended, written, read,
I wonder –

Is it action,
its simplicity, courage,
rush and surge
which truly transforms?

Not books in their stillness,
shut fast upon shelves.

And yet ... a phrase,
a half-forgotten conversation,
a potent submission turns into
subterranean weapons,
torpedoes,
            depth charges
erupting into action,
            here, now!

We descend to the street
brandishing placards in bold –

'You are
NOT
Powerless!'

During the Birchgrove years I was drawn to people living on the edge. I was impressed by their daring, their flouting of convention and, above all, the edgy way they lived their lives. I was indulging my own dangerous streak by knowing them: a form of living vicariously. Maybe I was too conventional to live in the dangerous wilds they inhabited.

So while some of my friends were falling off the cliff, I clung on. I was tempted to journey with them but always drew back. I never knew whether I was a coward or it was simply self-preservation.

I used to watch the poet Vicki Viidikas when she came to party at the Birchgrove house. Vicki was a waif-like figure, always on the edge of some crisis or going through a drug withdrawal: often withdrawn and then a sudden burst of brilliance. Despite her chaotic life, she kept writing, brilliant poems and short stories. Her tragic death a few years later did not surprise anyone. The flame of her talent remains.

There were a lot of visitors to the Birchgrove house. Bobbie from university days was a frequent guest, with her baby (fathered by the actor Arthur Dignam), and the eccentric and brilliant Adrian Hebe, who lived nearby. Michael Thornhill, the filmmaker, dropped in often. Mike and I became very good friends. He had already made his iconic film, *The FJ Holden*, and was putting together his first feature film, *Between Wars*. He'd nabbed Corin Redgrave, of the famous English thespian family, as the star.

I was to do some research for the film. When filming began, I stayed on, working frantically with Mike in breaks between filming to change

lines in the script (written by Frank Moorhouse) which the actors found unworkable. Budgets for independent films were small so a lot of things were done ad hoc.

Work and friendship and ideology were all mixed up together in those times. Being a feminist led me to work with some of the talented women at the Filmmakers Co-op, where they were creating a new and exciting genre of film. I knew some of these women and worked on three films, all on tiny budgets. Often I worked for free.

Gill Burnett, Darcy's ex-girlfriend, then married to Ross Poole, was making a film and Robyn Nevin was in the starring role. One of my jobs was to drive Robyn from Rose Bay to the set, a small flat in the inner suburbs. Most of us were flying blind, including the director. One day I was responsible for making the lunch. I forgot the boiling eggs on the stove and they boiled dry. I was sacked on the spot – from a job that wasn't paying me! I still have a knack for boiling eggs dry.

Another feminist film I worked on was called *Home*, directed by Robyn Murphy, a student at the nascent Film and Television School at Ryde. It was about young girls sent to institutions, otherwise known as 'homes', in the fifties and sixties. While researching the film and looking for 'talent', I met a young woman called Beryl. She was about twenty-five and had been working as a prostitute. She talked openly about her life and the institutions she had passed through: Parramatta Girls Home and the notorious Hay Girls Home. The subject was serious and intense. A young woman that Beryl knew re-enacted an episode that Beryl herself had endured: her wrists manacled to the seat in the carriage of the train taking her to far-off Hay.

Beryl and I became friends. For a while she stayed in the Birchgrove house. She had a strong intelligence, a forthright manner and a wonderful bluesy singing voice. When she sang 'Bird on a Wire', the famous Leonard Cohen song, it was a 'shiver up the spine' experience. When she sang that song she owned the bird and the wire, too. 'Like a drunk in a midnight choir' seemed written for her, her anthem; a plea to an absent god.

Her voice was so good that she played with entering a talent quest. I encouraged her, thinking it could become a new career and free her from prostitution. I was backstage pumping courage into her; her self-esteem was almost zero. But nothing came of it.

Then we wrote a script together – now I think a very bad script – about her previous life. Again, I tried to change her image of herself as someone who was doomed, 'a low life'. When on a high, Beryl had soaring confidence with strong views and strong instincts. A couple of years into our friendship, she told me she was Aboriginal. This hadn't occurred to me but added to my understanding of her.

When I first met her, she was pretty and trim and dressing to suit her compact figure. She was living in a smart modern flat in Elizabeth Bay. During the good times, no-one was better company. She was defiant, sexy, funny. Our friendship was stormy, with periods of love and mutual support then tense breaks, irritations, reconciliations. The last time I saw her, maybe ten years later, she was living rough around the Cross. In the poems below I called her 'Janice'.

Life Story
When I first met you
Janice
pretty pert sexy
small-waisted
you'd been pro-ing
        in Kalgoorlie.
Such stories to
widen my eyes.

You told them well.

Next I met you
rising star
hooker with brain
you were wild & strong

& angry.
You blasted the night
            with your singing

Next I met you
first hospital phase –
first white gowns
shuffling feet
glazed eyes
Help me Suzie
my friend Suzie

Next (there were
many meetings) we
worked and wrote
and lived and partied
together.

I lived through you
You clung to me

I tried to carry you
            on my back
You tried to trample me
            underfoot

We scared each other

We fell down

We parted

But I still saw you
all the time
in hostels
hospitals
bedsits
messy rooms
hospital
      corridors
on streets
on benches
in gutters

I still see you
You won't die

I turn street corners
dreading the sight
      of you

I cross the street
in case the body
on the bench
      is you

I avert my eyes
from a staggering shape
in case it's
      you

I see you more
when I don't
see you

Meeting
Twice in six months
on the corners of the Cross
me with my shopping
you grogged and mussy
We look at each other sadly
accept whatever it is
that must be accepted

I know you'll no longer
ring me in the middle
of the night
You won't chase me
with the obscene woes
of your story
You won't harry me
to the limits
of your distress

I am relieved
and desolate

I am free
and I miss you

When you die
will I know?

When it's over
will it end?

After we stopped meeting, Beryl would still often ring at three in the morning, crazy drunk. I finally asked her to stop ringing and she did.

Not long after, I moved to the country. Occasionally I caught sight of Beryl around the Cross. Once she said to me, 'Suzie' (she was one of the few people allowed to call me that), 'you are the fairest person I've ever met.'

I have never forgotten that, but now it rings bittersweet. I think she meant that I was not judgemental. That I gave people a lot of rope. But I wasn't 'being fair'; I wanted to save her and bring out her talents. I was youngish and naïve. What if it was meddling, disguised as friendship? All I do know is that we loved each other deeply.

Beryl died about twenty-five years ago. She over-balanced on her sister's balcony, in the inner city, reaching for a cup of coffee. I heard too late to go to the funeral. I paid for the funeral expenses.

* * *

My sense of my life, of dates, the length of time, events, evaporates like quicksand. I see something very clearly – I might even have a photo – but am I placing it at the right time? For instance, was the swimming pool party thrown when I came back from Holland on a visit or was it later, when I came back for good?

I can't believe that tumultuous time, starting in 1973, covered just three to four years. The events in the Push house, then the house in Birchgrove, could make for an entire memoir on their own. There is so much more I could dredge up from that time, the most tumultuous and vivid years of my life, but I'm not inclined to do so. Someone else would have made a liveable life out of it but I made only a mess. The dissolution of my marriage, the half-arsed and random affairs, the drinking and parties, the parade of people living there, replaced by other people living there, the two jobs with the film unit, and then the journey with the video centres, the rise and fall of the Whitlam government ...

If this was another kind of memoir, I would describe in more detail the political and social contexts in which I was embroiled. I am amazed that with my personal life in such disarray, I functioned at all. But in my working life I was reasonably effective. I achieved more than I thought I could.

My job at the video centre in Green Valley and then at Liverpool was also coming to an end. I had begun sharing my salary with Joan. Now I thought it was time to withdraw and leave the centre in the hands of local people. That had always been the idea. I remained the chair of Western Access, the new umbrella organisation for the centres. I discovered that I was a good, facilitating chair and a good lobbyist in Canberra in the fight to keep the video centres alive and funded.

When the news of Whitlam's fall came in November 1975, I was in Blacktown, then the most outer western suburb, in a meeting with the other centre directors. As we worked, we stayed tuned in to the radio. We knew that something big was brewing in Canberra. Then it came. The PM sacked! By instinct I ran out of the room and rushed into the street, sure that the revolution was starting. But there was not a single person out on the street on that bright hot Sydney day. There was nothing I could do.

I went back to the meeting. Everyone sat, stunned. Our world had come to an end.

Surely the momentum created by the Labor government would not collapse just like that? The Western Access centres lived on for quite a while. Once I had handed the job over to Joan, I was based in central Sydney, one of a group trying to get our first ever community TV station off the ground. That would have been a logical extension to the Video Access movement.

Retreat

I left the Balmain peninsula to live in Elizabeth Bay in the east. I found a small flat to rent. It was a relief to be alone.

The shabby old building housed a magnificent lift, a creaky, multi-mirrored creature from the turn of the last century. My flat had a little study on a built-in veranda, looking out on one of the city's prettiest bays. It was handed down from a line of actresses and academics.

My dear friend Noelle was living down the street. For the first time, since my first dog died when I was eleven, I acquired another dog, Jolie, as in the French *jolie-laide*.

Paul Thom, from university days, turned up in my life again. From a one-night stand he turned into a part-time lover. He was witty always and fun. He also encouraged me to be less intellectually timid and to build up my self-worth. Neither of was expecting it to be lasting. For once it seemed an affair that was benign to both.

The child question came to the forefront. The clock was ticking. Maybe I would never find the 'right' man, so there might be other solutions. Roelof, I thought, would have good genes and liked children. I asked him, in theory, would he donate his sperm, no strings attached? He was surprised and pleased. He said he would take an interest in the child if I wanted him to. But just asking seemed to settle me. My desire was not strong enough; the fear of bringing up a child on my own won out. The moment died.

I continued as the chair of the Liverpool centre and joined the push for community video in the city. More lobbying, organising, looking for money. Then another job came up. Rod Freedman, a budding filmmaker, sought me out. Would I be interested in making a video series with him on youth unemployment? I said yes, so I was back in the Lindfield compound of Film Australia.

There was a huge problem with youth unemployment in the mid to late seventies, and a lot of demonisation of young people out of work, the full moral panic. We found kids who could talk about their difficulties in a tight job market so that viewers would begin to understand their situation. The resulting videos were shown to Rotary clubs, schools and influencers in government.

In some ways I was back in my element. Back in the outer suburbs, working at the edges, trying to shift society's attitudes for the better. It was mildly useful work. I was accumulating experience in various fields but I still had no direction and only vague thoughts about the future.

* * *

My memory jerks around like a mad marionette ...

My little dog Jolie is run over in front of my eyes. She runs out on the road as I am about to visit my parents. The neighbours I thought snooty turned into angels of helpfulness as I carried my dead small dog in my arms.

Now I live in a flat at the top of Bellevue Hill, ten minutes walk from my parents. I own it. Why am I no longer renting my pleasant little flat in Elizabeth Bay? End of lease? Or, again, parental pressure to own a property?

The new flat is fine but can't be loved. The main bedroom looks out over red roofs to a boring bit of sea; the large eat-in kitchen has the same view. The living room is dark and I choose some unfortunate over-full curtains with a pattern of elephants, which make the room gloomier still. In the second bedroom is Noelle. I am still working for Film Australia.

It is not an unhappy time, just a 'hanging in the breeze' time. Hitting thirty-two, I feel the child-or-no-child ambivalence again. I join an organisation which partners 'at risk' kids with adults for mentoring and friendship, with a view to fostering or adoption. Maybe I can do that. I feel indebted, with a need to give back to counter my own privileged life. I meet with a young girl twice a week for a few months but it is not a good match.

OK, I am trying to be honest: it was not a bad match. But I am ashamed of the reason it broke down. In many ways we were well matched – she was about fifteen, the child of professional, well-off parents, but the family was so dysfunctional that she left home for good. The girl and I liked each other. She was intelligent, articulate. I eventually told the organisers I was not ready to take on the responsibility. Partly true but, to my shame, the real reason was that her body odour was overwhelming. I could not cope, especially in the car. I thought it might have something to do with the life-threatening illness she was living with, so I did not have the courage to bring it up. And I backed away.

I am still ashamed. Shame has a lot to do with stupidity, when common sense collapses. A kind of panic took over. I was plunged into a vat of hot embarrassment impossible to climb out of. Guilt, on the other hand, is out in the open. You can name your guilt, but the things you are most ashamed of barely see the light of day or are never articulated in print.

I veer back to the biological option: having my own child without a man. It is not too late. This time I think of Anton, repartnered and living in New Zealand on a university appointment. We are on good terms and write letters. On impulse, I write to him. Would he donate his sperm? No strings attached? I see now I was still attached to him. It took a long time to break our bonds. Wisely, Anton said no.

* * *

A kind of breakthrough in my thoughts about the future came when I was co-organising a conference on community TV with my friend Bronwyn Barwell, the director of Paddington Access Centre. My uncle died unexpectedly; a huge blow. My parents were overseas. The two families had always been close. My aunt and cousin were beset by grief. I was frantic with worry. 'Go and look after them,' Bronwyn said, 'I'll manage.'

I dropped the conference role and did what needed to be done. Once more a 'higher self' took over who made all the arrangements for the funeral, tracked down my parents somewhere in Europe, cooked for the whole family, conferred and counselled. The funeral over, my parents back, this well-functioning, efficient person vanished. Damn! Why could I not be like that every day of the week, always?

Somehow the family crisis acted as a circuit breaker. I decided that I needed to do something entirely different; something that might actually lead to a conventional, lasting career. One of my wider circle, Wendy Bacon, still a high-profile activist, got herself into law school. This was a major break away from the non-careerism advocated by the Push. Somehow it gave me permission, too. I had no real desire to be a lawyer but I thought it would be good for me to do something 'hard' and pursue it to the end. Some of my skills might fit. Maybe I would fall in love with the law.

In retrospect that was also my last unconscious stratagem to avoid being a writer. For so long I had stifled any thought of writing. I did not burn with any great idea for a novel. I wrote scraps and stopped, dismayed. They were second rate, borrowed, without an individual voice. As formless as myself.

* * *

I fear I will short-change you in writing about the next part my life. This section is not called 'retreat' for nothing. There is a period of more than nine years taken up by a long relationship which I find too hard to write about properly; so many road blocks. My heart starts to race and I can't bring those years into focus. After forty years, I still have not dealt with them.

I was around thirty-three, still working at Film Australia before starting at law school, when I met 'Rick' (not his real name) at a party in Balmain. Rick was a well-formed man, with a tinge of olive in his skin and greenish eyes. He looked good in a three-piece suit. He spoke with confidence, a perpetual undertow of irony in his rather attractive American accent.

Within the first half-hour our hands met. From then on, we could not avoid touching each other, lightly, delicately, the whole evening. We had a 'pash' in the car, like teenagers. I did not ask him in.

He rang five days later. Quickly we became lovers and settled into a serious relationship. Around the third date he introduced me to his child, then around three years old. The first meeting I remember as vividly as if it was today. Rick had some kind of ute and Sam was already asleep in the front seat. Rick handed him to me with a look of adoration on his face as if I was being handed the baby Jesus. Sam was a very pretty child with golden hair and light olive skin. I was immediately in love.

I was a plum ripe for the picking. On the surface this man seemed fine: good-looking, a quick mind, a few years older and the parent of an adorable child, and not averse to having another. The sexual attraction was strong – unusual for me and a lure to thinking one is in love. Rick, in his own way, was also looking for a berth, some stability.

But the currents underneath us were more telling: a last chance to have a settled relationship, a last chance to have a baby. Such was my desire to nurture this new love that I asked Noelle to move from the Bellevue Hill flat so Rick and I could have more privacy. So much for sisterhood, and even for friendship. The old paradigm of the supremacy of male–female coupling took over; I put my new lover ahead of my best friend. Looking for ballast not from within, but from someone else.

I fell pregnant, happily, early in the piece. Two months later I lost the child. An exchange at the hospital is burned into my memory. Not unkindly yet without thought, the nurse said, 'Did you really want this child, dear?'

I said nothing. I couldn't believe what I had just heard.

For months I woke up crying in the middle of the night. Secretly I mourned that lost baby for years.

I never tried to get pregnant again. If the subject was brought up, I would say that if a woman truly wants a child she will have one, no matter what. It's not the same for me. Besides, I had quickly fallen in love with his child. So I did have a child in my life; the circumstances were not ideal, but maybe it was my lot.

A few months later we moved into a big house a little further down the same street. It had been owned by Judy Cassab, the artist. She and her husband, John Kampfner, were friends of my parents and part of the Hungarian diaspora. Judy had quickly made a name in the Anglo art world. When I saw her house, she already had a buyer. I liked it a lot and exclaimed over the big black and green Art Deco bathroom upstairs. A gem, in good condition.

'You would not knock it out?' Judy asked.

'Of course not. I love it!'

'Then it's yours if you want it.'

The buyer who had wanted to be rid of the bathroom was sent packing. Judy lost a bit of money but the bathroom was saved.

The house was built on a steep block with a terrace garden out front. We painted the grey stucco pink. Under the windows, wooden shingles, a fashion from the twenties and thirties. It was a capacious house but not unmanageable. The two extra bedrooms had been made into a separate flat on the upper level.

My one brush with pop culture fame came when Daryl Braithwaite became my tenant in the upstairs flat, with his girlfriend, Sarah. Daryl was quiet, easy to be with. Sarah, a private school girl, had lovely manners and a quick mind.

This was the end of the seventies. At a party at their place I saw my first and only line of cocaine. After one snort, I thought, 'No ... not for me. Eating and drinking and some pot will do.' I was aware of my addictive tendencies.

In the new house Rick and I settled into a lop-sided routine: Sam lived with us half the time, half the time with his mother. Sam was growing, Rick was working, I was at uni, studying law. This would be my settled future: a new man, half a child, a new career in the offing. This was the package I sold myself.

The man I fell in love with was complex and slippery; he would affect an urbane manner, he could expound on any subject with learning and sometimes with wit, yet with a trace of contempt. There was something cat-like about him, more panther than lion, as he padded around the house. His hair was silky, his skin smooth. An underlying menace in his demeanour.

After the first year, when I sensed an implacable, unreachable wall around him, I wrote him a letter, wanting more honest intimacy between us. I got one small note back: 'I love and I hate and I don't know why.' This was a version of a quote from Ovid: 'I hate, and yet must love the thing I hate.' That's all I ever got about his feelings.

I heard many stories, often conflicting ones: of his past life in America (the locale sometimes changed to Canada), of a marriage with a Hawaiian-Japanese wife and two children, who never materialised. He also maintained that he was Jewish. When talk of marriage came up, the necessary paperwork to prove him a Jew never materialised either. We dropped the idea; it had become too embarrassing.

For a while he worked in a specialised field of fibre optics. He gave me the impression that he was the first in that field. I found out he was nothing of the kind. And so it went on. About four years into the relationship I realised that I could not believe anything he said.

He told stories about a neglectful and cruel father. As his own son grew into adolescence, he nagged and demeaned him constantly. He had adored Sam as a child. He now showed a mean and competitive side. He continually criticised and undermined the boy with cruel sarcasm.

He smoked a lot of dope, though many people did at the time. In some ways I can't fault his domestic behaviour; he washed up, took out the garbage. The routines of domestic life were all in place – we ate together, watched TV – but he was not there. When things were bad between us, he went into the next room, locked the door and read till three or four in the morning. I sensed his loneliness and isolation but found there was no way in. The mystery and absence eventually became a farce, and I could not believe it anymore.

What can I say except that it was a disaster – a nine-year disaster. I chose someone wrong entirely. We rarely quarrelled, only the occasional nasty flare-up. Neither of us wanted to rock our flimsy craft. But year after year I squashed the realisation that there would never ever be a meeting of souls or minds. No refuge or nourishment, just constant depletion.

* * *

I took refuge in my studying of law, its routines a relief from the wearisome life at home. I found the law a strange beast, almost exotic. It is a self-enclosed system with its own logic, a logic barely related to the outside world, nor to the logic you learn in a philosophy course. In my first year I fought this strange beast with my old weapons. My first essay was for Torts; I wrote an analysis of Dickens's *Bleak House*. I got away with it, and with a distinction.

But soon I began to understand that the only way I could get through this was to study methodically – for the first time in my life. I set up a study on the built-in veranda of the house and called my dog, Tessie, who 'worked' with me every morning when I wasn't at uni, often on case notes, each with its own card. Tessie loved the routine. In a way, it also saved me. The order, the sense of purpose and the company of my beloved dog. When I finally graduated Tessie would look at me: 'When are we going to our room?' It took her weeks to get the idea that it was over.

I got through all the 'black letter law' subjects which I forgot the minute the exams were over. My real interest was sparked by the electives: a pioneering course on Aboriginal Law run by Garth Nettheim, another in International Human Rights Law. These courses were much closer to my long-term interest in ethics and justice. I also liked Criminal Law because of the sheer interest and drama of lives gone wrong.

But clearly it was going to be hard for me to find a place in the law world. I staggered the four-year course over six years to minimise the stress of it. Maybe I did not want it to end. What the hell would I do after it had finished? The real challenge was to finish – a real degree, fought for, not doodled through as with the arts degree and the indulgence of the MA on Dickens, which had kept me going for years in Holland.

The students were mostly young men, with a good sprinkling of young women, just out of school. I was one of a handful of mature-age students. A mixed bunch. There was one ex-cop and other career-changers. I made some friendships.

My enduring bad memory was a signal of the times. Whenever a lecturer would venture ideas not related to statutes and black letter law, the young students would put down their pens and stare out the window. That's exactly when I started to wake up. I thirsted for the rationale and the ideas which backed up the law. I felt dismay and despair at the lack of interest of the young. In retrospect this lot of young people were going through an economic downturn whereas I had been in that golden generation with a welcoming job market. We could afford to dream and think.

* * *

Why did I stay with Rick for as long as I did? There were two stabilising and compelling factors. The first was the goal of completing the law degree. The other was my role in my stepson's life, ambiguous as it was. Sam's mother and I were wary of each other, and my view of her was distorted by my relationship with Rick. I knew that I should not play mother as Sam already had one. I was a kind of aunt, friend, mentor. My parents loved him – he was the closest thing they would ever have to a grandchild. The little chap would make things easier at family lunches on Sundays when he would splash in the pool and yell 'Look at me! Look at me!' over and over.

My parents did not like Rick but never said so in words. Most weekends we walked down to their place for lunch. With them he was usually urbane, polite. But there was an emptiness behind his pronouncements which we hid with family chat and watching young Sam playing in the pool.

Rick always ate well. When my mother plied him with more, without fail he would say 'Why not?' and hold out his plate with a Cheshire cat's grin. Years later, my parents told me that they hated that inevitable phrase, 'Why not?'

Sometimes the tensions would break the surface. I remember, with shame, once lashing out at Sam when I was at the end of my tether and he kept nagging me about something. We were in the black and green bathroom. I yelled at him and my nails raked his skin.

His alarmed mother rang me. Usually we kept a politic distance from each other. Much later, long after I broke up with Rick, she and I developed a real friendship. These days we love and respect each other.

As Sam grew from a beautiful, winsome child into a fledgling adult, trouble was brewing. His father loathed having his dominion and authority questioned. I tried to stand between them, to mollify

Rick and support the child. I didn't want to leave the child with Rick; I loved him. But I could not hide the growing bleakness. I'd finished my law degree. Now what?

It was many years into the relationship with Rick when I picked up the phone to hear Roelof on the line. I was taken aback – we had not been in touch for a long time. The Push was going through a period of decline. Victoria Street had been the apotheosis. Roelof had married – another bulwark of the Push belief system fallen – and had fathered two girls. He and I had never exchanged pleasantries. Now I could hear the strain in his voice. So straightaway I said, 'Roelof, what's wrong?'

He cleared his throat. 'Well ... I know you were always interested in children,' he said. 'Sue has left me. She's left the kids here with me. Umm ... would you be interested in coming to live with us?' And unsaid but clear, 'and take up a role with the kids?'

Not a romantic proposal, not even a proposal. But I understood where he was coming from. I was equally direct. 'I'm still with Rick,' I said, 'and there's a child here I need to be with. It wouldn't work. Besides, you're a bit too old.' (He was thirteen years older than me. Later I was embarrassed by this frank reply when I fell in love with someone thirteen years younger than me.)

He replied, 'Oh! OK ...' He was crestfallen.

We met a couple of times after that but we both knew it was a stab in the dark resulting from his panic about being left with two young children. As much as I admired and liked Roelof, it would be the same template – an older, more 'rational', charismatic man, his own emotional life locked up beyond reach.

Passing Time
Lectures, exams, study,
study, study.

Walk dog.
Cook meals.

Gee, I have a degree!
I can be a lawyer.

The child is growing up –
almost ten years

gone, gone, gone,
gone

One day I wake up,
rub the sleep from

my eyes and admit
that this false

life must end.

One morning I came downstairs, tired and listless. The Hungarian
cleaning lady was there. For years she came all the way from
Blacktown once a week, part of a tradition of Hungarian cleaning
ladies catching the train in from the outer suburbs and beyond to
clean for the Hungarian Jewish women of Bellevue Hill and Double
Bay. She had watched me silently all those years with Rick. E and I
knew each other well; we were close in our own way.

That morning I was not up to my usual chat. Suddenly she said to me,
'Why don't you leave him?'

I stared at her. 'I think I still love him.' The words sounded empty.

She said, 'I can't leave J (her husband, a boor who drank) and the kids. I have to stay. But you can leave.'

A neat summation of the class difference between us.

'Where would I go? And what about Sam?'

'He will be OK. You can go to your parents.'

Of course. They were just down the street. I left the next day.

After I left, I knew only three things: I could breathe again. I would never enter a heterosexual relationship again as I was so bad at it. Either I would live the rest of my life alone, although surrounded by some good friends, or possibly, just possibly, a woman I could live with in harmony might come my way.

When I left, Sam ran away a day later. He left a note which I have kept:

> Dear Sue
>
> I am not going home tonight because Rick told me it was my fault that you were leaving. I love you very much so please come home.
>
> Love xxx
>
> Sam

Rick found him a couple of days later at Bondi and brought him back to a house without me.

I lived with my parents for a few months. I tried to see Sam as much as possible. Eventually his father sent him to a boarding school. He was punishing both of us, I thought. He deprived me of the child I loved. And Sam was in exile, confused and hating the rigours of an all-boys boarding school.

It was an uneasy time, full of loss. After a while, Rick left the house. We made a financial agreement. I went back and shared the house with my friend Jane Harders. I felt like a survivor after the maelstrom: relieved, tired and happy to be alive.

I had graduated in 1986. Now I took on a job as a trial solicitor on a very long and unusual trial in Penrith. No-one knew my personal situation, not even my barrister, who I sat next to for months and months, yet Adrian and I developed a deep bond.

When I left, I was in my early forties and still trying to find a life I wanted to live. There is not much more to say except that the power of self-delusion can last as long as you want it to. Looking back, I am opaque to myself. I had been looking for a peaceful valley after the peaks and jagged edges of my Birchgrove life. But the valley I found proved to be a valley of snakes. And the peace was a false peace.

But nothing is ever wasted. The small boy I fell in love with as he slept in my lap the first time I met him is now in his forties and our bond remains strong. The law degree, even though I hardly put it to use, showed me I did have discipline and application, which helped me when I started writing. As for Rick, perhaps my long sojourn with him was my final growing up: to see the shackles I made for myself and, in throwing them off, to find what I truly valued.

Entr'acte

I notice I have written a great deal about the men in my life – not my intention at all! But inevitable when I think about it; the years between seventeen and forty-two were taken up with men, as boyfriends, lovers, mentors. The mystery and puzzle of them, their often baleful influence, the huge space they took up in the wider world. Most of my female friends were similarly preoccupied so it did not seem strange. It seemed the way it was. For me the field was littered with failure, most of which I blamed on myself.

When Women's Liberation got started I was happy and relieved. It was welcome but not new in my thinking. I never wanted to become a homemaker and conventional wife. I was already liberated, could stand on my own two feet. And one day I would find the 'right man'. That fatal last phrase was the flaw. I never really questioned my own deep-seated assumptions about men's and women's roles. I did not pay enough attention to the groundbreaking nature of the Women's Movement. I was only making a show of standing up for myself.

A few years after the breakup with Rick, when my life had changed radically, I wrote a sequence of poems about the major loves of my life.

In my long relationship with Anton we always met as equals. If anything, I had the intellectual edge. He was not sexist. It was not in his nature. Ironically, that was a kind of disadvantage. Unconsciously, I still thought that the man should have the superior intellect.

Three Loves
1.   *The Ex*
Big blond white-skinned
        already balding
a shambling sparkling intelligence
a curve of the arm
        (the only tanned part of him)
the head turned to one side
quizzical, quizzing
a fierce constant quenched
                        rebellion.
A strange tight European
kind of man.

        Courtship
Two scared little sparrows
who would be peacocks
huddling together.
Hovering at the edges
        pecking in the dust
pecking at each other
first gently then fiercely.

Where safety?
Where freedom?

        Together and Apart
In the days just before open marriage
and copious free sex
we lived together
half heartedly
in Bendigo, South America, Balmain
Holland, Annandale, in limbo, in pubs.
Fighting down curving streets
promising each other better times
freer times, more loving times.
Promising each other

till we parted, promises
    still on our lips.

    For me
only one Ex.
Many lovers, bogeymen
    friends
        some short sweet disasters
        a long ordeal. A jostle of
        sweet-sour memory
        but only one true
                Ex.

2.   *And one true nightmare*
Such a long bad dream
sleepwalking the years away,
such strain pretending happiness
to myself (and others)
smiling for my own benefit
speaking words of love
in a continuous and necessary
                      mantra.
    Willing a marriage, marrying wills
    forcing the fit, repairing leaks, damming dykes
        The slog of it!
And then nine years on
I woke up
on a morning somehow different

washed my face in cold water
gouged the sleep from my eyes
and walked away.

3.   *Some Years Passed*
I cleared the horizon
tasted solitude
breathed long and deep

and saw riding towards me
on a white charger
a Princess

my elegant blue-stockinged, riding-booted Princess
of a thousand daily acts of love
my widely practical, deeply romantic
heart's companion.

When I first saw my Princess
I confess I did not recognise her
my eyes so habituated to error
my ears so dulled
my soul disused.

  Further Miracles
occur from time to time
when the Princess wishes
(or occasionally of their own accord)
A fountain turns itself on
a smile escapes its prison
poems beckon around corners
and even the evening TV news
yields a drop of pleasure
when watched together.

Part 3
LANDFALL

I *really love writing*. I mean, I love a pen and paper. I love words and sentences, and the way you can knit them together and shift them around and pile them up and spread them out. I love the way that the raw material of an ordinary day doesn't start to reveal its deeper meaning until you've got the pen in your hand and you are halfway down the page ...

You have to believe, against the scornful trumpeting of your intellect, in the miraculous ability of form to create itself out of chaos. You have to hold the line through all the wretched days, months, even years that you spend *not* writing ... You have to believe that you're preparing the ground for something to manifest out of the darkness, to present itself, to be born.

Helen Garner, 'The invisible arrow'

The Ocean
At sixteen I wrote
"I think I'm flat
and that one day
I'll fall over
the edge of myself."

I laid down my pen.

I feared the sea
as once the mariners feared it.

They sailed on.
I was silent.

I watched the ocean -
unruly
dangerous.

I watched and walked.
I walked around, about,
besides, over, by
myself.
There was no edge.

I did not fall.

The ocean curved –
endless
marvellous

wave-words, salt-new
leaped from my tongue.

I picked up my pen.

Susan Varga

Jumping fences

If I live to be eighty, eighty-five, the first half of my life would have been blessed with good fortune. There was the rough start in Hungary but after arriving in Australia, no major tragedies, a lot of freedom, a life with few external impediments. Yet I was still thrashing about, directionless, often unhappy. Then, at forty-five, the two great hopes of my life finally fell into place. I started to write and I found love that I could believe in. Not before time my life was beginning to cohere. Yet my luck ran out in other ways. Tragedy and hardship were waiting for me but I became stronger to meet them.

Towards the end of 1989, I met and fell in love with Anne.

At Christmas that year I was staying with friends in Paterson, a lovely small town in the Hunter Valley. My hosts were Edith, a woman with whom I had a short affair while working at the video centre in Green Valley, and her partner, Robyn. Edith and I had remained friends. I was also friendly with Robyn, who had worked in the Health Department at Liverpool. Both had retired from the public service and they ran a bookshop in Maitland.

They often talked about a woman called Anne Coombs who lived near them. They thought I would like her.

On Boxing Day this 'Anne' dropped in. She was tall with long, long legs, longish reddish hair, and naturally elegant in a coltish way.

Her manner was forthright, almost tactless. I had never met anyone like her.

Anne, at thirty-two, was already a well-known journalist. After university, she started work at the *Newcastle Herald* before moving to the *Sydney Morning Herald*. She had been deputy editor of the *Good Weekend* and had already written a book about Mojo, a high-flying ad company made famous by its clever and still-loved jingles. We discussed her troubles with publishing the book *Adland*; the publishers were running scared that they would be sued by the main people portrayed in it.

In my city-centric life, that combination – a young woman living in Maitland, a smallish country town, and having an impressive career – was inconceivable. I was intrigued.

Anne's first impression of me was that I was an interesting older woman, an efficient and experienced barrister. If only. Neither of us had any idea of the other. She said she would contact me the next time she came to Sydney. She rang three weeks later, proposing we see a play together.

I knew that it was a date. She swears she did not. The play was at the Opera House, Strindberg's *Miss Julie*. On the way there, to my horror, I saw my parents coming towards us. Could they tell I was on a date with a woman? I wouldn't put it past my mother. Her instincts were acute. I introduced them. Nothing happened. We went in different directions.

During the play I felt a tingling awareness of the person sitting beside me. Anne and I had been more or less set up. My friends knew of her unhappy relationship with a woman, while she was still living with the man she had been with for eight years. She was beginning to think she might be lesbian.

Since leaving Rick eighteen months before, I'd been celibate and relieved to be so. I was not looking for anyone – certainly not for a man.

So when the first sparks started between us, I said to her, 'You're too early.' I was recovering from the cramping self-delusion of living with someone as alien and distant as the moon. I wanted more time before embarking on *anything*. It took me a little while to recognise that I had found a functioning human being, so different from myself and yet compatible. And this woman liked the look of me, in both senses.

After our first night together (around our fourth date) I drove home at dawn, a little hungover and dazed, changed clothes and then drove my stepson to the train at Central to start his boarding school term.

* * *

Anne was fresh territory for me. Her politics were leftish but were more based in the real world than mine. She came from a family who talked politics over the dinner table. She was also very Australian. What do I mean by that? Most of my friends were Australian, naturally, but some had migrant backgrounds or in some way were at the margins of 'Australianness'. Anne seemed rooted in herself, unselfconscious about who she was. We had very different roots; that attracted me but also scared me.

She blazed common sense and good judgement. We became friends quickly; it was the intrigue of opposites. The fact of a sexual attraction was a delicious extra pull. I realised that sex was no longer a test I had to pass. There was no danger; it was part of a continuum of growing love. She seemed to take me, with my neuroses and pretensions, with a pinch of salt, and still seemed to love me.

I was scared and hesitant. Her retort to my hesitations went like this: 'You are forty-five years old, Susan. Think of your choices: either me or some ageing bloke with a beer belly who will take you to barbecues.'

Not a subtle argument, but effective.

Yet behind her no-nonsense practical persona, Anne was a romantic. She sent me a dozen red roses of such quality that they lasted six weeks. Then came a present of pretty knickers. No man I had been with had thought of giving me a gift like that! Everything was turning on its head. I liked it.

One of the first things we did together was clean out my room in chambers in Macquarie Street. My abortive six-to-eight-month attempt at becoming a criminal barrister was over. I realised early that this was a man's game. Winning the game in the courts was the primary motivator. The ideal of justice came a sorry last. I had some of the skills required but not the appetite, the ambition. I was not cut out for it. Maybe if I had started younger ... Now I knew it was the wrong path. My soul was withering in that environment. I spent most of my time cowering in my room in chambers, drinking coffee and eating sticky buns.

Meeting Anne somehow tipped me into making the decision to get out. She helped me pile up the car with my few law books and other detritus. I wanted to take a few months off to find out what the hell I was going to do with the rest of my life.

About six weeks later, Anne came with me to visit Sam at his boarding school at Bathurst. We had exchanged a lot of information about ourselves but I still harboured a major secret. During the long drive I would tell her. No point in putting it off any longer.

Halfway up the Blue Mountains I said, under my breath, 'I have to tell you something. Something important.'

'OK.'

'But I need a drink first.'

It was eleven in the morning. She looked at me with puzzlement and dread. 'OK,' she said.

We pulled up at a pub. I wanted privacy so we stood in a hallway with our drinks. My double scotch trembled in my hand.

'For God's sake,' she said, 'spit it out!'

'OK, OK ...'

First a gulp of scotch.

'I have always ... wanted to ... write.'

I waited. Would she laugh? Such a risible, common ambition. Worse, be pissed off? I was encroaching on her territory, she who had already written one book and was working on another.

She hardly paused: 'Oh! Is that all? I thought you had cancer! What a relief. OK, so when are you going to start?'

My whole world shifted on its axis. This woman – possibly my life partner – was not only giving me permission but encouragement. *When are you going to start?*

'Oh ... soon,' I said lamely. A lifetime of doubts and delays fell away. *When are you going to start?*

Four months later I began *Heddy and Me*, the book I had been thinking about for twenty years.

* * *

Despite the excitement of our new love affair, Anne was determined to go to Paris as planned, to research and write about women writers and artists, mostly lesbian, in Paris in the 1920s and thirties. We had two months together before she left.

At the airport, waiting for her plane, she looked at my untidy nails and started to file them, as if we had known each other for decades.

We corresponded fervently. And after a few weeks she asked me to join her in Paris. I did.

On the plane I bought a small string of pearls for her. She says I was wearing a pink shirt and a grey skirt just above the knee as I came down the escalator at Charles de Gaulle. I had lost weight from the sheer excitement of being with her.

It became an unplanned honeymoon. We lived in a small two-room flat in Montmartre owned by Anne's friend Mark, an Australian pianist, who practised there. The main room was mostly taken up by his grand piano. The toilet was so tiny that I couldn't shut the door without banging my knees. In the bedroom was a single mattress on the floor. We found an African migrant market and bought a double foam mattress, carrying it home on our heads. We were happy.

I enrolled at the Alliance Francaise to brush up on my French but I often missed my morning class; the double mattress on the floor was too enticing.

Anne wanted me to go to a famous lesbian nightclub which only opened after midnight. I wondered what strange world I might be getting into. I demurred, mostly because I didn't want to stay awake so late, but also because I was scared. It didn't help that Anne had given me Djuna Barnes's novel *Nightwood* to read – an intense, dark work about the lesbian underworld of the twenties in Paris. Would it be like that?

I wanted a broader life. I had escaped the 'married-to-a-Jewish-doctor' ghetto and did not want another walled-off society. Nor did I want to brand myself as a lesbian separatist. Neither did Anne. But this was a darker, romantic, adventurous side of her that I was yet to understand. For all my rebellious youth and my Push connections, I was a nice middle-class Jewish girl from the North Shore, hesitating about finally 'jumping the fence'.

After a month in Paris we took off on a driving trip, destination: Venice. On the way we spent an enchanted week in the Dordogne. The small hotel was owned by two older women, sisters, seemingly fragile, silent, but welcoming. The old house, their family home, was simply and elegantly run. The food was unpretentious. Perfect.

Our room overlooked a long wisteria walk and a garden wild with roses and clematis. There were only two other guests. Time had treated the eighteenth-century house kindly. The woodwork and furniture were polished to a sheen the colour of sunshine.

The surrounding meadows leaned towards a clear stream. We took a picnic down there one day. Apart from the odd car passing by, the only sound was birdsong. We rolled ourselves in our blanket and had a honeymoon cuddle.

I am embarrassed to write about this time. It sounds postcard-picture perfect. Yet most of us have known the enchantment of the first few weeks of love, where the real possibility of a new and happier life might be dawning. It is a wondrous time but crumbles into cliché in the writing, which would be even worse if I tried to write a poem about it. It may turn to dust.

Venice felt organic, a natural wonder. The weather was showery, the churches dim and not too crowded. We did the minimum amount of touristing, simply walking the streets, marvelling. We met a lonely Sasha Soldatow, the writer, eking out his time on an Australia Council grant.

There was one bumpy jolt to our idyll. As one does in Venice, we hailed a gondola. The gondolier, a jolly young man, handled Anne in gallantly and then turned to me: 'Now Mama!'

'No! Partner!' said Anne crossly, quickly. But the gondola ride had lost its magic. I was mortified.

(It was not to be an isolated incident, mind you. People often sense a closeness beyond friendship between us yet it never occurs to them we might be lovers. Sometimes they say 'sister' – better for my self-esteem, naturally – but usually it is 'mother'. Assumptions die hard. Even now, with equal marriage legalised, it still happens, if not quite as often.)

After a few days in Venice I had to go home, leaving Anne to go back to France to finish her research. Back in Oz, missing Anne badly, it didn't take me too long to decide to make a future together. She came home a few weeks later and moved into my new house in Randwick. One day she arrived with two suitcases and her dog, Scruffy. The irrepressible Scruffy and my gentle Alsatian, Jed, became inseparable within days, as did we.

After a few months I told my stepson about Anne. I asked him, 'Did you guess?'

'No,' he said. He was not very interested – he was fourteen – 'but she's OK. She likes animals.'

And that was that.

My parents adjusted after the first shock that I was in a relationship with a woman, remarkably well given their age and the world they grew up in. I asked my mother the same question: had she guessed?

'No,' she said, 'I didn't guess. But is it Anne?' Mother was always instinctive.

And then after a pause, 'If it makes you happier' – as if that was a near-impossible goal – 'then it is all right by me.'

My father: 'Can't you just be friends?'

'No,' I told him. 'This is different.'

He was puzzled and a little sad. 'I won't be dancing on tabletops tonight,' he said.

Yet he was lovely to her from the start. They liked each other. Mother was cooler. She sensed her loss of power over me. There was no point in trying to manipulate Anne, as she had done with many of my friends. Anne scotched that very early. To my relief they established a healthy mutual respect.

The nicest reaction was from my Hungarian cleaning lady. Nothing was said after Anne moved in. E was cautious and polite. But after a few weeks, without discussion, Anne's freshly ironed nightie appeared on the other side of the bed, along with my own. She was accepted.

Our friends coped in their different ways. Sometimes the path was bumpy; some of her friends thought maybe I was a scheming older lesbian, whereas mine thought she might be a young adventuress taking me for a ride. But on the whole it was a relatively easy transition. This was 1990, not the sixties or seventies. Neither of us had grappled with teenage angst about having the 'wrong' sexuality. Neither was totally inexperienced nor surprised about the change. I was forty-five and she was thirty-two. We were spared the worst of the experience of 'coming out'.

I could say that becoming a lesbian was a wonderful revelation and solved everything. But it was more gradual and nuanced. In my teens I had no idea the possibility existed. I remember a schoolfriend pressing her leg against mine and puzzling about what it might mean. In my twenties, an occasional experiment. But nothing to shake the fixed idea that I would eventually meet 'The Man' and maybe have children. In my thirties, a more serious affair with a woman, Edith. When it ended, I scuttled back to the next man.

Exactly where I fitted on the spectrum of sexuality I did not know and eventually did not care. I had not been a secret lesbian hiding my true desires. I never secretly lusted after a woman (well, once after a bit of pot, but it was a mild case of lust) but I have always found them more physically and aesthetically attractive. Slowly my fantasies turned more to women than to men. I became disillusioned with what men had to give and tired of not being able to truly enjoy sex with them, let alone achieve orgasm.

The important thing was that my emotional and spiritual being was extended and enlarged by being with a woman. I was more at ease, more myself. With Anne it seemed natural; our sexual exchanges were relaxed and easy. There was no boundary between love and sex; they intermingled without thought. Above all, no power-play, no threat – real or implied.

From then on, men became friends. Most of them have been homosexual, although not all. Precious friends, with all their complexities and subtleties. To this day, I can find a (rare) man attractive but don't need to act on it.

I can't say, though, that all my sexual problems ceased and I became orgasmic and free. My inhibitions were too long engrained. But sex was now fun, truly intimate and pleasurable, and integral to our love and life together. I felt for the first time that I was embarking on life with a partner in every sense.

Halfway through the arc of life I could go forwards, armed.

* * *

Since childhood, once my mother deemed me old enough to understand, she (and to a lesser extent, Dad) told me stories of what happened in the war years and how the Holocaust had engulfed Hungary in the later stages of the war.

She also gave me vivid pictures of her childhood days. The family's different abodes: first the flat in the middle of Pest, crowded with four children, the grand piano and the massive potted palm, two icons treasured by my grandmother. Then in a more prosperous phase, the villa her father built in genteel Buda, where she had her own room with a Juliet balcony; the apricot tree laden with summer fruit each year; the hill where she and her brothers would toboggan in the snow.

Of their faithful Alsatian, Caesar, who followed their car for miles after they left him behind when moving back to Pest. Then the awful years when her beloved father ruined the family with his gambling, when they moved to increasingly down-at-heel flats as her mother scrimped and saved to pay off debtors. The nights when there was no bread on the table. The rolled-up carpets she had to take on the tram to the pawn shop. The humiliation and misery of her teenage years.

Eventually, she met my father. She was well off again and embarked on a life as a comfortable young matron. Her first child was born in 1941, the second (me) towards the end of 1943 when the situation of Hungary's 600,000 Jews was deteriorating rapidly. They hoped they still might escape the fate of the Polish Jews and others in surrounding countries, hearing shocking, unbelievable rumours of wholesale carnage. But Hitler crossed the border in early 1944 when I was six months old. She told me what happened after my birth, in vivid scraps, like light shows or playlets adapted for a child's ear. From an early age I knew it was a gripping tale begging to be told.

From my early twenties, whenever my mother recounted her story of the war years, people would say to her 'you have to write it down'. Her reply was always, 'I'm waiting for Susan.' This was a promise but also a burden to me and, as years peeled away, an ever-growing guilt. I wanted to write it but the task was replete with complication.

My mother and I had been locked in battle since my adolescence. Much love but some mutual dislike and a constant push and pull of our warring values. She was a powerful personality and her world view was black and white, no ifs or buts. My world was full of many confusing shades of grey, shot through with occasional vivid illuminations and bursts of inspiration.

The tension between us hardly ever slackened. When would I show the promise that had radiated from me as a child? In her eyes I had not acquired stability, or children, or a 'career' worth mentioning – the last, being the law, just another waste of time. So I had to find some rapprochement with her before I started writing. I needed a secure place within myself to withstand her encroachments. Another consideration was that time might be running out. She might lose her clarity or her enthusiasm. She was seventy-three before I thought myself finally ready.

The other reason I'd put off the project for so long was because it involved facing the multiple conundrums and horrors of the Holocaust. Every Jewish child of survivors has to contend with this. We carry the residual and complex guilts: why the Jews, why the enormous scale of carnage, and why did we and our parents survive? What guilt should the next generation carry? How to live with this atomic cloud hanging over our lives? How to heal our damaged parents and ourselves?

When Anne came to live with me I was finishing renovations of my new house in Randwick. I reserved a back room looking out to the garden for a study. It was time.

The book, *Heddy and Me*, as I eventually called it, had been lurking for so long that I had no trouble finding my major themes. Heddy's story would be the backbone. Other themes would be the long-term impact of the Holocaust, the uprooting of lives from one side of the world to the other in emigrating from Hungary, woven through with my troubled relationship with my mother. During the writing, other themes arose: the way the process of recording Heddy's story would change my relationship with her, and my parents' reactions to my love affair with Anne.

First, I needed to get Heddy's story down in her own words – in Hungarian. She spoke good English but was more relaxed and colourful in her birth language. Migrants often adopt, if unconsciously, a distorted persona in learning a second language; the one they think locals want to see and hear.

I began to visit her once a week with a small tape recorder. We sat in the formal dining room on the corner of the antique Spanish table with a delicate but large Japanese screen behind us. During the following week, I'd transcribe the Hungarian into an exercise book in

English. It was a painfully slow exercise but it had one good effect of getting to know her story better and better as well as the way she used language, her quirks of speech.

Every week we met at the same time and went through exactly the same routine. I wanted her to treat the project as I did, with discipline and not as a form of self-indulgence. If she got off the topic I cut her short. When the hour and a quarter was up, the session was over.

I set my own strict rules from the start because I wanted complete control of the final result. I would listen and try to accommodate her but would not guarantee her requests. She understood and agreed.

I was lucky she accepted my strictures. Her flow of words never stopped, except for one time, when she broke down about her brother Pali's death in Russia. Even then, I pushed her to keep going.

The process took six months.

Next step, Budapest. I needed to spend real time in Hungary. Anne and I planned a long trip: a look at Vienna, then three months in Budapest, with trips to the countryside, visiting all the places Mum had talked about.

This was the journey I had dreaded and anticipated all my adult life. Now I had a partner whom I loved and trusted. She was keen to come and understood the backstory. Now I could be *excited* to go back.

Return to Hungary, 1990

Since my family's departure in 1948, my only brief visit to Hungary was when I was about nineteen. Back then, in the early sixties, the Communist regime had softened; after the Hungarian Uprising of '56, some adjustments had to be made to calm the populace. The outside world labelled the changes 'Goulash Communism'. The relatives called it 'a lukewarm bath'.

Small freedoms made life bearable. Small enterprises were allowed. Many people could afford a basic holiday house at Balaton, the big inland lake not far from Budapest. But it was a grey, cramped life. People spoke in whispers, looked over their shoulders in public places. Cautious humour and acid jokes were some relief.

Back then I hadn't related much to the remaining family, living in dark flats with ill-fitting furniture, immersed in the humdrum of survival. My cousin Robi, a couple of years older than me, looked like Elvis Presley, and we had nothing to say to each other. I felt myself to be Australian. I had no real ties to this grim, battered city and no feeling for a tiny landlocked country in Eastern – not even civilised Western – Europe. I was sulky, put-upon.

In 1990 we arrived to a sweltering summer. The previous year, the Berlin Wall had come down and the Soviet empire in Eastern Europe with it. Budapest was waking from a long period of hardship and unwanted isolation. The city seemed half asleep, as if the Communists might come back at any moment. Many street names (Lenin Square for example) had been crossed out, changed back to pre-war names. Saint István, patron saint of Hungary and her first king, was everywhere. But as jobs disappeared and the social fabric disintegrated, we saw sad people standing in the subways, selling cans of peas, two bars of soap, pornographic magazines.

Among the new parties springing up was a 'youth' party called Fidesz, which demanded that its members had to stand down by thirty-five, to be replaced by younger people. Its popular but scandalising poster showed a photoshopped Brezhnev and Erich Honecker (the East German leader) in a passionate clinch, and underneath, a picture of two young attractive Hungarians in the same clinch. The slogan: 'Which do you choose?' Its leadership was a collective of young men and women, among them charismatic Viktor Orbán. Their party seemed like a breath of fresh air, liberal and inclusive. But over the years we watched Orbán become a powerful leader and swing the party ever more to the right, the rule about stepping down at thirty-five long abandoned.

Living in Budapest in the summer and autumn of 1990 brought the city to life for me in deep and scary ways. I could not disown or ignore my birthplace any longer.

Towards the end of our stay, Heddy and Gyuszi joined us. I went with Mum to many of her old haunts and homes. Those three months changed my feelings about Hungary radically.

When I think of Budapest
I think of 1990.

The communists gone
The city's heart
and limbs still numb

In the former Jewish quarter
we rent a flat, two sparse rooms
a make-shift kitchen, a cold water tap.

Outside our building, a billboard in praise
of false teeth – black mouth, yellow molars –
grins and creaks at passers-by.

In a small square a tiny restaurant
serving Jewish-Hungarian food.
The customers know the pretty waitress

after thirty years of cheery smiles.
The owner, in a short white coat,
doctor-like, stands by the till.

He doesn't speak much but his sad
eyes take everything in –
the kids fighting in the square,

mothers resting under plane trees.
The old ghetto survivors huddled
in the shade.

In 1944 the ghetto was sealed off
from the city. There was nowhere
to bury the dead.

The square was crammed high
with Jewish bodies rotting in rows
waiting for liberation.

Did You Know
that Eichmann's plan, to clear Hungary
of every single Jew (the capital being

the richest prize), was thwarted?
He had finished in the countryside –

all Jews deported, dispatched.
Then Hitler recalled him to Berlin

so his work halted at the city's outskirts
and some of Budapest's Jews got to live.

But two months later Eichmann
was back. The death marches

re-formed, filing towards Auschwitz.

The Central Synagogue
In 1990 the congregation is sparse.
Yet on a Saturday a huddle of
teenage girls in their Sabbath best
skitter to the gates.
By the door pimply boys
lounge about in wait,
as boys do, the world over.

Journeys with Mother

Mother arrives from her posh hotel
bringing delicious 'pocaga'
filched from the breakfast buffet.
She beams, showing off her prize.

We are walking through her past.

Yesterday she took me to see
her old girls' school where Jew
and Gentile mixed as one.
Outside school, the barriers
stayed, spikes up.

Tomorrow, we will knock
at the door of my father's flat
where he read his books
and waited for a wife to appear.

Years passed – his mother
had given up hope.
In a coffee house he met my mother,
fresh-faced, 21, deep-blue eyes,
light olive skin. No make-up.

Seven years later,
the night I was born,
my father wept for joy.

He saw me once again
on a day's leave. At dawn
he kissed his wife and left.

She watched him, helpless in his
ill-fitting labour camp uniform
until he disappeared.

Childhood Home

Tall heavy doors open to a narrow
courtyard. Cast-iron railings gird
the balconies from floor to floor.

I hear the clatter of children,
past and present, their feet
hammering, voices thrilling.

On the fifth floor Mother knocks
on the door of her childhood home.
A worn-looking woman answers.

They are about the same age
yet Mother radiates the
easy life of the West.

'I've lived here alone
since the War,' the woman says.
'My husband didn't come back.'

Mother nods. All Jews know
what that phrase means.

In the kitchen rows of bottled
pears and peppers on a shelf.

'For the winter,' the woman says.

Mother nods again.
'We did the same, before ...'

I know little of my father, Feri. He died well before I had a chance to form memories. He was born in a village to a family of rural feather merchants who had fled the pogroms in Germany the century before. There were three Schwimmer boys. The middle son died young. Feri, the youngest, was a frail, sickly child with a head of golden curls.

He was coddled by his mother, who feared losing another child. In his teens he was sent to a TB sanatorium high in the mountains. He grew up shy, quiet, awkward, bookish, dutiful. Being dutiful, after finishing school, he trapped himself in the family business.

In time, the family became wealthy and set up in Budapest. Feri bought his own flat, worked in the business, read his books at night.

My Father

1.
is a handful of photos, facts
wisps of anecdotes.

A few phrases drifting
through time like fine smoke

He lived a modest life. But liked
good hotels and a well-cut suit.

When he finally married, at 35,
everyone from the village was amazed.

'A girl from Budapest!
And beautiful too!'

On honeymoon in Capri, sitting up in bed,
he read of the first anti-Jewish laws.

'That I have lived to see this day,'
he said, and wept.

2.

My father mulled over fleeing Hitler;
South America? Or even Australia?

(I have seen his books,
carefully underlined)

but couldn't bear to leave his mother.
Her arthritic knees

(which I have inherited)
crippled them both.

So they stayed, rooted
                in their earth.

Feri died in the Fertőrákos labour camp near the Austrian border
sometime in late 1944. Back in Budapest, Heddy had no news of him
and no means of obtaining any. Finally, a man showed up wanting to
speak to her privately. He had been in the next bunk to my father in
the labour camp.

Feri had been ill and depressed for weeks. He entrusted his friend
with an address (at my uncle's flat so as not to endanger us) and sent
this message: 'Tell my wife that I love her and the children very much,
but I died.'

He laid down on his bunk that night, the man said, and was found
dead the next morning.

My mother was grieved but not surprised. 'He was too sensitive,'
she said to me, 'and not strong physically. I knew his chances were
not good.'

Heddy's wartime experiences were very different; she was made of
different stuff.

Mother's Wartime Transactions

1.
'Pick the apples from our tree!'
her neighbours call out.
'Store our apples!'
The open truck jolts away,
bound for Theresienstadt.

2.
A hundred Jewish men,
forced labourers, crammed
in her storeroom out the back.
Little food. No water.

They come to her door.
'Please, post our letters.'

They tell her what little they know;
what towns in the East have fallen;
the swirling – unbelievable – rumours.

3.
'What can I do for you, handsome Madame?'
asks the sergeant at the police station.
'A permit to leave,' she says,
bribe at the ready.

He looks at her with kindness.

Later, when events turn, it's
'a permit to stay'. This time,
he does not want a bribe.

4.
To peasants outside the village,
Mother says, 'Take our furniture
and linen. Keep them safe.

If I don't come back
they are yours.'

5.
'Hide your jewellery in my backyard,'
her friend, the local doctor says.
They dig up the earth on a moonlit night.
'Remember this tree, my dear.'

6.
On the run with false passports.
A rented room in a ragged village.
The young family is kind. Together
they hull corn in the long evenings.

After the war, she seeks them out
to thank them. Did they ever
guess? Shyly, they say,
'We think we always knew.'

7.
At last the Russians!

They chase the Germans
from village to village
like so much dry hay.

But with liberation comes rape –
she and her mother –
in the same room.
Afterwards her mother says
'Never mind, my darling,
this goes with it.'

'This' – the rape
and the abortion after.

8.
Good news. Across country,
Feri's village already liberated!
So in deep winter, snow
thigh-high, she hires a cart.

At the other end of the village
more family, too afraid to leave.
Three-year-old Robi sobs,
pleads to come with us.
His mother clutches him tight
The cart lurches forward.

A lone Russian soldier
stops us. Mother
holds up the baby.

He waves his arm. 'Davai!'
Everyone knew that Russian
word of salvation.
Davai! Go!

9.
Pitch black night. Bombs overhead.
A barge crammed with fleeing people.
A soldier next to my mother says,
'Give me the baby to hold; I'm a deserter.'
She hands me over without a word.

10.
Starving Budapest is liberated.
Heddy rides on top of a train
to the city, a suitcase filled
with lard, ducks, flour, sausages.

She arrives home, suitcase empty.
Money to live on for months.

11.
The household goods are returned
Heddy sets a table –
the best linen, glasses, china.
Sits down with her mother to eat.
They toast each other.
'To survival! To life!'

In 1990 I met my cousin Robi again. Robi had changed since the early sixties, as indeed I had. He no longer looked like Elvis. He had a grown-up daughter and was into his second marriage with a Christian woman, Rózsi, who I instantly liked.

We met at Gerbeaud, the grandest of the old coffee houses which the Communists kept going as icons of times past. This time, Robi was eager to claim me. He talked about our grandmother, her special scent. '*Illat*', he called it – a bit like 'fragrance' in English. I had the same beloved *illat* embedded in my nostrils. I was half won over.

'When we were in hiding,' he said later, 'in that village, in Kisláng, there was a big German who came to the well in the backyard. I was so frightened. I wept when Heddy took you and Jutka away in the cart. I begged to be taken with you.'

'You felt left behind?' I asked my cousin.

'Yes,' he said. 'Then all of you left for Australia. And I was stuck here.'

I started to open my heart to his.

185

My parents stayed in Budapest for a few weeks. It was a rich time. The four of us enjoyed the complicated pleasures of the city. We became closer.

When they left, Dad said to Anne and me, 'Take care of each other.'

It was a kind of benediction.

New ground

Back in Australia, in my newly set up study, I started writing in earnest. I had three short pieces already written, piles of transcript, and I had done most of the reading. In Budapest I kept a journal which would become the basis for the last part of the book. Lots of new material. No going back now.

I was finally writing and Mr Lowry could no longer haunt me. For so long I had dreaded turning out mediocre. What did I have to say to the world? Maybe, one day, when I had sorted myself out better, understood the world better ... In the meantime, I cultivated a silly maxim I would trot out: 'If you can't be a Dickens or a Dostoevsky (two of my idols from early reading days), why bother? The world does not need another mediocre self-serving author, blah, blah.'

Fear of failure silenced me, even when I started to know *what* I wanted to write. That, and the knowing voice of men, rational, intellectual men, in my head saying, 'What would you have to say? You're just one of many – an intelligent, not unattractive woman, with uncertain opinions and no direction. So keep mum, keep your head down.'

Yet I always had used words as my secret weapon to get through whatever I was facing. I wrote fluent and passionate essays which got me through exams in English and History, without much fact or real argument. At university I sometimes wrote an essay marked as 'elegant' or 'brilliant'. In my working life, I wrote submissions and became fluent as a lobbyist and speechmaker when the need arose.

I enjoyed anything to do with words but I rarely wrote for myself. If I tried, a black mantra blocked me quickly: 'no good, crap, lame, no, STOP'. This self-dismissal was automatic and swift, and kept me imprisoned.

Do I regret starting so late? There is no point in regretting it. If you don't know who you are, you don't have a voice and you can't write – not well, anyway. Having a voice is everything in writing. It was a pity it took so long, but there it is. Once I started, I was free.

* * *

A few months after starting the book, I showed Anne the first draft of two early chapters.

'Not bad,' she said, 'but the tone is not right – rather twee.'

I was devastated. Twee! But after a while, I felt happy. She would always tell me the truth. I went back to work and got rid of twee.

The book took me four years to write and up to fifteen drafts. Every morning I would approach my desk, scared and excited. The wonder and relief of writing has never left me. My friend Sasha Soldatow, one of the few writers I knew, said, 'Words on the page!' Getting something down, anything at all, to work with. Every morning, to reassure myself about writing bad stuff, I wrote a little motto before new words: 'Everything can be changed!' I could make it better next time around.

I have always been fascinated by the way each word changes the meaning and shape of a sentence; the choice of one particular word instead of multiple others, then their order – what is ahead, what follows behind; the subtleties of punctuation to pace and the layers of a sentence. And the delight of a paragraph as the sentences pile up. A paragraph can be a mini short story, it can be a bridge, it can be simply expository, it can be purely atmospheric or it can be an ending. So many possibilities. With each successive draft I embellish, polish, enlarge, riff. Or cut, cut, cut. Reshape, add, subtract. Then start over again with the next draft.

Writing a book is not unlike building a house. At first the scaffolding then the overarching roof, then different rooms with different purposes. One room too many? Another too large? Windows to look out to a bigger world. Is the house fenced off, inward-looking or opened out? Decisions, decisions.

As I write, words start to think *for* me. I can expand a small thought, make it vigorous or more beautiful. It is a two-way process; the word and I, coupled in a dance. On a good day I can access that 'higher self' which used to elude me. In that way, it is an addiction.

I am in love with words, feel privileged to work with them. I take the privilege seriously by never writing for myself alone. I try to grapple with the human condition (sorry for the cliché), to observe and comment beyond myself, to send a signal, however weak the beam, to other people.

Despite my obsession with words, I rarely use a dictionary and only as a last resort. I have always hated them. As a child, English was a voyage of discovery. I came across the sense of words quite quickly but sometimes painstakingly. Looking in the dictionary was cheating. Discovering their meaning was a private joy. I was not going to hear any of those words at home. I was the voyager, my parents waiting on the shore till I returned with new words. Even now I never look up synonyms – I wait for the right word to find me.

This 'voyage' was partly due to circumstance. Migrant children were always interpreting for, or correcting, their parents, a strange reversal of roles. I remember when a Spanish cleaning lady came for her interview with Mum. She brought her six-year-old child with her to translate both ways. (She got the job and was with my mother for thirty years; they developed their own ways of communicating and trust.)

While I picked up everyday language from friends and school, more complex words were only accessed in books. Thus grew my love of the English language. Not that it was an exclusive love; later I began to appreciate the meaty strength of Hungarian and gained more proficiency in it. I always loved the sounds of French, in its elegance and precision. I regret not pursuing the opportunity to make myself fully at ease with it. I parlayed Dutch, a difficult and interesting language. A smattering of South American Spanish – passionate, dark, a great language for poetry. Yet English is my companion and the basis of what I do. Every day it is the medium and access point to all things, second only to life itself. I don't like to play with it as many others do, however. I'm not interested in crosswords or puns and I'm hopeless at Scrabble. For me, it is still the words on the pages of books, the way they make sense out of life.

* * *

I had not thought that I would finish the last parts of *Heddy and Me* living in the country. Anne introduced me to the pleasures of a country house on her small acreage at Maitland. And ever since reading Mary Grant Bruce in childhood I had fantasised about living in a rural setting, riding horses and writing in solitude, though I never thought it could really happen.

In 1992 we returned from a quiet beach holiday in Queensland and caught a taxi from the airport to our Randwick house. The taxi emitted foul petrol fumes, combining with a thousand odours of the city. Anne, who liked the city only for short spells, said, 'Let's get out of here. Let's look for something in the country.'

'Great idea,' I said.

The idea had never seriously occurred to me until then but I surprised myself. I was ready for it. Maybe we were acquiring some confidence as full-time writers and could leave Sydney and its charms – mostly the harbour and its brash energy – and find a quiet country place conducive to a writerly life.

We both liked the Hunter, north of Sydney. Anne had been born and raised there, but it was too hot in summer for me. I was not keen on the second choice of the Southern Highlands, either; it made me think of retired stockbrokers and the nouveaux riche. But the prices were in a lull there and its closeness to Sydney would make the transition easier.

The agent was meant to take us to a pretty old cottage that we had seen in the ads but said instead, 'I'll just take you to this other house first.' When we saw the place, there were three instant blows to the heart: the first, a view from a high hill of a momentous mountain gorge. The second, three early yellow daffodils nodding beside a bucolic oval pond. The third, inside finding two rooms perfect for studies and, wonderfully, at opposite ends of the house.

We tried not to show that we were in love. We tried to look at other houses but really the deal was done.

The house was on twenty acres. It was called Keil-na-nain, Gaelic for 'Copse of the Birds' – so named by a Scottish doctor who built it in 1952. The 1950s was not my preferred style, yet we found the house a constant delight. Though it was in solid brick, they were old mellow sandstock bricks. Everything about it was slightly askew: windows in unexpected places with bits of wrought iron around them, wrought iron arches laden with clematis and wisteria, old carriage lamps at the garage, four twisted chimney pots brought from England.

Inside, red cedar doors, long windows. A tiny, narrow dining room with an equally tiny fireplace in the corner but long windows overlooking the garden and pond. We decorated its walls with peasant plates brought from Hungary. My table, which I'd schlepped with me since Birchgrove days, just fitted in the room.

On the south side our studies also looked to the pond, where wild ducks landed and fat yabbies lurked. From a kitchen window, an old camellia flowered, tricoloured – pink, red and white – for months.

A corridor from the front door curved slightly in two different directions. A gun cupboard in the hall quickly became a bookcase. The fireplace in the main room was ungainly and built for roasting Viking feasts, but made a mean fire, warming most of the house.

Quite near the house was a caretaker's cottage. Then a large tin shed, half of which made a guest cottage. Our small settlement of houses and sheds nestled on a ledge: steep country above, steep country below. A track curved up to a paddock from which the ridges of Morton National Park spread out in splendour. The main driveway from the front gate ran beside a patch of remnant rainforest.

The garden showed the influence of famed garden designer Edna Walling. Although planned, it had a wild untameable quality. A big rockery faced the house; it took years to uncover its many paths and

stairs as we tried and failed to tame the garden's wilful ecosystem. It was crammed with old azaleas, rhododendrons, verbenas and maples. One year we counted twelve types of daffodil. At the rear, a crazy-paved sandstone terrace with steps leading down to the oval pond, its sundial also a little askew. The spring-fed pond had its own sand-filtered cleaning system and a little slope to allow dogs and the occasional human to step in. At the end of the pond, a golden ash tree mirrored itself on the still surface.

It was an enchanted space; everyone who visited there felt it. I felt the enchantment every day I lived there, even in less happy times. My parents, wedded to cities, felt it, too. My mother would make an obeisance to the flaming orange mollis azalea near the front door then wander around the house noting every detail. My father looked around, inhaled the air and said, 'Never sell this place,' then retired to the sunroom to read the newspaper.

When we moved in, we agreed to give ourselves two years before reviewing our flight to the country. The deadline came and went. We spent three months renovating and getting rid of a few monstrosities, like carpet creeping up the sides of the king-sized built-in bed in the main bedroom. Then we settled into a routine of productive work. I needed two more years of writing before finishing the book.

Halcyon Days
Every room gives on to wild gardens
each with their tangled beauties

Our doors remain shut.
The phone unanswered

One of us makes coffee.
Next day, the other

An exchange of monosyllables.
A bird note. A rustle of leaves.

Lunch: we talk in the kitchen,
if asked, about work done, or not.

The afternoon drive to
the post office and shop.

Early evening, we tend
old horses in the paddocks.

As we walk the dogs
a fine mist descends.

Wombats come out
from their homes.

The sun sets beyond white gates.
An evening scotch as night arrives.

May the gods continue
to grant more Halcyon Days.

Of course the country idyll had its flaws and bad days. Sometimes I felt cut off, lonely. One evening in the first year, as winter started to bite, I drove to a swimming class in Bowral, the biggest town nearby. In the twenty-five minutes it took to get there I saw not a single car on the road. I drove through heavy mist, then dense fog. It felt as if I'd come to the end of the earth.

Today, there is always traffic on the road, just not (yet) Sydney traffic.

* * *

Doris Lessing talks about everyone having a myth country. Where is mine? The places that have marked me? The grimy streets of Budapest, the longing and fear embedded in the buildings? The backyard in Willoughby with the mulberry tree, the carpet of jacarandas at Willoughby Public School, or my first encounters with the Australian bush with Anton? The loneliness of the flat long fields of Holland?

At Keil-na-nain my worlds come together. In my study, as I start to work – a hard joy this writing – I look out to a nissa tree colouring into autumn, beyond that a tall untidy gum, and beyond the gum a stand of bush with glimpses of the mountain range beyond. For me it is a necessary synthesis: the autumn colouring, the daffodils emerging, is Europe; the gum tree and the bush beyond is Australia. Both are deep rooted.

Here I feel a new freedom. This is my myth country. Another piece of the puzzle of being.

* * *

I finally finished the book. After a couple of rejections, Penguin took it with enthusiasm and *Heddy and Me* came out in 1994. The publishers thought that little needed changing. 'If it ain't broke, don't fix it,' one editor said. Penguin was promoting biography that year and chose *Heddy and Me* to head their list. As I entered a major bookstore in the city I saw prominent dump bins with my book featured. I could not believe it. It was a dream run for an unknown.

The book sold over 12,000 copies and had good reviews. It was translated into Hungarian and German. I have not had the same luck again. But I was a writer at last and, it seemed, not a bad one.

* * *

The life of writers living and working together helps relieve the isolation that is a writer's lot, but is often hard as well. Living with another writer is complicated. We talk about our different problems, we critique each other with profit and generosity. But inevitably there is friction, too, when one is going through a high and the other is in the writerly doldrums.

For the first years we were mostly in sync. After *Heddy and Me* came out, Anne's milestone book, *Sex and Anarchy*, her detailed and wonderfully readable account of 'the rise and fall of the Sydney Push', was published in 1996. It garnered much praise and healthy sales. It remains the definitive account of this important intellectual stream in Australian society.

In the early days of Keil-na-nain, when Anne was writing *Sex and Anarchy*, George Molnar would come to spend weekends with us. He was generous with his time and knowledge, talking about Push philosophy and social theory, and what Anne should be reading. Once he drove down from Sydney with us. We had picked up a new kitten from our friends June and Jan Gibson. In the back seat, George sat cradling the little kitten, crooning his new name – 'Samm-ee, Samm-ee, little kitten, little Samm-ee' – the whole way, in heaven.

He stayed in our guest flat, where we provided him with breakfast. But he appeared on our doorstep, saying 'What's the point of visiting if I have to have breakfast on my own?' Then he talked and talked!

After our long-ago affair ended, George and I remained in touch only fitfully over the years. I saw him at Push gatherings or campaigns, on the streets of Glebe, or in the Fisher Library. I was always pleased to see him but always dreading, too, that he would still condescend to me, talk AT me, and deflect anything personal with one of his bad jokes. While I was writing *Heddy and Me* my worst fears were realised. I ran into him outside the public library in Macquarie Street. He was in the public service by then, reading philosophy on the side.

What are you doing? he asked.

Writing a book.

What about?

Umm ... Hungary, the war, my mother.

He gave a derisive snort.

Not another professional Hungarian! Isn't Riemer enough? (Andrew Riemer, academic, critic and writer.) And there's others coming out of the woodwork. I strongly advise you to desist. Just resist the temptation.

I was hugely deflated but also angry with him. How dare he! All my old bitterness against his influence on my life rose up.

I finished my book, nonetheless.

Some time after it was published he phoned me. He'd read it and wanted to talk. I went to the appointed meeting like a martyr to the stake. How long would I have to suffer his diatribe about all the things I'd done wrong, misunderstood, failed to address?

He began.

First I have to tell you that I found only two factual errors.

Oh.

He expatiated at length on one of the errors, to do with the correct word in Hungarian for a horse's thigh. Another error was a date, although he admitted he could be wrong.

Then he said –

This is the third book I've read by friends of mine in memoir form – one was Germaine's. Yours is the best.

Oh.

Now don't ever tell me again that you can't do something. (An allusion to the days he used to try to teach me logic and I'd wail that I could never do it.)

And then he told me, so wistfully and simply, about how my description of my uncle Pali had reminded him of his favourite uncle, who, like mine, was handsome and clever and delightful company and, like mine, was killed in Russia during the war. When George was a child, seven or eight years old, his uncle used to play chess with him. They'd go for walks together and discuss life. His young uncle smoked a pipe and smelt and felt good to be near. And then the war came and he went into a labour camp and was not seen again.

I don't know why I didn't ask George more about the war years then. He probably would have told me what happened to him between the ages of ten and fifteen, during the war and its aftermath. He might even, by then, have had some insight into how that awful time of hunger and fear and the subsequent years as wandering refugees would have affected the precocious adolescent who arrived in Australia in 1951 with his mother and grandmother.

But I was still overawed by him – and amazed that he had confided in me something so deeply personal. For that meeting, it was enough. As usually happened with George, that rare moment of intimacy and insight was buried under the weight of the public George.

I had one other glimpse of this side of George later, perhaps eighteen months before he died. When he was visiting Anne and me at the farm, he suddenly asked when we were going to Hungary again, maybe next year? Until recently, he said, he'd never wanted to see Hungary again but he had been tentatively thinking he might, just might, go back. Would I let him know when we'd formulated our plans because 'I might go with you?'

I was flabbergasted, touched and horrified. Could I stand such large amounts of time with George? I prevaricated and put the question in the too-hard basket.

* * *

Of the many visitors who came to see how we could live in the boondocks, so Sydney-centric were our friends, in our first years at Keil-na-nain, one new friend came more often and stayed longer. I think we met Margaret at a party at Sasha Soldatow's in Bondi. The three of us clicked.

Margaret McClusky was then well known for her best-selling novel *Wedlock*, a biting satire on Sydney's upper echelons, which made her name quickly. Since then, she had been in the writerly doldrums and fiddling with various projects, including a de-cluttering business. She reckoned she knew the subject well from personal experience.

She was a biggish, raw-boned woman who commanded attention. At her best she was excellent company, with a quick mind, acerbic wit and a wide range of interests and ideas. She peppered us with faxes (this was the early 1990s): little poems, anecdotes, her life story. We tried to keep up.

Her mood swings were extreme. She would often plan to visit but would change her mind at the last moment. She could be very erratic, pushy and high maintenance. I still have a poem-fax sending up her attempt to kill herself at The Gap. She managed to make it both poignant and very funny.

Margaret's pattern seemed to be intense engagement followed by abrupt withdrawal. It was a rich friendship, despite its drawbacks. It ended abruptly when Anne decided not to ask her to her fortieth birthday party. We were never forgiven.

A few years later we saw in the newspaper that she had died in a fire in her flat. I will never know whether the fire was accidental or not, although that was the finding. Her death still haunts me.

Here is a poem she faxed me for my birthday. It gives a taste of her humour and depth.

17/10/1995
Such tiny feet
To carry you all the way
From Holocaust to
Hornsby High
And even further
To
The grace of love
Compassion
Self knowledge
Distinction
Are there any greater virtues?

(Duck collecting, perhaps
At which you also
Excel)

(The 'duck collecting' was a longstanding joke about four motherless ducklings we were trying to save in our pond.)

While *Heddy and Me* was being assessed, Anne and I went to the first Gay and Lesbian Writing Conference, held at Rozelle. I remember it well for two important reasons. First, someone from Penguin told me, by inference, that the book had been accepted. Second, I left a boring session towards its end to see what the broadcaster Robert Dessaix looked like in the next room. I had listened to the Books and Ideas program on the ABC for years, and its outstanding presenter with his distinctive voice. Now I stood at the back of the room peering towards the person on the stage. It was not Robert Dessaix – it was Robert Jones! My old schoolmate, the irrepressible Robert Jones of forty-five years ago at Artarmon Opportunity School. It had to be him: the same hazel green eyes, the olive skin, the compact zinging energy.

When we were both in our late twenties, I ran into him at the Stables Theatre. He seemed somewhat diminished then, a little remote. No spark of our old rapport. This time I went up to him after the session – he was surrounded by admirers – and said, 'Robert, I think we know each other.'

One searching look, then his eyes dropped swiftly to my name tag. 'Susan!'

Pause. Then he said, 'What would your mother think if she knew I was here?'

Ah, I thought, Heddy's powerful moral authority after all this time. I said, 'It is all right Robert. She knows *I* am here.'

We did not fall into each other's arms, not then. I guessed that Robert had been more scarred by coming out as a gay man than I had been as a new lesbian. It took some time for both of us to let our defences down. I learnt how he came to change his name from his first book, *A Mother's Disgrace*. In fact, Dessaix was his real name; his birth mother was of French descent. How much better it suited his persona.

We rebuilt our friendship slowly. I think he was bamboozled by my parents' desire to see him again. My mother had a radiant look of finding a lost child. My father insisted on giving him financial advice – the only form of male affection he could latch onto.

Over time Robert and I have re-found the affinity we had as children. Strangely, our lives have run in parallel. We had both tried marriage and failed it; both 'jumped the fence'; we started writing at the same time, first published in the same year, and wrote first books about our mothers. We were even placed 'first and second' in a writing prize, as if we were back in primary school. Despite writing novels (two each), we are both essentially writers of memoir, nonfiction and essays.

Robert and I don't see each other much; he lives in Hobart and I in the Southern Highlands. When he goes to Sydney he sometimes comes down to see me.

When I was in my teens, Mum fell pregnant, to her surprise. She thought it was too late to have another child. She didn't tell us then but later on I found out she had had an abortion and the child would have been a boy. If I'd had a brother, I sometimes think it would be someone like Robert. A little younger than me (even though in fact we're almost the same age) but brilliant, ebullient and sparkling. Someone who keeps me on my toes.

* * *

The ten years after Anne and I moved to the country were probably the best years of both our lives. We continued to love our twenty acres with a passion. We were both writing with some success. We also started working on social justice programs – another deep need for me. We travelled. And every time, coming home to our small piece of country was a joy and revelation. I tasted happiness.

We did sell Keil-na-nain after twenty-five years. The steep slopes were making my crumbling knees worse, and even Anne was finding it harder keeping cattle and horses on the steep paddocks.

In the last two years of her life, Anne's mother lived there, savouring the days, the bounteous flowers changing through the seasons, the benign vistas, the scabby gum towering above the Japanese nissa resplendent in its autumn coat.

Place is vital for our need of beauty, essential to our sense of serenity and knowing that we are truly at home. I had that only once, at Keil-na-nain, wrapped in its ball of magic.

Magic or enchantment is fleeting. It appears and vanishes at random. I love the house I live in now, created by us both, combining many features we have liked in other houses. It suits us so well. But I believe the best spaces happen when some magic brings everything together, not by artifice or trying. At Keil-na-nain the magic was in three early daffodils and a house we never would have seen unless an agent, unbidden, took us there.

Holland and Europe, 1993–1994

Sometimes unexpected strands of your life can come together, like intersecting railway lines. Twenty years after leaving Holland, I was back for an extended stay. Anton and I were long since divorced but still in touch and friendly. This time I was with Anne. Having lived together for four years, we trusted the solid foundations of our relationship.

We were in Holland for different but complementary reasons. I wanted to reconnect to the country and the family that had so influenced me when young. Anne was in the research stage of her book *Sex and Anarchy*. She needed to interview people connected to the Push then living in Europe: Frank Moorhouse in France, Gordon Barton in Italy. Others, like Germaine Greer, Clive James, Lynne Segal, were just on the other side of the channel. We decided to use Amsterdam as our base and rented a basement flat for six weeks from an expat Australian composer, Jon Rose.

I was waiting nervously for the proofs of my first book, fiddling with ideas for the next and writing poems. I had never written poetry before, apart from a few schoolgirl efforts. Before leaving Australia this time, a suite of poems about the family in Holland started coming out, triggered by the impending visit. Now, back on Dutch soil, visiting the ex-relatives in the north of Holland and in Friesland, the poems kept coming.

I Remember
that in the mid-north
of Holland
aka the Netherlands
where the bitumen
and the footpaths
are reclaimed
from the sea

we sat,
ex-husband
and I
over Dutch cognacs
in a huge café
carpets on the walls,
tables quite empty –

contemplating
our future.

We walked home
to his parents' house,
the icy streets
quite empty.

We climbed the stairs
to iron beds
side by side
like shallow graves

At the white window
the future,
its hands clumsy
with cold,
beckoned

and I remember
that I shut
my eyes tight
against it
and slept.

The Family Farm
Before I came back
the eldest brother
sent me a photo
of his wife and himself

outside 'Kooihof',
sitting on deckchairs
among the fuchsias
and the potting mix.

'Kooihof'. Just the name
lifts my heart in memory.
His mother long dead,
his father killed by a car,

he's now head of the family,
solidly seated, so rooted
in his earth, he can smile
just a little.

The White Bridge
Twenty-two years on
other people live
on the daughter's farm

by the sea.
The white bridge
is gone.

Holiday huts
in rows by the dyke.
The pub no longer

so far.
Roads better
cars faster.

But the same harsh wind
harangues the dyke,
hurls herself at the sea.

The Daughter Revisited
Illness has ambushed
this ageing woman clinging
to a slippery life.

When she is better
when the pension comes
(in two years)

when she has overcome
The Operation
(she has always
overcome everything)
then the World Trip
to faraway places

where everyone else
has already been while
she made obeisance to Duty.

She always had
large visions
in a tiny world.

I wish her big balmy
seas, blue skies, white
shores without end.

The Iron Beds
The same iron bedsteads
now in the daughter's house.
The worn sideboard too

stashed in the spare room,
the stolid chairs and table
of a thousand exact meals

The photograph on the wall
the clock in the next room.
Not much else.

Yet my landscape is
littered with their memory.
I was not here to bury them.

I nod over my shoulder.
See, I came back,
I tell them.

They are alive inside my head,
smiling, admonishing, always kind.
We are happy together.

But when I leave
the flat earth
and wide water
swallows them whole.

The Village of Painted Furniture
In the wind-whipped streets
the small houses huddling
close to their canals,

the sea always close.
Water
without end, water

No-one about. The painted
furniture remains unbought
the café owner taken by surprise.

Yet when summer warms
the painted shutters
and the pretty pot plants,

the little worlds beyond
the shining windows,
will still be shut
against enquiry,

close-drawn as
the heavy drapes
drawn for death.

I later sent Dorothy Porter these poems, asking if it was worth my
keeping on. We had met with Anne and Dot's partner, the novelist
Andrea Goldsmith, at a feminist book fair in Melbourne in 1994. She
wrote a terse but useful note which I kept for years and now can't find,
though I remember what it said. Yes, she said, it is worth keeping on
going. Always listen to the 'breath'. Make sure the reader knows who
the people are and their context. I revised the poems with this advice.

Some years later Dorothy Porter died at the age of fifty-four. A great
personal tragedy for Andrea and a tragedy for Australian literature.

Despite her loss Andy, showing steely courage, has continued her distinguished career and has also been a supportive friend to me, personally and professionally.

* * *

Back in Amsterdam I met my niece, whom I had last seen when she was four.

The Niece at Twenty-six
At twenty-six
a fresh shyness
hangs about her still

The same blond wisps
full mouth whispering
sibilances still

and an (imaginary)
little girl's hand snakes
into mine, in friendship

We settled into our curious basement flat in the inner suburbs. The double bed, just an extension of the living room, was jammed against the front window. We could see hundreds of feet going past on the pavement as we lay in bed of a morning, comforting and mesmeric. In the dark hallway was a big bathtub in a kind of cupboard. We used to lie at either end and giggle in the steamy dark warmth. Just a couple of steps up from the basement, off the kitchen, was a tiny backyard, a blessing on sunny winter days.

This was my first time living in charming, sophisticated Amsterdam. Anton and I had been based in a northern province and in Utrecht – another Holland entirely. It was winter again (in my mind it is always winter in Holland) but there was virtually no snow in the city. There were none of the famous canals nearby, but it was an appealing district just the same. We walked in a large park not far from the flat, admiring the ducks and the civility and sober mien of the Dutch. We often ate in a cheap workman's café nearby, filled with silent men.

I was happy to be back in Holland. I had always admired its people: their deep questioning of life along with a very practical approach to everyday living; the melancholy that lay under the extreme order of their lives. And despite the lack of space, or because of it, the beauty they created everywhere, in the smallest garden, wood or public space.

There was also much which made me mad, as it had done years ago: everything and everyone in its right place and the complacency and smugness that went with that. Yet Amsterdam was looser than the provinces, always had been. In some streets the fuggy smell of dope was predominant. Middle-aged dropouts and second-generation hippies were everywhere. Everyone spoke good English. Even the supermarket staff spoke excellent English. That made me mad in a different way – mad with envy for their excellent education system.

As we settled into the rhythms of the city, poems about turning fifty – living half a century! – were on my mind.

Turning Fifty

In my rented basement flat
I hear the shoes of passers-by
click, tap, scrape & shuffle
past my window
as I stare at old age
     over an ever
            smaller hill
and contemplate
the lessening options.
The larger possibilities.

Winter morning

Death sneaks in
one winter morning
sidles into bed
makes me move
over and make room

We should be friends
she says
so she can teach me
to live my life
a little better

Will she grant
a tranquil end
I ask her
or hurl me
fierce and frantic
from my life?

She won't say.

She knows
I'll bargain with her
scold her
send her to sit
on the sidelines
many years yet

She doesn't mind

We have such time
she says,
to get to know
each other's little ways
do we not?

I Dream
of always missing planes
the train always in the

wrong direction, always
one step behind the
safe step, the one
and only step.

Worse.
I dream of
my loved ones
starving, calling.
Predators
muscle in.

I dream of the
multitudinous
possibilities
of loss.

I wake in
a warm room
my arm flung
hotly over
my beloved
& my dream
slinks away
red-eyed
into grey morning.

A Women's Dance
A tribe of women
at ease
for a night
as if
the long
ice age
of no place
(except as
wife mother daughter
in men's houses)
had never
happened

as if
in every other street
of Amsterdam
it wasn't business
as usual
in a postmodern
post-feminist
world.

Amsterdam was such a civilised place. It seemed impossible that Yugoslavia was not far away, on the same continent, and tearing itself into pieces.

I had always believed in the promise of Europe, with its profound cultural roots, its proud and magnificent buildings and institutions, its diverse society yet with common shared values. That promise was always sitting on the horizon and turning into a mirage. Now the latest example was the violent disintegration of Yugoslavia. Maybe Yugoslavia was the real prototype, not progressive, organised Holland.

Europe
1.
In this, my grey Europe
of six languages on the
      cereal packet

(what was once) Yugoslavia
feels far away, muffled
by vast distances

a comic opera turned
      bloody
           not Europe at all.

2.
In this, my grey Europe,
the movement of peoples
is on again –
thrown out of one
ex-country
      over another
ex-border

Offered to
Malaysia
    Norway
Australia
    any place
from which to nurse
old hatreds, nurture
new loathings
    weep curse
        and dream
        of a home
        found only on
        suddenly useless
        maps.

3.
In Amsterdam the shops
are full for Christmas
(only five shopping days left)

People step gingerly
along slippery streets
linger by glittering windows,
buy last-minute gifts –
spicy iced 'stollen'
& baubles for the tree

& wonder what they
    might have done
    might still do
        for Bosnia.

4.
On the streets
at midnight
the stutter of gunfire
the shriek of bombs

Rockets whistle past
my cowering window
the night aglare
with angry smoke

I wonder where
the birds flee
whether the weeds
will catch alight

I imagine the dead
even before they fall.
The maimed and wounded
flooding in.

But it's just thousands of 'bungers'
thrown on the pavements of Amsterdam
for the Brave New Year of 1994.

5.
Is it possible again
in this my grey Europe
my old heart's centre
not to know –

or if we know,
not enough.
And if we do
know enough –

we don't
care enough.
And if we do care,
it's not enough

to stop the
slaughter.
As the lights go out
on Europe, again

again

In our last weeks in Europe, I joined Anne in visiting Frank Moorhouse in France and Gordon Barton on Lake Como in Italy. I knew both men from our Push days. At university I worked part time for a while for Barton, who had set up the transport company IPEC, and later the Australia Party, in his headquarters, then a corner building in Forest Lodge, a stone's throw from the university. I was a dogsbody, doing whatever job was needed, as a couple of other Push girls were. I never got to know him well. He was an unashamed capitalist, with libertarian overtones. The Push was free to use his fax machine and printer for their pamphlets and campaigns.

As for Frank Moorhouse, I watched him enter the Push as an uncertain Nowra boy, then become a force in his own right, before branching out as a writer. The Push was ambivalent about this development but was secretly proud of his success. Now, a little lonely, holed up in the French countryside, writing his magnum opus, Frank was the perfect host. One night he took us to a truck stop diner; we ate a meal unimaginably better than any served up at a truck stop in Australia. French truckies knew and liked their food.

For Frank Moorhouse
In a small French town –
the epitome of
a small French town –
sits the ageing author
the wildness merely lurking
in the eye, the hand steady
on the glass, these days

and I sit opposite –
no longer timid.
My dearest love
at my side

while he instructs us
on the eating of the
soupe au poissons.

'The crouton,' he says,
'the fish paste,
    the cheese,
        into the bowl,
            just so.'

Lake Como, Italy
1.
The lake is glassy under a pigeon-wing sky
until rain pings, scattering its vast calm.
It knows it is beautiful, even on this grey winter's day.
The rich, in their manicured villas on its shore
make obeisance to it. The far-off
ring of mountains pay homage,
doffing their snowy caps.

Today, a dull day, all gaiety spent,
pleasure-craft moored, tourists gone.

Gordon Barton lives in a small house,
a view of the lake from his study.
He is old now. Deaf, withdrawn.
A benevolent Lear becalmed
on a foreign shore.

His daughter comes home from the supermarket.
Efficient, kind, living her own mysterious life.
His son in Milan, visits between business trips.

Gordon in his study, tape recorder on,
is transformed.
Geysers of stories pour from him –
Push gossip, business deals, politics,
the zest and zeitgeist of his times.

When he pauses, his eyes swivel to the lake.
It stares back, implacable, hard as glass.

2.
Interview over, dinner done,
the lake a black presence
outside, the TV news
is turned on.

From Australia the Black Friday Fires
blaze from the screen.
Scenes from Dante's Hell
lick our horrified faces,
leap to our trembling eyeballs.

We watch in silence,
acquaintances no longer –
just fellow Australians
so very far from home.

                    Black Friday, January 7, 1994

A child survivor

For many years I thought I had no personal business with the defining event of the twentieth century. I bought my mother's line: I was only a baby; I had no memory of it. Then we came to Australia and led a normal life. End of story.

I thought my job was only to take into account the effect of the Holocaust on my parents. And to try to comprehend and manage the scale and horror of THIS THING that had taken my father, uncle, my stepfather's two children, his first wife, his parents and most of his siblings, among millions of others.

None of this fully hit me until I entered high school. Till then I'd promoted (unconsciously) a story that was acceptable to everyone: wicked Communists took over Hungary and forced us to flee. That was part of the real story but a relatively small part. The Holocaust was still taboo subject matter – too close for anyone to look it fully in the face.

The conundrums I faced when beginning to think more broadly about the past seemed immense. I was not ashamed of being a Jew. Many post-Holocaust kids were. They thought that Jews must have done something really wrong to be persecuted in this way. I saw through that myth early, but I did not want to be defined by Jewishness either. I dreamed of being cosmopolitan, creating my own persona, freed from labels. But the war's shadow followed me around. The accident of being born in 1943 was never going to leave me.

It was only when I went to a child survivors conference in Montreal that I became enlightened about my real self in the Holocaust years. In 1992, as I was writing a late draft of *Heddy and Me*, I got a phone call from my cousin Erika, living in Canada. Erika was the child of Heddy's half-brother Pubi. She was organising one of the first child survivors conferences. I was intrigued. I flew to Canada to attend.

I just squeaked into that territory, being born only two years before the war ended. Other child survivors were aged five, ten, twelve and so on, and more conscious at the time. Now we were all being acknowledged. We, too, had suffered and been traumatised, marked for life. This was a huge shift of perspective for me. I was no longer a guilty outsider looking on, trying to comprehend my parents' experience. I was a participant. For the first time I looked at my own situation and its effect on me.

> Everything I have known and written about shifts focus. It is only a small shift, like viewing a scene through the tracery of a tree, then moving a few inches to see the panorama clear. But having made that shift, I see I have to claim a part of myself long disowned. I am excited and very frightened ...
>
> *Heddy and Me*

* * *

At the conference I listened to many child survivors. One woman stood out. She was a tiny, neat-looking Polish woman, very shy, very self-contained, who spoke unexpectedly at the end of a session, in a faltering, lightly accented voice.

Almost immediately the room fell silent. Her voice and her story stayed with me.

Sophie Talking: 1

When I got home to
my town in Poland
there was nothing

The Germans took
the heavy albums
with all the pictures

I was frantic for
the pictures of
my aunts
my beautiful mother
all of them

I wrote to my uncle
in Canada for
some pictures

He sent me one,
one only
picture
of all my life before

so I carried
in my head
all the pictures

When I went to
the new country
I asked my uncle
for more pictures

But he said
there were
no more

My uncle died

His son asked me
'Do you want these
photos? I don't
know who they are.'

He threw me a shoebox
of pictures
of my life

All of us –
my sweet small aunts
my mother
        beautiful
my father
and his walking stick
        the children

One picture
torn in two –
my parents
on their wedding day

He let his children
play with my pictures!

I screamed to my husband
'Why is my daughter
sitting with my parents?'
'It's you,' he said, 'you.
Be calm.'

Now every night
I put the pictures
by my bed
near the shoes
        ready.

Sophie Talking: 2

When the thunder came
like the bombs before
I got up
and stood all night
by my children's beds
watching them sleep

The doctor said
'you are normal
don't worry'

Today
when the thunder starts
like the bombs long ago

I put on the shoes
grab the pictures

and I run to the empty room
where my children
used to sleep.

Sophie Talking: 3

They want to copy
my pictures
for the museum

for the future
they tell me
so it cannot
happen again

But I can't let them
take my pictures

Every day I must
see my dear ones
in the pictures

all together
all alive.

Talking at last
What did it cost, Sophie,
this talking at last?

Not to your sympathetic
educated girls
nor to your pups of grandsons
those loving licking boys

not to a patient husband
in a happy marriage

but to a roomful of
strangers
at the very end of a long hour.

You thought grief
could be catching,
sealed it in the centre
of your body
bound tight by bones
flesh sinew muscle skin
will

until in a roomful of
strangers
at the very end of a long hour
your small voice begins.

Maria Tumarkin says in her book *Axiomatic*: 'A survivor learns how to be alive and dead. A child survivor is a particular kind of survivor: an expert in doubleness. And a child who survived in hiding ... is in its own category.' I turn back to that time in hiding, not long after I was born, and try to piece together my part in the unfolding disaster for the Jews of Hungary.

I was lucky to be born at all, as everyone told Heddy to have an abortion; it was not a time to bring a Jewish child into the world. Even Feri agreed. But Heddy was determined to keep me.

Now I can look at my sister and myself as living beings, rather than burdens my mother had to bear. The Russians bundled us into the kitchen when mum and our grandmother and aunt were raped in the next room. On the barge crossing the river we were terrified little souls as the bombs dropped in the night. The tension and fear would affect any child; in my case through imbibing the sounds, actions, atmosphere, through my pores; for my older, fully conscious sister, the terror would have been all-consuming.

Our first years on earth were ones that no child should be put through. Of course, that applies to any child in wartorn circumstances. I am against the exceptionalism of many Holocaust survivors who see the Holocaust as unique. The scale and systemic nature of it may have made it unique but in terms of cruelty and racism there are many parallels in history. You don't have to look far. The decimation of Aboriginal people was widespread, in the open and brutal. But we Australians have never owned it, as the Germans, to their credit, have. We continue to hide from our history.

We children were lucky, too – we survived. Although our mother's love was fierce, she did not have the energy or opportunity to give us any psychological protection and to provide security in which to develop normally. Both of us, in our own ways, grew up fearful and damaged.

All this swirled in my mind as I became an adult, along with the troubles of everyday existence. Periodically I saw a psychoanalyst and eventually I worked out that nothing was really wrong with me, except that I had had a lousy start in life, mentally, emotionally and physically. In that I was by no means unique.

After the conference in Canada, a whole new strand emerged in my last drafts of *Heddy and Me*:

> I started to find this other child, who was hidden for so long. She was not the undamaged child to whom nothing happened, who had been spirited away to safe, bland Australia.
>
> I know who she is now. She is a child who survived the War, at the outer edges of the Holocaust. I can trace her through who I am now. She is my fears, my sense of displacement, my omnipresent sense of threat. She is also my resilience and accommodation, my will to find meaning and to make things work.
>
> Two words are used often to describe the personalities of child survivors: 'dissimulation and adaption'. So it was in the post-war years, and so it remained. So it continued into the immigrant years. Changes of identity, half in one world, half in the other. A child, yet not, a Jew, yet not, an Australian, yet not.

Even though the defeated Germans left in April 1945, it took a long time for life to become 'normal'. Heddy took over what was left of my father's business; her mother looked after the children. 'Normal' only started to happen again when I was over three, when my stepfather came into our lives. By then, there are pictures of me and Jutka kitted out as middle-class kids, smiling for the camera.

* * *

After Anne's and my first visit to Budapest in 1990 came a love-hate relationship with the country that lasted a long time. The city's streets and buildings called me, rich and textured, laden with associations. We wanted a small outpost to come to each year to drink at the potent fountain of Eastern Europe. Our friend Kati found a tiny jewel of a flat in a courtyard building in Liszt Ferenc Square, a few yards from the music academy and a short walk down the main avenue to the Opera House and our favourite coffee house, dating from the turn of the nineteenth century.

Our little flat had high coffered ceilings befitting a mediaeval monastery. But its glory was the two tall windows looking out into the courtyard, where, in spring, slender trees budded into the tenderest green. In the centre of the courtyard a disused fountain trailed ivy. The courtyard was bound by the sturdy but graceful arches of our apartment building. The flat was barely more than a big room with a huge-tiled stove customary to Eastern Europe, now converted

to gas. A small cave of a bathroom which, when lit, showed glass shelves dusted with glossy blue and green glass pebbles. (I still have a handful.) At the back of the flat a tiny kitchen with two stools for eating, and beyond that a small space which might have been a maid's room. It fitted nothing more than a bed. Anne had to hop over me to get to the bathroom.

The flat came fully furnished; the owner was into shabby chic before it became fashionable. It was our nest and foothold in Europe. For a decade we went to the flat almost every year, snatching six weeks here, three months there, and in between renting out to music students from the academy. We were immersed in the city. We took our writing with us. We had our favourite markets, favourite coffee shops. We made some friends, and became fond of the remaining relatives. My cousin Robi and I found some mutual ground – our fear of Heddy's wrath, as an example – and became close in our own way. His wife was one of my favourite people on this earth. She did not know how to discriminate between Christians and Jews. She simply poured love on people dear to her.

Back in Sydney, Heddy and I sat side by side sweating over the Hungarian translation of *Heddy and Me*. There were many mistranslations in the text. I could sense when the word was wrong but my Hungarian wasn't good enough to find a replacement. 'Find me the word, find me the word!' I'd demand feverishly. Eventually we nutted something out but she got the butt of my bad temper.

The next year the Budapest book launch was held in a wonderful bookshop at the end of our square that carried Hungarian and a few English titles. I spoke, in a mixture of halting Hungarian and English. My parents were there, remnants of our family (including a beaming Robi and Rózsi), my mother's old schoolfriends and our new friends.

We had made two lifelong friends, one Jewish, one Christian – both very different but both devoted to the ideal of Hungary emerging from the ravages of war and revolution and the grey domination of the Soviet state to become a stable democracy, as it had never achieved in its past. We were watching as a new Hungary developed and often we were there to witness key events.

In 2004 we were there when Hungary was admitted into the European Union. Suddenly it was no longer a struggling eastern state but was allowed into the light – the charmed civilisation of Western Europe. A huge crowd gathered in the city's biggest square, waiting for the countdown to midnight. Our friend Réka had tears streaming down her face. To her, once a young Hungarian-minority refugee from Romania, this was Hungary's crowning achievement. Such jubilation! Hungary had taken its rightful place in Europe.

In 2006 we wanted to have Anne's fiftieth birthday celebration in Budapest and invited friends in Europe and England and a couple from the Antipodes. The enduring image of the party was the surprise Réka had organised. Once the guests had their glass of champagne, Réka threw open the shutters to our romantic shadowy courtyard and a gypsy trio burst into 'Happy birthday to yoou' in

their strong Hungarian accents, their deep voices resonating through the courtyard. Réka had rehearsed the three men all afternoon on the banks of the Danube.

Politics with a big P raised its head that weekend; it was also the fiftieth anniversary of the 1956 uprising against the Soviet regime. There were clashes between people with opposing views of what the uprising had meant: violent scuffles, cops everywhere, and tear gas seeping through the streets. I heard people say that underneath the idealistic and nationalistic rhetoric of the anniversary the ultra-conservatives and anti-Semitic forces were trying to get the upper hand again. Some of our guests were caught at the edges of the fracas and were scared; others were excited by the drama.

After the first few years, getting back to Budapest became harder and harder. And after ten years we decided to sell our beloved little flat. Events kept me away from Hungary for the next thirteen years. My focus was unwaveringly back in Australia.

Writing from the imagination

The first book was done. The next peak to climb in my new 'career' was writing a novel – something I could pull from the imagination. I was scared silly. Was I up to a different skill set? I had no ideas to speak of, or none that I liked. A novel was *not* something I was dying to write, except in theory. I had no plot or theme, or even subject, as I had in *Heddy and Me*.

In this dull, flat period, I started to write poetry. My years in Holland were on my mind. I also went to a creative writing class. I was not proud – anything to get me started again. The novelist Sue Woolfe was my generous teacher. She told me, out of class, that she liked my first Dutch poems.

In class she gave us an exercise which took my fancy: two people on a train. What if something, anything, connected them? Months later I re-read what I had written then and thought, 'there is something in this'. I wanted to follow these two people. With that, I was away.

I had two vague themes: the first was about how people whose families fail them can find a more meaningful family of choice to sustain them. The second, to create a complex picture of Australian life: Christian and Jewish, country and city, black and white, gay and straight, working class and middle class; and to explore the cross-currents between them. I had no plot to follow; I simply followed my nose.

* * *

Jane is the Australian-born child of a Hungarian Holocaust survivor, Sylvia. She is unhappily married to Luke. Sylvia is very much a matriarch, loved and loathed by Jane, and tolerated with deep affection by her niece, Beth. Beth lost her parents early. She is more free floating and less conventional then her cousin Jane, both in her career path and choice of lovers. She is leaving the city to find a life in a small country town. Beth buys a cottage in Tralalba, my fictional town. There she meets Rosa, an older woman, living alone, running a nursery. Her neighbours are Dot, a single mother living on the margins, and her son, seven-year-old Kenny. And so the story begins.

I particularly wanted to set most of the novel in a country town. I had spent enough time in country towns to develop a deep affection for them, for both their architecture and their people, who I found often less superficial than city people. Beneath their stoic and sometimes monosyllabic speech, they dug further into the big questions of life. They could be more generous with their time and true affections.

I had so many images to choose from, big and small, when writing my fictional Tralalba: Forbes in the central west of New South Wales in my youth, where my father invested in a big property and where I fell in love with the landscape; or the outback towns in central Queensland when backpacking with Anton; or the Bendigo of my twenties; or the outskirts of Maitland when I first met Anne. Later, the small towns in the Southern Highlands scattered towards Canberra. To me the cities seemed transplanted copies of European cities, whereas the countryside felt real, unique and truly Australian. In the country, strangely, I felt more at home.

I loved writing about the town in the novel. After moving from the city, Beth invites her aunt, Hungarian Sylvia, to visit her in her new home:

> As Beth drives to the station, she tries looking at Tralalba through Sylvia's eyes. She sees the town's battered hoardings and sagging

pub verandahs, its shiny new supermarket and botched shopping mall. Just another nondescript, wide-streeted Australian town, redeemed only by some lovely old trees in tangled gardens.

As Beth gets to know her neighbour, Dot:

The paspalum sticks to her legs as she walks across the yellowing paddocks. Once through the waterless creek-bed, there's a better view of the Carruthers place. The house has so many out-houses and additions that it's hard to tell which part is the original dwelling. Old kitchens and sheds and laundries sprawl out the back and sides. There are two tacked-on verandahs used as sleep-outs, and the original open verandah is weighed down by a hoary potato vine. Relics of former inhabitants litter the yard: an old Holden with its doors off, a rusting copper, a mangle (still in good enough nick to fetch a decent price in an antique shop), rolls of wire, and the remains of a once-handsome orchard. A love-seat creaks under a tree, the stuffing coming out of its cushions.

There was another by-product from the writing of *Happy Families*. Once I got the story down and was writing my second or third draft, I became dissatisfied by the lack of depth in some of the characters. I started writing poems about them, their 'back story' and inner selves. All the characters were imaginary but of course with bits of people I knew, or knew about, as well as bits of myself. Others came to me from nowhere.

I was in familiar territory with Sylvia, a dominating older woman from the Old World, seared by war and the Holocaust. She started out as another Heddy figure but became quite different quickly, as fictional characters do. In a sense her story was what might have happened to Heddy had she not succeeded in keeping her daughters alive.

Sylvia Part 1

Good Girl
Sylvia was always a good girl.
There was no way out
but to be good for Daddykins.

The best hiding place is in the fold
of the brocaded curtains. It's close, dark,
a heavy dark smell. Sylvia's legs tremble.
Her forehead is moist. Her socks
cling to her ankles. Will Rózsi or Ági
find her?

The door swings open. The parquet creaks.
It creaks in a Daddykins way.
The curtains shiver.
The room is full of dark dust.

Mother in the Buda Hills
Holiday, holiday
              three whole months of holiday.

Mama's languorous limbs quicken.
              She walks through the lilac grove
past the count's mansion, down through
              the long grass to the village
for some eggs and a chat.

Father doesn't come till the weekend.
He comes on the Friday night train from Budapest
              The Bull Train the women call it.

Mama puts more combs in her hair
when he comes
tightens her belt, sets her mouth
clears her eyes of light

takes Rózsi in her arms
Sylvia by the hand
Ági trailing behind

and walks sedately down the hill
listening to the train's far whistle.

Sylvia meets Imre
at a ball.
Young women in waiting
their futures thoroughly imagined –
      spacious apartments
      solid husbands
      chic clothes
      brilliant children
      obedient maids
      soirees, cafes
      silver coffee sets.
The list spools effortlessly
in their heads as they eye the room.

Imre asks Sylvia to dance.
He seems to fit the bill.
Who is Sylvia to see further,
imagine a Hitler?

Married Life
A red-gold curl escaping the chignon
A light beam on the deeply polished floors
The perfect almond-crescents.
A giggle with the maid, also young
Small gaieties with nowhere to go.

Sylvia checks the manicure, her heels,
looks in the mirror.
Is the baby showing yet?

Daughters
Through daughters Sylvia redeems her life.
Daughters are her highway to salvation.
Through daughters a vision can be fashioned
Through daughters, dress, taste,
food, flowers, books
can be regulated.

Daughters filter light.
The ways they stand at windows
gives pleasure.

Daughters are a key.

If Sylvia had borne sons instead of daughters
there would have been no need for keys.

Her sons would have battered down any door
picked up huge armfuls of the world
and carried them back to her hearth.

War Time
Every night before bed
she plays a game with the children.
'My name is ...'
Two chocolates and a kiss if they get it right.
A disapproving frown if they don't.
Third time wrong she slaps them
across the face, turns
from their dilated eyes.

She will come for them soon
she tells them, she and Daddy
as soon as the troubles are over.

They'll be brown as berries
she tells them
from their holiday by the lake.

My name is ...
Two chocolates and a kiss
if they get it right.

Holocaust Blues
Where are my children?
Given away

Where is my husband?
Disappeared

Where are my children?
On the train to a camp

My sisters in hiding
My friends dispersed

I am a ghost walking
walking the room

calling their names
but not out loud

Out aloud I practise
my own new name.

When the War is Over
Sylvia is angry with the children
        because they don't come home.

They must hate her
        for teaching them new names.

They love their new parents in America
        much better.

That is surely where they have gone – America.

In America they are fat, happy, carefree.
Maybe they still think about her at bedtime
        just as the lights go out.

Perhaps they remember the chocolates
        and the kisses?

She is angry with them for a whole year.
It's easier than grief.

Sylvia accepts Imre's death –
She understands that men die in wars
and of privation.
They even die in concentration camps.
That's incontrovertible fact.

And children die too, of course
of diphtheria, accidents on the ice
acute appendicitis, or even still
of TB. But they are not
led by the hand into gas ovens
especially built for the purpose.
No.

And even if it were true
she would never have let it happen
to her children.
Never.

The children are fat and happy
in America.

Part 2. The New World
For a whole year Sylvia is crazy

Then she buries her memories
acquires a passport stamped 'never to return'
packs her suitcases

and from one day to the next
stops talking about the children.

Sylvia's Loss
When Sylvia lost two daughters
she thought God had thrown her life
onto a rubbish heap
and left her there to scavenge
amongst the rags and tatters.

She thought that if she had been better,
God might have looked the other way
& left her the children.

But God, being as it turned out,
the cruellest of all beings
left her alive and alone.

So Sylvia of the rags-and-tatters
packed her memories in a suitcase
and went off to the New World.

Where she married Henry
had another child,
made up her face at a mirror
in a quiet room
and went to sleep every night
(after reading five pages of a book she chose carefully)
at ten-fifteen sharp.

Emigration
When she left for the New World
Sylvia changed her name
to accommodate a new life.

Just a small change of spelling and cadence.
Szilvia became Sylvia
along with a new tight little mask
a new tight little laugh
a continental sparkle
a European style
so sophisticated, fascinating.

Even Sylvia's goodness
acquired a different moral value.

Sylvia's Revenge

An ordered life
others around her neat and tidy
and good, if possible.
          If not, disciplined.

The cushions straight,
the garden clean
          roses clipped –
or better still, no roses –
too many diseases,
black-spot, mildew,
fallen petals.

Australia

When she first saw Australia
the very light seemed clean
the dead safely buried
the murdered mostly black and
          not spoken of.

She thought things could be done
fences built

She saw a new flat canvas
on which to paint herself in tasteful colours

and her energy was as boundless as
the new continent.

The Right Colours

Henry was in the right colours.
A hint of warmth in his beige and grey.
Nice polished black shoes.
She soon cured him of his weakness
for yellow socks.

Many years later
feeling more secure in this safe
yes, safe foreign country
she permitted a red-patterned tie.
Quite dashing, really
with his well-brushed slowly
silvering hair.

Part 3. Sylvia Redux, Aged Seventy

Sylvia and Henry

Sylvia and Henry sit on the terrace.
He sips a modest scotch and soda
she a thimbleful of vermouth.

The azaleas in rude bloom
the pool blue, the sky clear.
A well of light before sunset.

When she gets up her chair scrapes.
He starts, lovingly watches the trail
of her dress across the lawn.

She picks leaves off the grass
tweaks a dying flower

He sighs in fear.
His breath blows gently.
He taps his fingers together.

From across the garden
she can hear the tiny tapping.

Poor Henry. Worrying.
Worrying himself
to an early death.

Sylvia in the Garden
Back bent, but only in the garden,
Sylvia allows a little mellowness
a small rambling.
She likes the droop of fuchsias
their passionate deep skirts
their feathery endings.

She likes the multiple delicacies
and sweet scalloping of hydrangeas
(so prized in Europe, massed in
the best florists.)

She likes the hellebores
the pinky greens & greeny pinks
trembling into silver

Winter roses they call them in English.
She hears their music
as they bend to the wind.

Picture Sylvia
Straight backed, slim.
She walks a little stiffly,
       feet firm
chin slightly raised
(her profile is best)
her proud nose more Roman
than Jewish, she likes to think.

Her lips often thin
with disappointment
but tremulous, pretty
       when she laughs.

Her skin, a languorous sheeny white
now creased in a thousand wrinkles.
But Sylvia never looks old,
just more distinguished.

Her hands, elegant and manicured
gesture perpetually.
       When she laughs
they quiver & play helplessly on her chest.
       When she's angry
the little finger clenches.
       When she's happy
she sits with her feet a little
       apart
    just a bit shocking
showing stocking to mid-thigh.

Sylvia's Hair
is a poem in itself.
Not auburn
    or flame
        or carrot
But a pale
    pure
    red.

Red in long silky trails
    as a child

Demurely clasped at her neck
    at fifteen

Dyed blond
    during the war

Cut short
    for Australia

Allowed to go grey at seventy
    (not a moment before).

Sylvia and Memory
There are those who nurture memory
    water and stake it
    finger its hothouse blooms
    wear the whitest gardenias
        in their buttonholes.

There are those who take
their pet memories
out to lunch.

    Not Sylvia. She buries
    her memories, builds walls

with barbed wire
big locked gates

How often she thinks of
throwing the key away
but can't.

At night, in her dreams
she scales the wall
cuts the wire, unlocks the gates
digs up the earth
& dances with the dead.

Most of the novel, apart from Sylvia, came from the Australian part of me. That was a great relief and a new freedom after the backwards pull of the Hungarian elements.

After writing a raft of poems on various characters in the novel, I wove some of the material back into the book, in prose. I now think they were the liveliest parts of the novel. Yet I did not take the hint this offered me until much later.

A strong image came to me of a woman, Dell, who my 'heroine', Beth, might fall in love with. Dell is the daughter of Rosa, the owner of the nursery where Beth works part time. Mother and daughter have been estranged for many years. Dell lives in Western Australia and is married with four children. She only comes back to Tralalba for a reluctant visit when Rosa falls ill. That's when she meets Beth.

I had written a lot about Rosa, now for Dell. In my mind's eye she is blond, attractive in a cramped and subdued way. Her 'feel' is sharp, consumed with some half-realised fear. She is living a suburban life which she deep down hates. Meeting Beth, whose life has been more expansive and varied, changes her irrevocably. These poems gave me her back story and a stronger sense of her.

Dell as a Child in Rosa's House

Dell lives in a street lined with willows.

     Rosa is never cruel, Bill always kind.

The boys tease her

     but not unmercifully.

There are yabbies in the creek

     bare legs in summer

     her friend Sandra down the road

There are bananas and apples

     on the sideboard

     Jatz crackers in the jar

     by the stove

     burnt chops steak chicken casserole

& a roast most Sundays

eaten in silence

     in the dark dining room.

The quiet afflicts Dell.

     Where is everyone?

Her mother shuts herself in the small room

     beyond the kitchen.

Dad is at golf

or taking the boys to footy. She wanders

from porch to kitchen to lounge room to bedroom.

Who is she?

In the daytime, books from the library

populate her world.

But at night ...

Dell on the Verge of Puberty
The hint of violet in Dell's eyes,
hair lingering in tendrils
                    on her young neck
            assault Rosa.
She twists the bright hair
                into tight bunches
avoiding Dell's eyes.

When Dell grows breasts
        Dad becomes distant
            suspicious.
Will stares and gropes her
in the bathroom.

And that blank space inside her
grows to fill her whole body.
Her bones sing to her
        a dull song of misgiving.

Dell's Secret
Sandra defects in favour of the boy-mad crowd
                leaving Dell under the jacaranda tree
in the farthest corner of the playground
                reading novels.

Her brother Will is coming
                into her room –
he's a vast secret crushing her life.

She wears out her library card
        but fails English.

Writing compositions
is impossible
    now she's
        vacated
            her body.

Dell Tries Self Help

Stops washing her pretty blond hair
lets it hang in rat's tails
greasy around her neck
eats to get plump, grows pasty
avoids light

Will is not deterred.

So she grows rail thin again
teaches her violet eyes
            to repel intruders
marshals her features in a perfect imitation
                    of calm

and just before leaving town
gets herself a perm –
a steely helmet of tight bright curls.

Children

Dell has three children and another on the way.
She revolves around the Hills Hoist
turning in the windy backyard
    by the swings and sandpit.

The oldest starts primary school.
    She makes sandwiches in batches.
She's got a little stockpile
ready in the freezer.

Some days she hates
the relentless sunshine
the violent blue sky.

Doug is a nice man.
He conspires with Dell
to damp down her fires.

When he feels her tremble
in the night, he tells her
it's only a nightmare, or overwork.

But watching her face inert
in front of the TV
            he is afraid.

Getting Older
At Twenty
Dell already looks older –
            her mouth thin with the effort
                        of controlling it
            eyes hooded with hiding
            her fine hair brittled with perming
            back hunched in permanent defence.

At Thirty
she is considered good looking
in a crabbed kind of a way.

At Forty
she is too thin, brittle boned
tightly held
            her body hoarding cold seeds
            of disappointment.

But Dell's Eyes

contain clues
she can't control.
Their colour deepens
to a tender violet
& for an instant
they overtake her face
radiate her cheeks
quiver her mouth
so that she has
to turn away
& order her eyes
to stop talking.

Meeting Beth

at the hospital gates
Dell can control
hand, voice, mouth
          but her eyes elude her.
They can't look away.

Falling in Love

And so Beth and Dell fall –
an apt phrase, Dell thinks –
          falling
                    plunging
                              an arabesque
                              a tumble
a somersault

                              a leap
                              in the
                              dark
trusting in the lover
to break the fall with eager arms.

When I look back on *Happy Families*, I was under-ambitious. I just wanted to see whether I could write a novel. I enjoyed making it and enjoyed the new skills I learnt, but I took no longer or deeper view. The book I produced was competent, well enough written, readable. But no great fire in me came alight, no overarching idea, and it showed in what I produced.

My publisher at the time described it as a middle-brow book. That wounded me then. I was moving to a plainer style – no pretensions, nothing fancy. Maybe I overdid that. More likely, she sensed a lack of real passion both in the prose and plot.

With a bit more luck I might have gained a wider readership but the book was mostly ignored, despite some nice reviews. Then came a surprise bonus. A year after the novel came out, when I was still licking my wounds, I got a call from Vision Australia inviting me to their awards night in Victoria. No-one had told me that *Happy Families* had been translated into Braille and had come out as a talking book, the latter read by the renowned actor Helen Morse. The Vision Australia yearly awards worked on a different system; their librarians chose ten books each year to be translated into Braille and made available as talking books. Then the books were voted on by the readership. *Happy Families* won both Braille Book of the Year and Talking Book of the Year, despite competition from established writers such as Elizabeth Jolley.

I did not know what to make of this and still don't. Maybe just because of its simplicity of style, the novel came to vivid life for vision-impaired readers. Whatever the reason, it was a nice boost to my flagging self-confidence. These awards have a special place in my heart.

* * *

Around this time, I enrolled in a poetry workshop run by Wollongong University. Ron Pretty, poet and academic, was to head the week-long course. To get into the course, you were expected to have had a significant number of poems published in good poetry journals, so I sent them out. I hated the process – trying to divide poems, which I mostly wrote in series; trying to keep track of what I had sent where. It was a bitty task and I lacked the organisation to do it properly. I only realised later that it was relatively easy to place the poems for publication.

I enjoyed the live-in workshop and re-met Joanne Burns. She and I had seen each other in Push and related circles. Jo is a brilliant and highly individual poet, recognised as such since her twenties. She was there as a teacher. At the desk checking in, I met Lesley Lebkowicz, still known then as Lesley Fowler. She became and still is my mentor, with her fine mind and honed poetic skills. The week lives in my memory as the three of us bonding like school kids, keeping close to each other in our sleeping quarters and forming lasting connections.

My class at the workshop was taught by the American poet Carol Frost. She was a hard taskmaster and did not like most of my poems. Many other participants were serious poets and I felt like an amateur in their midst. I thought I was not meant to be a poet.

Later, in Broome, where Anne and I spent a year, I wrote a few poems but sent them only to Lesley. As always, her forensic eye improved what I was writing. After that I stopped writing poetry until fate brought it back into my life many years later.

Broome, a different Australia

By 1998 Anne and I had been living together for nearly ten years. We were both writing full time on our twenty acres in Bundanoon in the Southern Highlands. So far we had managed to survive as two writers living in one house – no easy feat. There were a few periods of jealousy and conflict when one was in a low while the other was riding high, but generally we were each other's best support and mentor. Now we were contemplating writing a book together. Would ego, styles and ideas clash in dangerous ways? A big risk for any relationship.

Our idea was to spend a year in a country town and write a portrait of it, through its people, locale, politics and its relationship to the wider Australian community. But which town? We even talked about the town nearest to us, Bundanoon, but decided that wasn't wise. Wagga was a candidate, too, for a while, as was Gulgong, the town featured on the ten-dollar note. Or maybe a town in Tasmania, the island state as its backdrop? But no town we looked at took fire with us. Then we went to Broome on a holiday.

Until then my knowledge of northern Australia was nil. Broome grabbed me by the throat and changed me forever. Everything about it appealed and challenged: the heat, the colours, the remoteness, the intensity of its life and politics, the wonderful eye-catching mix of people. Everything I knew about Australia was being overturned in this town.

On the second day there, a Sunday, we rounded a corner and saw cars everywhere. I thought it must be for a football match but it was the turnout to the Catholic church. We slipped inside and stood at the back. The atmosphere was different from anything I had experienced. The mixed-race population of Broome – Malay, Chinese, Aboriginal, Filipino and Anglo, and mixed in all combinations – was there. It was a *Missa Kimberley* mass, the hymns sung in Kriol. The choir of little girls, old men and respectable matrons sang lustily, accompanied by a couple of guitars. The bishop, a tall robust man, preached on land rights and delivered a few pointed blows at Pauline Hanson, who was then in the ascendant. The congregation drank it in.

After that hour in the Catholic church we knew that this was the town we wanted to write about. Not only was Broome a physically stunning place, where at every turn you saw aqua water meeting red sand, but it also had a frontier quality, with its history of pearling, isolation and extreme heat. Then there was the mix of races, seemingly living in harmony. Despite its tiny size, it had a strong identity and vitality. We made plans to get back there within months.

* * *

We started the journey from Goulburn in New South Wales, following in the tracks legendary cattle barons the Duracks had undertaken more than a hundred years earlier, through Queensland, the Northern Territory and into the Kimberley region, then finally to Broome. It's only when you travel by car to Broome that you understand its extreme isolation. Its nearest town to the north is Derby, nearly three hours away. In the south is Port Hedland, more than six hours drive. Perth is a long, two-day drive. From the Southern Highlands it took us ten leisurely days to get there.

In those days, when you first drove through Broome it seemed to be gone in a blink; a long street with some shops and then nothing much else. A few straggly streets without curbing, a lot of red dust. Hidden behind the bougainvillea and shaded by palm trees, old Broome pearling masters' houses, built with tin and with wide, wide verandas against the relentless heat. Once you got your bearings, you could find the fabled Cable Beach and its resort, fifteen minutes from the centre, the mangrove swamps and the long jetty out at the port.

At the end of the twentieth century, it was still a small town of about 5,000 people. Its tourists came in the winter but the real Broome emerged only when the tourists had gone. We arrived in May, meant to be the beginning of the cooler dry season. The wall of heat hit us nonetheless.

Perpetua Durack, who we had met on our first trip, had found us a house to rent, next door to her place. This house was famous in the town's folklore as its garden had been the crucible for the creation of Jimmy Chi's musical *Bran Nue Dae*. It was a true Broome house – tin roof and walls, wide shuttered verandas, and two small rooms in the centre of the house where people could shelter from the cyclones. We had a bedroom in a corner of the veranda, with a chest of drawers and a bit of curtain acting as a partition. The house had many charms, but for us pampered southern women it was a shock. We were not ready for the rag-bag of furniture and random belongings stacked haphazardly about. We struggled to find a spot we could work in. Fine red dust covered every surface. Perpetua, used to outback northern ways of living, could not understand our worries.

We loved the outside loo, with its luminescent green frogs immobile in the toilet bowl. The garden was lush and cooler than the house. Donny, the owner, raked the paths lovingly but was deaf to our pleas to do something about the house.

Then came the rats. After dusk they jumped from the palm trees, leaping through the eaves, skittering through the bedroom towards the kitchen. The night when a rat landed on the bed broke Anne. The next night we escaped to a small motel and started looking for another house to rent.

Eventually we found a less romantic but practical small house not far from Town Beach. It had low ceilings and a hot, hot kitchen. But it had airconditioning for the unbearable days, of which there would be many. It was more suburban and tidy; the reticulation gave people green lawns and shady gardens.

Once settled, we got into the rhythm of the town fairly quickly. We told the locals our plans and began finding our 'characters'. It was a lively time. Apart from struggling with the heat, we were falling in love with Broome.

Broome Time
Broome time
is sitting on the veranda
thinking, on and off

Broome time
is bougainvillea in long bright arcs
suburban streets tipped in turquoise
ceiling fans and sweat

In Broome time
a plane flies low over Sun Pictures
scrambling the plot

Broome time
is elastic...
long... loose... elastic...
is iced coffee at Bloom's
a beer at the 'Roey'
cavalcades of colour
down Carnarvon Street

Broome time
heavy with pearl fever
development greed
old cruelties

Broome time –
a frangipani dusk
the 'retic' ticking on each night
oiled floorboards, mozzie coils

a breeze off Roebuck Bay

Broome Time...

It was an intense yet languorous year. Languorous because the overwhelming heat enforced a different lifestyle: walk or exercise by 7am, then by 10 o'clock it was too hot to work (unless you had the aircon blasting) or do anything much until the evening. Then the 'retic' came on to nurse the exhausted plants and grass back to life, and it was time for a very welcome drink.

Intense, too, as we became immersed in the town's life. Fairly soon we found the people we wanted to concentrate on for our book, people who would give us different aspects of Broome life. We divided them between us depending on our own interests and the connection we had made with them.

We told everyone that this book was not about Broome's history, as everyone assumed. It would be an account or portrait of the present-day Broome, through their eyes. We made it clear we would record every long interview, and always kept the tape recorder on the table. Sometimes we followed people where they worked or played.

Anne was interested in local politics and council matters from her time as a journalist. She met a young dynamic man called Kevin, who was from an Indigenous and Chinese background, who was making his mark on the town as a promising pollie. Another was Lyn, a councillor and businesswoman, an ex-socialite from Sydney who for a time ran a fish and chip shop in Broome. Another was Pearl Hamaguchi, married to a Japanese pearler, a powerful matriarch with a clutch of strapping sons, mostly working in the pearling business. Pearl had deep roots in the town's history.

We picked eight main people between us plus a large cast of minor characters. A couple of people we both got to know. Gordon, or Gordy, was a criminal barrister with flowing hair who retained the manners of an outback larrikin despite his long, manicured nails and habit of tossing his peroxided hair skittishly in court. He defended an endless line of young Indigenous men for petty crime.

Damien was his 'Bosie' – a beautiful, tall Aboriginal man with a mane of curly black hair past his shoulders and an insouciance and flair that charmed Gordy and most other people he met. Only in Broome was such a pairing possible; not only possible but liked and accepted.

Gordy was taken up by Damien's family. His relationship with his mother-in-law was deep and affectionate; she would stroke his long blond hair as he lay with his head on her lap in front of the campfire.

Gordy was fond of bringing his domestic life into court arguments: 'I can see how this would happen, Your Honour,' he would say in a domestic violence case. 'Why, last night, when Damien and I had a fight ...'

'That will do, Mr Bauman. Move on.'

'Yes, Your Honour,' grinning and flicking his hair. 'Now, in the case of Brown & Jones ...'

Gordy was a good lawyer, a very good lawyer.

Another of my people was Vanessa, a young health worker who was working towards a university degree which involved travelling down south every couple of months. Her father was Timorese and her mother Aboriginal. She was lively and had a keen mind and strong opinions. Vanessa had two lovely kids with a white mineworker. She was a bit guarded with me, protecting her privacy, more alert to the potential dangers than some of our other interviewees.

I had always been interested in the workings of religion, so I followed the Bishop of Broome, Chris Saunders. He was also known as 'the flying bishop' as he flew around his huge diocese, the biggest in the world, in his single-engine plane. He loved to fly. We went with him once when he flew up to visit communities on the Dampier Peninsula. As he flew over Lombadina he dipped his wings to say hello to the handful of people who lived there.

I was taken by his forthright manner and his overt political stance on land rights, with the ominous emergence of Pauline Hanson that year. Every week I went to the 'bishop's palace', a darkish place with mismatched furniture, to interview him. We drank bad coffee and smoked. He was a companionable person, intelligent, complex. He went out of his way to promote and laud the mixed races living in harmony in the 'Broome way'.

He liked to cook and once invited us to dinner. It was getting late and he was a little 'tired and emotional'. When the food finally came out of the oven he dropped it all on the floor. No-one was fazed; we ate the remains and had more drinks.

He was a man who made friends and enemies in equal measure. He had been in hot water with the Vatican a few times. I wonder whether only in remote Broome could he get away with his style of leadership.

Perpetua Durack became another of our characters. Perpetua was running an art gallery from her home in a gracious old pearling master's house, showing a mixture of Aboriginal and Anglo Australian art. The gallery took up most of the house. She 'camped', as she called it, in two small rooms at the back. She was the daughter of the artist Elizabeth Durack and the niece of Mary Durack, the novelist. The Durack connection was part of the folklore of the Kimberley.

Perpetua was a fascinating mix of hardiness and practicality combined with a ladylike gentility and hesitance. I think her persona was a mask to hide her shyness.

She had a bond with Mary, another one of the people who Anne got to know. Mary was one of the leading younger Indigenous women. Her family and Perpetua's had known each other for generations, often in a master–servant relationship. Another common bond was the Catholic church and the loving ties that the older Indigenous women had with the nuns. The bond between the nuns and the Catholic women they had raised was a potent strand of Broome life.

We remain friends with Perpetua and Mary today, and with Gordy; we telephone every now and again. We maintained friendly relations with Lyn although we have not been in touch lately. She has settled in Tasmania, a long way from her stylish Broome house with its cool spaces, where she would pad about barefoot in floating outfits. She and the Bishop were dinner-party friends, although I think she didn't have a scrap of religion in her. I don't think the Bishop worried about that.

Stephen Baamba Albert, an actor and performer with a reputation that extended beyond Broome, was a talented and charming man. He came from an old Broome family and had been married to Wendy Albert, a white ex-nun now running the town's good bookshop. Wendy was one of our gate-keepers whom we showed the finished manuscript to. Baamba gave a lively interview, full of anecdotes of Broome life and his long relationship with composer and writer Jimmy Chi. I noticed, though, that as soon as the tape recorder was stopped he became closed off and dismissive, his professional amiable manner gone.

Broome was so intense that every now and then we needed time away. Once we went on a small boat cruise with three other couples on a mum-and-dad enterprise called *The Tropic Rover*, sailing the Buccaneer Archipelago.

These Islands
These islands have secrets,
I know it –
    a little cache of lizards
    unique to one of them
a nest of nasty rocks
    for silly sailors

    an outcast pirate's bones
a horde of half-remembered dreams

a pair of not-so-secret hermits
    in a sodden paradise
(trinkets for tourists
    home brew on show)

We watch and watch
these islands
so similar and spare –
their secret selves
    hold fast.

About halfway through our time in Broome we took a break, time to digest, and flew back to the Highlands. We had a couple of weeks there in mist and rain, cool air, Anglo faces all round. Another planet, not just another country.

That started my fascination with living different lifestyles in different parts of the country.

* * *

When we arrived back in Broome a black and white puppy was waiting at our gate, one ear cocked, his expression saying, 'Where have you been?' We found out that he lived next door with some boorish people who neglected him, occasionally throwing him curried chicken bones and forgetting to fill his water bowl on the hottest days. There was a hole in the fence which he dug deeper and deeper until he could get through the fence easily and then he spent most of his days with us. How he loved to be let into the airconned house where he would sit on the cool tiles at our feet.

After a while we asked the neighbours if we could take him for walks. It became clear they did not care about him so we took him over. Eventually he became our third dog at Keil-na-nain, after Scruffy and Jack. He loved the cool climate of the farm, never forgetting his first ordeals in Broome. He bounded around our twenty acres in glee. He adored Anne. When she was not in his sight he became anxious and agitated. He was our beloved dog for eight years. But that is another story.

Broome had changed in our absence, emptied of the last tourists. It was quiet, brooding; the build-up to the wet season was well underway. The mangoes were ripe and lush on the trees. It was time for the annual Mango Festival. Some local had dreamed up the festival as a way of keeping everyone sane and diverted in the long weeks before the relief brought by the wet season.

Not long before our departure, at Christmas, a cyclone was bearing down on Broome. Here is a passage from *Broometime* to give the flavour of that tense time:

The main street in Chinatown has been closed off for the Christmas party. There is hardly a tourist to be seen. They've all fled because of Cyclone Thelma – still Category Five, still coming directly at us.

Broome is almost back to being a black town tonight. Kids are running around with balloons, the food stalls – particularly the Thai – are doing good business, and a few traders (fewer than usual) are trying to get some Christmas sales. With Chinatown cordoned off, the main street is one big comfortable promenade ...

[On the stage, Baamba and Jimmy Chi are singing with the Pigram Brothers.] They sing their hearts out, united in the music. They sing full-throated and full-hearted with the unpretentious musicality that is the hallmark of the Broome sound.

And the songs they sing! All composed here, for and around this little town.

> Just one step closer, don't throw me away
> and carry me back to my town by the bay
> When the darkness is falling at passing of days
> won't you cherish the memory of my town by the bay?

The crowd stills. The unspoken hangs in the air – that this could be our last night together in this beloved place.

* * *

We spent almost a year absorbed and immersed in Broome then we went back to the cool of the Southern Highlands to write the book. It was a risky process, writing a book together. We had been apprehensive whether our relationship would stand up to the inevitable fights over content and style. Our solution was to never blend our voices but to keep our individual voice and pursue different things, which we would braid together into a narrative. It never came to blows; in fact, it wasn't too traumatic. Possibly both of us blunted our own styles in order to blend in the book and that may have taken some of the zest and vigour out of it. The fact that we did it and had made decent compromises with each other only strengthened our relationship.

We were about to leave for a final trip to Broome, to tie up odds and ends, when Sasha Soldatow rang with the news of George Molnar's heart attack. He was sixty-five.

George was lying unconscious in hospital. Carlotta, his long-term girlfriend, neighbour and friend, rang me. Would I come up from the Highlands? There would have to be a decision about turning off his life support. George had no family and, somehow, because we were both Hungarian and Jewish, she saw me as surrogate 'family'.

A small group of people gathered at the bedside. George looked good, really – pale but otherwise sound. He had three or four tubes coming from his mouth, he was hooked to machines, but the nurses were keeping him as clean and dignified-looking as possible, and they treated him tenderly, calling him by name, as if they knew him themselves. They said he was deeply, irreversibly unconscious.

We stood around his bed, touching him, aimlessly smoothing his sheets. Then we took turns to be alone with him. I sat by his bed and held his hand, touched his wiry hair and found myself talking to him in Hungarian. We had never exchanged a word in our first language before. I had heard somewhere that hearing is the last sense to go. I thought that it was possible, just possible, that if he could hear and understand anything, he could hear it in his mother tongue. I spoke to him like a mother, in vague little endearments and reassurances: 'Kisumuifu, minden jo lesz, majjd fogod lattni. Tudod hogy szerettlek ... itt vagjok veled ...', 'My little boy, everything will be all right you'll see, you know I love you ... I'm here with you ...' I said anything that

came into my head, in some hope that he'd hear a comforting low murmur, something that would make him feel good, peaceful and calm about leaving us.

I missed the funeral as we couldn't get out of our commitments in Broome. Andre Frankovits and Anne thought I should write the obituary for the *Sydney Morning Herald*. So I started working on it in Broome, sweating under a ceiling fan, feeling lost, marooned, away from this tribal event.

A week after the funeral, I was surprised to see Germaine Greer in an outdoor café in Broome's main street. I overcame my fear of this fierce ex-Push goddess to ask her how the funeral had been. She confirmed what I had already heard: the curious lack of respect that his oldest friends had accorded George, telling stories, most of them not flattering.

I finished the obituary with this:

> George Molnar was a series of paradoxes: he adored children, but had a vasectomy in the prime of life; having a mind fabulously suited to philosophy, he abandoned it for many years;

269

quintessentially a Jewish intellectual who couldn't hold a drink, he tried desperately to fit in with the hard-drinking, womanising and gambling habits of the Sydney Push.

Much of the loving tenderness within him was expended on his adored cats, though as he got older, sometimes humans as well.

He had no family, but when he died he was surrounded by his friends from the Push, who will remember him with a potent mixture of irritation, bemusement, admiration and love.

The day this came out, I got a fax from Helen Garner, who I had met only a few weeks before, telling me that she had never met George but after reading the obituary she felt as if she had known him.

I cried a little when reading this. I thought maybe I'd done George proud.

* * *

Broometime was published in 2001. The book came out in March, height of the wet season. There was to be a launch at the bookshop in Broome.

The first sign of a storm brewing was a phone call from the barrister Gordy as we changed planes in Darwin.

'Maybe don't come, girls, it's getting a bit hot here.' He did not mean the temperature. 'Think again.'

We got the same kind of message from Lyn Page, but we were already on our way. How bad could it get?

Our launcher, Pat Lowe, writer and wife of the famous artist Jimmy Pike, knew what was brewing so she changed her plans. There was to be no nice conventional introduction – after a neutral sentence or two, Pat opened it to debate by the crowd. Anyone could speak. Most had not read the book and the speculation and rumour had run rife. We answered questions, mostly hostile, as well as we could. We stayed calm, as the invective and accusations of us having betrayed the town grew torrid.

We were standing on a covered veranda outside the bookshop, the crowd was on the pavement and street below. One man leapt onto the veranda and stamped on a copy of the book: 'This is what I think of this bloody book!' I crossed my arms in front of my chest in unconscious defence.

It was a steamy hot night. Everyone was dripping sweat. There was a sudden drenching downpour, lasting a good ten minutes. Not a soul moved; everyone was riveted by the drama.

After it finished, one of the 'characters', incensed at seeing his words in print and worried what his mother would think of his account of his childhood, accosted Anne, spitting in fury. We were shocked and shaken.

Afterwards, one of the older women, an Indigenous Broome matriarch, approached Anne: 'Come and have a cup of tea with us tomorrow,' she said.

She and her sister sat down with us in her house. They had read the book and liked it. They patted our hands. 'Don't take it too seriously,' they said. 'Most people around here are not readers, love. It will die down.'

The next day the *Australian* took it up on their front page. They kept the story going almost every day for two weeks. Our first crime was that we had called Broome 'dust-laden' and had described rats in the ceiling of our rented house. One journalist described us as 'lesbian seagulls who had shat on Broome'. We eventually got an apology from the Press Council for that.

In Broome there was an unofficial ban on buying the book. The bookshop kept it under the counter and sold it in brown paper bags. The library had a huge waiting list for it although people swore they would never read it.

Our agents, who should have been there for us in this situation, were not seen for dust. When we left to go to Perth for an event for the book, we faced another tirade from a young firebrand from Broome.

We were devastated. We had expected some sort of reaction but nothing of this ferocity. So what led to this disaster? It's impossible to untangle the many strands of objections and reactions. Some were petty and came from people barely mentioned in the book; others were major.

Some thoughts: we underestimated the hothouse nature of a small town and the spreading reverberations of every word. We were fascinated with the complicated multiracial family structures of many Broome people. But in dwelling on this, we had touched a raw nerve. Writing about who was and was not Aboriginal not only hurt feelings but also had big financial implications in native title claims. People were happy enough to talk about their heritage in person but not so happy about seeing it in print. We were perhaps naïve and not sensitive enough to all the ramifications.

We were also writing in a genre not common in Australia: contemporary reportage or narrative nonfiction, talking about the everyday lives of living people without aliases. We were aware of the danger of using real names in real time so we had suggested insurance to the publishers. They said there was no need. The book was fine. Our editor made only a few minor changes. Only my cautious father advised us to take out insurance, just in case.

In the wash-up we realised we had made two serious cultural mistakes that were not picked up by our gate-keepers who had vetted the book. The two incidents had previously been published in the local press so we thought they were on the record and could be talked about.

But both involved young children, one named, the other not named though identifiable by inference locally. We published an apology in the local paper.

The book was selling well but it was decided to withdraw it and revise for a new edition. Some changes were made. It was only after the second edition was published that a lawsuit was brought. A minor figure objected to a statement made, not by us but by one of our protagonists. The dispiriting repercussions dragged on for months.

There were radio and TV interviews, opinions for and against, letters to the papers. Some invective, occasional praise. Peter Craven, the critic and cultural commentator, was a late entrant into the controversy. After the first edition was withdrawn he wrote: 'The charm of the book is the frankness of the talk the authors elicited and the deep enchantment and strangeness of the world they encounter which clings to this story like a sweaty shirt. Let's hope it gets a re-run.'

My hope is that, in time, the book will stand as a loving portrait of Broome at the end of the twentieth century and as a useful social document.

* * *

It was twenty years before we ventured back to Broome. Much as we loved the town we felt anxious and apprehensive every time we thought about going back. In 2018 our friend Perpetua was launching a book of her mother Elizabeth Durack's letters in Broome. She wanted us to come. We slipped into town without notice. Within two hours we found Gordy, then Mary. With both, it was as if we had never left. We also caught up with Pearl Hamaguchi. She chatted to us as of old as she fed us sandwiches. About the book, she said airily, 'You shouldn't have taken it so seriously, girls.' Then she moved on to other matters.

Part 4
FATE

She said that life was a series of losses, and I would learn to make my peace with that in time.

Bernhard Schlink, *Olga*

Music heard so deeply
That it is not heard at all,
but you are the music
While the music lasts.

T.S. Eliot, 'The Dry Salvages'

Dark times

Still traumatised by the fate of *Broometime* it took us some time to get our bearings. Seeing the love that our Broome dog, Boy, had for his new cool surroundings in the highlands helped a little, as did the support from staunch friends.

I had an idea forming for a new book. There were three overlapping Hungarian lives on my mind; one was called Rózsika Schwimmer. I heard about her through a Hungarian Jewish man living in Bundanoon, a retired classical musician, who was related to her. My birth father's name was also Schwimmer and Rózsika was born in the same small town as he. So there was a good chance we were related. But much more interesting was that Rózsika, born around 1880, emigrated to the United States where she became a mover and shaker in feminist and peace circles. I later learnt that she bequeathed a huge archive of her work and personal letters in several languages – Hungarian, German, English and French – to the New York Public Library. During World War I she persuaded Henry Ford, the founder of the famous car company, to donate large amounts to fund a 'peace ship' to try to end the war.

The second Hungarian who interested me, again from a strange coincidence, was a man called Lajos Kassák. Born twenty years after Rózsika, Kassák came from a poor, working-class rural family. He left school at eleven and was apprenticed to a locksmith. In his late teens he discovered his talents as both a writer and artist and became renowned in both fields. Here in Australia I had never heard of him. One day, browsing in a shop in Queen Street, Woollahra, I noticed two pictures on the floor towards the back. As I came towards them, I thought 'Central Europe, maybe Hungarian'. They were modernist collages, signed with the Hungarian named 'Kassák'. I was right!

The shop owner had come across them through another unusual story: in Melbourne the grandson of a woman who had lived in Paris in the 1920s found the pictures in an old suitcase. The old lady had acquired the collages in exchange for meals when Kassák was down and out

in Paris. They came with her to Australia and were forgotten at the bottom of the suitcase for fifty years. The dealer did some research and found a small museum in Budapest dedicated to Kassák. I visited on my next trip to Budapest. The elderly curator could not credit that the Kassáks had made their way to far-off Australia.

I bought the collages; they are among the best art we have. More and more intrigued by this man, I hunted down his autobiography in Hungarian. I began, very laboriously, to read it. It amazed me that he began an autobiography of a thousand pages at the age of thirty-seven! I liked the daring and self-confidence that drove him to write about life when still so young. He called it 'One Man's Life'. It was lively, frank, eschewing the pompous literary style of many Hungarian writers. He also broke new ground with a famous poem, the Hungarian equivalent of T.S. Eliot's 'The Waste Land'. As an artist working in the twenties he was cutting edge and in touch with many of the European avant-garde.

The last of the Hungarian trio was to be my friend and ex-lover, George Molnar, not long dead. George was born in the thirties when Kassák was middle-aged. He came to Australia as a teenage refugee after the Holocaust. I thought his brilliant brain, strong personality, his radical politics and varied interests were worth writing about.

My book idea was to write three long essays about their interlapping lives stretching from the 1880s to the 1990s, threaded through with the themes of exile and creativity. Rózsika and George were both uprooted from their homeland, both Jewish, whereas Kassák, although not Jewish, was in exile from his working-class roots and battling to find his place in Hungarian artistic life. I knew the nascent idea would take a long time and much research, but I started nibbling at its edges. At least the project was about dead people, and mostly not about Australia. I would be safer. The wheel was turning back to Europe.

Anne was feeling disillusioned with writing about contemporary Australia, which was her chief focus. *Broometime* was the second book that had got her into trouble (the other was her first book, *Adland*). She branched off, following another talent and interest. Most of her time over the next two years was spent designing and project managing the building of three houses on a piece of land in Bundanoon.

In July of that year, we took a holiday in Bali. I had never been there before. In the back of a tourist van in Ubud taking us to a gamelan performance, we met two young Americans, both thirty-three. One of them, Jared, was polite and chatted with us. The other, CJ, was silent, thinking that we were boring middle-aged housewives on a holiday without our husbands. Still, we warmed to each other. A few hours later, over a meal together, it dawned on them that Anne and I might be a couple.

'That took you a long time,' we said.

'Oh. Well, we are, too,' they said.

'You don't say,' we said. '*We* knew that the first minute we saw you.'

A close friendship formed quickly. Twenty years later, we meet as often as we can. 'The boys' settled in New Zealand. We've spent time together in the US, in Hungary for Anne's fiftieth birthday, and often in various parts of Australia and New Zealand. Our four personality traits intersect fruitfully and in constantly changing ways. It has never mattered that I am little older than Jared's mother. They have supported us hugely in dark times since, and I think we have supported them, too.

* * *

When in 2000 Inga Clendinnen published *Writing the Holocaust*, I read it with respect and admiration. For many years Inga was an academic known for her work on the Mayan civilisation in South America. In this book she set herself the task of reading the vast literature on the Holocaust and trying to make some considered observations and conclusions on this calamity. It was a broad-minded and scrupulously fair book. I sent her a fan letter, written from my non-religious, marginally Jewish perspective. She wrote back warmly. I sent her *Heddy and Me* and we became friends.

I remember our first meeting at our Elizabeth Bay flat. She was just recovering after the first major assault on her health; she climbed five floors with her small knapsack on her back to have tea with us. She had a strong, handsome face (in her youth she was outstandingly beautiful), a confident, unpretentious manner and a deep understanding of people. Talking to Inga was pleasure.

One encounter some years later sticks in my memory. She was coming to Sydney with her husband, John, a philosopher, and staying with John's friend David Armstrong, Emeritus Professor of Philosophy at Sydney University. Armstrong asked her who else she wanted at dinner and she said, 'Susan and Anne'.

I knew Armstrong from university days; he was a friend and mentor to Bobbie Gledhill, so I had met him often over the years. David had also developed a warm friendship with George Molnar, his neighbour in Glebe. In the 1970s they had been bitter enemies during the 'philosophy wars' at Sydney Uni. George had not long died and that evening David spent a lot of time talking about him, how they had wonderful discussions on philosophy despite their strong political differences.

I sat around Armstrong's table with Inga, John and Anne wondering, as one does, how the many strands of one's life cross and re-cross. It was a lively evening, but the thing I most remember is that after dinner Inga and I drew aside into a quiet corner and talked about the tragedy unfolding in my family. How kind and quiet she was with me, almost motherly.

I found her an admirable woman yet no saint – she could be a formidable enemy, as when she crossed swords with Kate Grenville over what Inga saw as an abuse of history in fiction.

I was lucky to know her.

* * *

In my first memoir, my mother, Heddy, Dad and my birth father, Feri, were in the foreground, framed by their life in Hungary and the effects of the war. In this book I have kept Mum and Dad mostly in the background. My own lifespan and times as I grew up and matured in Australia are the focus. Not that my parents retreated once I became an adult; we are talking about a Jewish family after all! They did not politely fade into the woodwork as many Anglo parents do. Emotionally and financially they continued to hover. It's only towards the end that I ever played the adult, as their powers waned.

Ever since he came into our lives in 1946, Dad was our standard-bearer for survival. The Holocaust wrecked his former life, wiping out his wife and children, his parents, most family members. Yet he pulled himself together after a period of disabling grief, married Mum, and took on Judy and me as his own children. In Australia he started a new business career and eventually made enough money for us all to live in comfort.

In 2001, in June, we celebrated Dad's ninetieth birthday in Berlin. The irony of the location was not lost on us. Hitler was long dead and Dad was alive and kicking and having a fine dinner with his family.

The following year, with Dad ninety-one and Mum eighty-six, they were both well and pursuing their lives. Mum retained most of her fabulous energy. Dad was still working part time most days – he owned and managed commercial buildings – although the office mostly ran itself by then, with two dedicated staff, Pat and Chris. Sometimes he was found sleeping at his desk, or in the car while Chris (his secretary since she was sixteen) ferried him around to inspect properties. Yet his appetite for life was still strong. He was respected and liked. We were not worried about him. Somehow we had stopped worrying; he would go on and on. He seemed invincible.

I remember them both coming to Melbourne and beaming at an awards night when *Happy Families* found some belated success. When the *Broometime* debacle occurred, they were alarmed but supportive. Later, I found a shoebox of cuttings. Mum had followed the whole thing – the bad and the good.

* * *

Like millions of people the world over, Anne and I watched again and again as the planes flew into the twin towers in New York. Everything changed from that moment on. In Australia one of the far-reaching consequences of that horror day was a hardening of attitude towards people from the Middle East, and a demonising of refugees from that region. Then the *Tampa* stand-off soon after, when the captain of the MV *Tampa* was prevented from landing 433 refugees, mostly Hazaras from Afghanistan, whom he had rescued at sea. That led to Prime

Minister John Howard's arrogant and infamous, 'We will decide who comes to this country and the circumstances in which they come.'

One afternoon in October, the month after September 11, Anne and I were sitting in our lounge room in Exeter talking with our good friend Helen McCue, all of us frustrated and angry with the callous, narrow-minded reaction of the government. What could we do in a small place two hours from Sydney?

'Think global, act local' was our thinking. A month later, having got together a working group of locals of various political persuasions, including someone from the National Party (an encouraging sign), we staged a public meeting in Bowral. A big banner on the stage optimistically proclaimed 'Rural Australians for Refugees' (there were ten of us at that stage). On the walls of the hall we hung two slogans: 'Put yourself in their shoes' and 'When you know the facts, you will open your heart'.

To our amazement the hall filled to capacity. Over 500 people. On the seats we placed our ten-point plan. We got some good national media coverage and within a day came a stream of emails from country people all over Australia, including one from Gulargambone, New South Wales: 'I thought I was the only one to think like this.'

'How can I set up a RAR group in my town?' 'Can I join? What can I do?' It was my job to answer them. I answered each one in a personal way – so many isolated people, feeling lonely and helpless, wanting to take some sort of action to help refugees. They just needed encouragement and advice to make the first steps.

We had stumbled into the first days of online campaigning and I was building a membership soul by soul. The irony was that I was a technophobe, constantly battling with my computer, a battle the bloody machine almost always won.

From the beginning Anne, Helen and I made a good team. Helen knew how organisations worked and was a canny strategist. She had worked as a consultant for the United Nations and set up the union movement's aid organisation, APHEDA. Anne was good with handling media and at understanding the politics. I was a 'people person' and like a dog with a bone once I knew an idea was a goer and the cause was just. We were lucky, too, that we could stop our other work over the next few months as the movement we had started with that hall meeting snowballed. In the first six months, ninety RAR groups sprang up around the country. At its peak there were 120 active groups.

For the first few months I was fully engaged in the development of RAR. It was one of the most exhilarating times of my life. Dad would often joke: 'I was vunce a refugee Miss Varga, can you give me a little attention?' I laughed; that little joke was so typical of him, but I did not take it seriously.

Dad had had one or two health scares in his eighties but he bounced back. His brain was still sharp. He still played a bit of golf and went to his beloved bridge (he was very good at bridge) twice a week. Mother, as always, was Dad's energetic supporter, kept an immaculate home, travelled with him and maintained contact with a big circle of friends and, of course, her daughters.

One day in March 2002 Mum dropped Dad off at the Double Bay bridge club for an afternoon game. He was halfway through a rubber when the cards dropped from his hands. He toppled sideways from his chair, felled by a major stroke. His shocked bridge partners followed the ambulance to the hospital. 'He had a really good hand,' one of them told my mother later.

The stroke was so massive that Mum and I agreed with the doctors that there was no point trying to keep him alive. He could not speak. He was paralysed. His only movement was to raise his good arm in a gesture of despair and frustration.

He lasted three days until my sister arrived from London. A few hours later, he died, in the few minutes when no-one else was in the room. He made his exit quietly.

I had no idea that a great wall of grief would hit me on his death. Dad and I had always got on well but our bond had never been intense, just affectionate and easy. We never had anything in common – no interests or ideas. He was practical, benevolent, a good businessman and an indulgent parent. I was the dreamer and idealist and eventually a writer. We respected each other. Neither tried to change the other. It was very different from my fraught relationship with my mother. I thought Dad's eventual passing would be sad, of course, but uncomplicated. It was not like that at all. His death blindsided me, unmoored me. I realised he was the single rock on which our precarious family stood.

Immortal father

After 90
the years spiral upwards ...
a mysterious bargain made
                    with fate.

Then death rushes roaring in –
snatches my immortal father
from his clothes
                    & disappears him

The funeral happens.
Normal days come.
They go. A month arrives.
                    Then six months too.

I stand still, mouth
agape, waiting for the fall
                    of a footstep.

Dad's death happened without warning, despite his great age. Some weeks after the funeral we decided to go on a ten-day trip to New Zealand that we had previously booked with Jared and CJ. They had been living in Japan a few years and we were to help them decide whether they could emigrate to New Zealand. We were going to tour the country to find a place where they might settle.

Heddy was appalled that I would leave her and Judy so soon after Dad's death, but I needed a break away from the clamour and shock. CJ and Jared were empathetic and supportive and I was relieved to be somewhere else.

One night I was unable to sleep. I got up and crept out of the hotel in a small town, and started to climb a hill behind the hotel, in complete darkness, sobbing and wheezing, my throat constricted with grief.

Dad was gone. Dad was gone.

Although I rang Mum every day, my guilt at having left her grew apace. Why was I here and not at her side? I cut the visit short and flew back.

Once I was back, I realised that my few weeks to mourn Dad fully were over. I was forced to shift my focus onto Mum. It became clear that her grief was beyond 'normal' bounds. I know there is no such thing as 'normal' grief. It finds myriad ways to express itself. But in Heddy's case the alarm bells started to ring very early.

Her body expressed its grief in a very dramatic way. She had always been a robust woman, strong boned, energetic, extrovert. I always felt pale beside her, more like my father, Feri – shy, introverted, prone to illness. Now I saw Heddy, the heroine of the war years, fading before my eyes: lost, inconsolable, thin, ill. All in a matter of weeks.

Her descent was so swift. She plunged into a deep depression. Her physical condition deteriorated very quickly, too. I started to go with her on an endless round of appointments: doctor, grief counsellor, psychiatrist and other assorted therapists. Apart from her doctor, she dismissed them all.

'Nice people,' she said, 'but they can't help me.'

But her GP was sure to find a 'cure'.

'I've got over the shock of my husband's death,' she said to him. 'I accept that he's gone. It's just my body has fallen to pieces.' Then she would enumerate all her bodily complaints, desperate for a medical solution. She tried everything – diets, new pills. She developed new symptoms. Months passed and no-one could come up with a 'diagnosis'. It was as if grief was killing her.

Later, I wrote:

There was an early sign of what was happening. You became afraid of swimming. You, who had always loved the water. Swimming was your meditation, your yoga. You swam a strong smooth stroke.

Remember how you taught me to swim? Breaststroke of course – it was the only style I ever liked. It made me feel calm and secure. I have a memory of swimming towards you when I was small, reassured by the calm beauty of your working arms, the serene angle of your head. I'd swim into your arms.

'Little ducky,' you'd say.

'Big ducky,' I'd say and cling to your neck.

You swam into old age. Still a strong smooth stroke.

After Dad died, I took to the water. It seemed to help more than anything else. I encouraged you to swim, too.

'It's too cold now,' you said. 'Maybe when summer comes.'

I found a heated pool and spa near where you lived and took you to see it. You told the receptionist all about your husband's death. She showed us the pool, which was first class. You cast a cursory glance at it.

'I'm afraid of the water now,' you said. 'I don't know why. What if something were to happen to me?'

You'd changed, and not just temporarily – irrevocably.

* * *

The first suicide attempt came about three months after Dad's death. She swallowed about fifty pills – sleeping pills, antidepressants, whatever she could find. In hospital they pumped her stomach out. When she woke she was furious that she had not died.

Eventually we persuaded her to go to the Northside Clinic, which dealt in intensive therapy for depression and other mental problems. It might break her from her bleak routine and downwards spiral at home. She hardly slept or ate. I would find her at 11am in her little dressing room, staring at the mirror, still half dressed. Her depression lifted a little in the late afternoon but there was still a long evening to get through.

She agreed to go into Northside but after two days she fought like a tiger to get out again and got her way:

'No, I'm leaving. My bag is packed.'

We argued for an hour, more. The doctor was brought in. 'I can't force her to stay,' he said.

I pleaded, I begged, I bargained. 'You have to stay. Here they can adjust your medication, make sure you sleep, give you support. At home it will be the same torture as before. Just for a week! You promised to give it a week. For once, you have to obey ME.'

She began to cry like a hysterical child. 'You win,' she said and started taking off her clothes, oblivious to who else was in the room. Half in bed, in disarray, she got me to pull her pants off and help put her nightie on – my proud, self-sufficient mother.

Back at home, a relative, a lovely woman of cheerful disposition, a few years younger that Mum, volunteered to stay with her, cooking lovely meals to tempt her appetite and trying to lighten her mood. All to no avail. Her weight dropped from a size 14 to size 8.

Next the doctors recommended ECT. They said the procedure had changed over the years and was not as barbarically administered as in the past. Still, it seemed like a last terrible resort. She spent six weeks behind locked doors: I could visit her most days, although I dreaded going in.

> She often wanted to walk with me. We paced the narrow pink-walled corridors. Up, down, turn. Up, down, turn. We joked that we were strolling on the promenade beside the Danube. Which tree-lined avenue will we take? The one on the left or the one on the right? It was our only joke, but we enjoyed it. I took her insubstantial arm gently, feeling how close the bones were to the skin, how little weight she had left to lean on my arm.

On discharge, she seemed improved and went back to her beautiful flat, determined to start again. But soon the same round of symptoms took hold of her. She maintained she wanted to die and she started to plead with me, nag me, to help her to do it again 'properly'.

In the six months after Dad died, she made three suicide attempts. Two more with pills, secreted all around the house. Each time the doctors saved her and remarked how strong she still was physically, then discharged her, despite my pleas to keep her safe in hospital.

* * *

Rural Australians for Refugees continued to grow as my family life exploded. I stepped back from a leading role, though I still went to meetings and chaired a couple. I kept thinking that the nightmare would end soon and Heddy would start to get back to normal. The constant guilt I carried struck both ways: was I deserting the 'cause' to pursue my own small tragedies? Or was I letting my mother down by not concentrating all my efforts and time on her?

After our relative Evika had to give up on her, my life-long friend Liz generously offered to live with Mum as her carer. I was trying on and off to keep working on the book idea, so after much consideration Anne and I flew to New York as planned months before. I spent three weeks in the New York Public Library working on the vast archive left to the library by Rózsika Schwimmer, one of my three Hungarian subjects. It was a productive break, with Anne helping with reams of photocopying in the library. But I was consumed with guilt and anxiety every day away.

Mum finally persuaded me to help her in her third suicide attempt. I tried to find the right combination of drugs. But again she survived, again her stomach was pumped. To my horror the doctors were happy to let her out, on the condition that she had home-help twenty-four hours a day.

Within days she had dismissed all the helpers. She would not abide these people in her house. She swore to everyone that it was all over; she was back to her old self. I found a Hungarian housekeeper. She settled down with the housekeeper whom she liked, and seemed to get on with her new life. Her voice on the phone sounded fine. I tried to stay away. I had run out of choices; I had to believe her and resume my own life. Anne was, by then, thoroughly pissed off with the amount of time I spent with Heddy and my obsession with her.

I stayed away three weeks. Nine months had passed since Dad's death. One morning Mum showed an unexpected visitor around the flat and had a cup of tea with her. The visitor found her cheerful, bustling, chatty.

After the visitor was gone, she told the housekeeper she was going to see her optometrist and would be back soon after.

Then she took a taxi to Edgecliff station and threw herself under a train.

* * *

It was Friday the 13th of December. My dear relative Evika rang as dusk fell. Anne was at the stove cooking dinner. I lifted the receiver.

'Suszika, I have to tell you something. Mum is dead. Mum has killed herself.'

'How, Evika?' I said, dully.

'A train. She went to Edgecliff. She asked my son to identify her. She left a note in her handbag.'

She had thought ahead to spare me that. I was grateful.

I rang my sister in London. 'Sit down,' I said. 'Evika has just rung. Mum has died. A train.'

No-one thought
'The last person ever!
So positive, so lively.'
You fooled us all.

In truth you had not changed,
just turbo-charged your will
for your last big project.

Kali, black goddess of death,
fierce, enormous, invaded you,
I a crawling pygmy, clawing

at your feet, frantic in praise
of life. But what use
a living-loving daughter

but to help achieve
your one obscene goal?

I am not angry, mother,
you fought so fiercely to die.

Your Wake

Your wake, so long, stormy,
    left us bewildered,
        without resolution.

In the wake of your death
    a tide of guilts and griefs
        engulfed me.

They pooled into a lake,
    big enough to last me
        the rest of days.

Trapped in your wake, threshing
    in dank detritus, sinking in
        treacherous silt –

all to make good your story,
    your death less
        unbearable.

Mother-grief

I don't regret your passing.
At 87 you had earned
the right to go.

Yet for years I worked
to explain the inexplicable,
side-stepping drowning grief.

Finally, mother-grief arrived,
gentled by the smile from
the particular blue of your eyes.

Our quarrels, battles of will,
ancient ghosts, puppet shows.
Empty battlegrounds now.

I miss the crook of your finger.
The way you wore a shirt.
You carried off big earrings.

I miss your cooking.
I miss your mother-voice,
its pure load of love.

Grit
You had real grit.
In death you passed
a small portion on to me –
a grit I never knew I had.
Thank you, dear mother
for an unexpected legacy.

I have little memory of those first years after Heddy's death. In January 2003, a few weeks after the funeral, some good friends organised a trip to Vietnam for us; all we had to do was get on the plane.

A jotting from my notebook: 'How death crept up on Dad and snatched him. How it tempted, teased and mocked Mum.'

'Did her hands freeze in those
last minutes, as they did when
the Germans came?

I think you were not afraid
this time – simply busy,
in action.'

I could not settle when we got home. Anne and I were not in sync, to
put it mildly. So I spent the month of May alone in a seaside cottage
at Gerroa on the south coast. Anne went on a road trip for RAR,
visiting detention centres and RAR members, taking Boy with her
for company.

I slept a lot and gazed at the sea and jotted fragments in a notebook.

Enough
To hear the lilt of her voice
        would be enough.
To touch the back of her neck
        would be enough.
To see her walk straight, sure,
        would restore the world.

In my rented house with its blue-painted walls decorated with sunny
posters of Greek islands, I thought vaguely of my future life. I could
resume my book about the three Hungarians. But now that subject
seemed as distant as the moon. My present overwhelmed everything.
Writing about anything else was impossible.

I read a lot and I came across this sentence by Marcel Proust.

> One makes so many commitments in life that the time comes when,
> disappointed at never being able to keep them all, one turns to
> the grave, one summons death, death which comes to the aid of
> destinies that are having difficulty fulfilling themselves.

This sentence, stately and profound, seemed to apply to mother's
state of mind beyond the obvious grief of losing a husband. That was

a huge blow in itself but I think (not that Heddy talked about this then, at least not to me) that all the events of her life began to haunt her inner world. The humiliations of poverty when her beloved father gambled all their money on horses; her adolescence was fraught with penny pinching, visits to the pawn shop to sell the family carpets, and frantic pleas to the butcher or grocer to extend their credit a little longer. I often wondered whether that time scarred her as much as the Holocaust had.

Heddy loved a challenge; she always rose to them. Her life story attests to that. But when Dad died, somehow that vim and determination left her, disappeared altogether. Her mind and emotions turned to death; the only prospect which could release her from the nightmare her life had become. It was the only thing that invigorated her. Death became her last great challenge and to fight that dark force proved impossible.

That last day she planned very carefully. But did she think that throwing herself under a train would not leave permanent trauma on all who loved her? She was never a cruel woman but I believe that the death wish gripped her in a vice and propelled her to her end.

It is now, unbelievably, almost twenty years since, and only recently have I begun to think of her without the way she died stamped on the forefront of my brain. Only now can I think about her whole life, her triumphs and her magnetism, her loveable traits, her fierce love of her daughters. Only now can I begin to miss her and feel the strength of the love between us. Judy and I composed her gravestone together. I contributed 'A remarkable woman' and Judy added the phrase 'Our eternal love, Judy and Susan'.

With Dad, it was the suddenness of his death that shook me. After I got over that, I could weave his little sayings and jokes into the fabric of my life. I could think of him easily. I could summon him, figuratively, for his advice and comfort. With Mum the aftermath was much more complicated.

* * *

That month by the sea on my own became the basis for the second part of a book eventually called *Headlong*. Slowly my diary and notes began to turn into a fictionalised version of events, starting from when Dad died and followed by the months of Heddy's decline until she finally managed to kill herself. Part Two recounted the years after; the confusions and intensity of grief and the constant questioning of how her life came to this extraordinary end.

After that month I met up with Anne, finishing her RAR road trip. We met in Brunswick Heads on the north coast, our first time there. Then we drove through southeast Queensland, trying to heal our rift before returning to the Highlands.

I remember an exchange between us, just before the third suicide attempt, when all my time and attention was on Mum. She said, 'I want to be first with you' and I said, 'Sorry, but just now you're not.' I thought that she was being selfish; she thought I was rejecting her.

As we lived through each suicide attempt Anne had acted with strength and common sense, supporting me in all things. But in the aftermath she had to put up with me day after day as I went to my writing room and came out ragged and drained. I was frozen in time. I was working doggedly to make some sense of Heddy's death and to make a real contribution to the debate on the right to die.

I was no longer a functioning partner. I was withdrawn, irritable, out of tune with my partner's needs. The worst thing was that I did not even know it. Our arguments were terrible.

Art and literature often do not mix well with everyday life. Maybe I was performing a kind of penance for not succeeding in saving my mother's life. I wanted to resurrect her, explain her, keep her alive. Now I wonder why I tried so hard to keep her alive. Would it have been more humane and tender to let her have her way and simply be loving and empathise, as my sister tried to do.

I believed, and still do, that dying was my mother's consistent goal and it was her right to make that decision. The only question left behind for children, family and friends is: would the person who commits suicide have felt the same strong need to die the next month, or the next year, if only we had succeeded in keeping her alive?

I think every family of a suicide lives with that unanswered question for the rest of their lives.

Transitions, 2004–2010

I may never know whether writing *Headlong* so soon after Heddy's death was a good or bad decision. Most days, for five years, I relived each suicide attempt: the decisions, conversations, aftermaths. Writing it was not 'cathartic' as many presumed. I was too caught up, obsessed with doing the best job I could. There was not much room for plain, healing grief.

There was much activity in the real world apart from writing, but in my memory of this period the book cast a pall over everything.

If I'd started it, say, ten years after the event, I would – I think I would – have written it differently. I would not have put the reader through four attempts to die. I would have condensed all the details of her decline. Even though I fictionalised the novel, I was still telling 'the truth' in essence. It was a hybrid novel, never making a true transition into the freedom of fiction.

Nonfiction would have been my natural preferred choice. But the privacy of family had to be maintained. That and the antiquated laws of our country would have had me sailing too close to the wind. Fiction it had to be.

The book was published in 2009, six years after Mum's death. People who read it found it a powerful book. The problem was not many people read it. It sold a mere 2,000 copies, despite good reviews. As one agent who rejected it said, 'It's very well written but I don't want to go there' (that is, to the terrain of suicide and death) 'and I think other people will feel the same.'

It was a wounding but frank judgement and she was proved right. Perhaps the subject matter was too confronting. Even now, I hesitate to give the book to someone as a 'present'. Why put them through it? But there were many good reasons to write it. Among them, to try to break down the barriers and taboos around death and suicide.

My attempt to help shift that made little mark. *Headlong* was welcomed by euthanasia supporters and the softer 'right to die' movement. Yet Heddy was not a perfect poster girl for euthanasia as she did not have a terminal illness. She was ill, beyond doubt, but there was no agreed diagnosis. She was simply determined to end her life because her pain, both physical and mental, was unbearable. Is that not enough?

Mum chose the railway tracks only because she had found no easy legal way to die. Legislation had made the 'right' drugs very hard to procure and even if you managed to get them, things could go badly wrong.

In the larger picture, *Headlong*, I believe, was up against a reluctance to talk about death, far less suicide; death is a big shibboleth in our society. It will take many more years of discussion, less timidity and more breakthroughs in legislation (there are some already). Poll after poll shows that, for many years, a huge majority of people have supported the right to choose how and when to die. They understand that the wish for death can be as valid as the wish to live forever. One day the politicians will catch up with them.

* * *

I see, in having sent my father off to his death on the page, that I have once again skirted around the dark side of him and buried it. It is time, many years after his demise in 2002, to put a stop to that.

The mildest depiction of the darker side of Dad was that he was a man who couldn't tame his libido. In that he was not alone among the male sex. That would account for the rumours of his extramarital affairs, despite his adoration for his wife.

I myself had a brush with his worse side when approaching adolescence but was relatively lucky. Maybe Mum had an inkling of danger because she became watchful as Dad became sexual around me. She supervised his sexualised behaviours. For instance, he wanted to have 'neck parties', which would involve me lying on top of the bed while he nuzzled my neck. It was meant to be a kind of joke, and to indulge him. Mum would stand at the door of the marital bedroom and after a few minutes say, 'That's enough.'

It was a queasy part of 'family fun'. Another 'fun' thing was having a bath together. He had to put on his bathers – I was growing breasts by then. I think I had my swimming costume on but I can't be sure now. Again, Mum would hover near the bathroom. I was a naïve child, maybe twelve. I just thought it was icky and weird. And after a while I refused to play.

In my adulthood I watched with unease the way Dad squeezed and pummelled my stepson's young flesh. I believe it was harmless but it was borderline behaviour.

Then, years later, I was appalled when a dear friend told me that Dad had attacked her sexually more than once in his office, even risking being discovered by the staff. I had to step in then. I told him forcefully that it had to stop. He agreed, sheepishly, but I saw no signs of remorse or horror at his own behaviour, just embarrassment about being found out.

Yet everything else I have said about him – his kindness, mildness, benevolence, generosity – is also true. I did not stop loving him. Go figure the complexity of human behaviour.

The effect on my own sexuality was to make me wary of sex, never quite letting myself go. What sordid and dangerous path would it lead to? The result: long-term sexual unhappiness.

I bring these events up reluctantly after a long period of silence because many families have similar stories lying buried. For centuries men have felt themselves entitled to proposition or force sex on women or girls, including their wives, whenever they have the opportunity. My guess is that every second girl has had an uncle, a stepfather, a father, a brother, a grandfather, a neighbour who took 'liberties' which traumatised and confused them. In my case, as well as Dad, there was the neighbour's gardener, who lived two doors down, trying to entice me into his room. I escaped before any real harm was done. For centuries women and girls just put up with it. They buried it. In the twentieth century, as women's power gradually increased, our silenced and timid voices became stronger. In the twenty-first century, this canker at the core of family life is rising to the surface. Maybe another 'Me Too' campaign will eventually explode the issue and force real change. But I wonder whether the silence, the secrecy (and long-lasting damage), will ever be eradicated. This vein runs very deep in all societies.

The last few years have seen an erruption of horrifying stories of institutional child abuse, especially in the Catholic school system. This disaster came very close to us in 2018. Among Anne's closest friends were Mark Wakely and Steven Alward; all three met as cub reporters at the *Newcastle Herald*, an incubator for talented young Novocastrians. Mark and Steven formed a binding relationship, lasting thirty-eight years. Both forged excellent careers at the ABC. Both men were respected and liked. All seemed well in their world.

Not long after marriage equality was passed (Steven and Mark had waited and campaigned for it), they planned their wedding. Anne was to be a witness. The morning after she and Steven had been discussing the wedding music, Anne received a call from a detective who then handed the phone to a distraught and bewildered Mark. Steven had killed himself overnight.

Anne and I spent the next three days by Mark's side, as he commenced the struggle of his life: how to live without Steven and how to make sense of this hideous tragedy. No-one could believe it; they had a wedding imminent, a long and loving relationship, and were at the beginning of a delightful retirement.

After some time and much research it became clear that the reason for Steven's suicide (if not the only one) was the endemic child sexual abuse by teachers and priests in Catholic schools in the Newcastle area. Steven had been obsessed by the findings of the royal commission, often staying up half the night to read the reports. And he felt guilty, complicit, because for a long time he had defended a priest who turned out to be one of the worst offenders. He was deeply depressed by the number of suicides in his school cohort. But he never said he had himself been abused. After his death it came to light that he had.

The evening after talking to Anne about the wedding plans, Steven got another call. He talked for a long time to the brother of a schoolfriend who had killed himself. During the night, while Mark was asleep, he took his own life.

No-one who knew and loved Steven can recover from the shock of his death. Yet his is one of many tragic stories of lives blighted or cut short. The betrayal of trust and innocence by priests – men of God and 'Fathers' to these boys – is another dark hidden seam in our society.

Again, one hopes for change, real change, but can it happen without demolishing the institutions that have bred the abuse?

* * *

Everything changed when Heddy and Gyuszi died. It was a hard and complex time, but this new parentless life also turned out to be immensely productive, brought about directly and indirectly by their deaths.

Much of what happened demands a different kind of narrative, involving a public part of one's self, and it is hard to avoid sounding self-serving or, worse, preachy. So I will only sketch two ventures which took up a big part of our lives in these years. One I have already talked about, the creation of Rural Australians for Refugees. The other was the establishment, flowing directly from Dad's death, of the Becher Foundation.

But first: my sister and I decided not to continue with Dad's business, as he had hoped. Joseph's daughter, my cousin Suzi, now took over her half of Varga Brothers. Over the next two years Judy and I sorted out how to close our half and sell off the assets, dividing them between us. There were long sessions with staff, accountants, lawyers and others. Neither of us had a head for business so it was hard, brain-breaking work. The complex structures and evaluations took a big toll on our fragile relationship.

Once we had finally finished with the business, a cautious friendship grew between us. Our parents had hoped for this rapprochement but both had, albeit not consciously, set us against each other. The new friendship grew uncertainly for a few years, then withered. But lately, to my relief and happiness, it has been revived. These days we aim for affection and civility, knowing our bond is deep and important but easily upset.

Finally, I was financially independent, and not before time, at sixty! Now I could put my money where my mouth was, by putting a big slice of my inheritance to good use.

Most of my life I struggled with my feelings about money. Our first ten or so years in Australia were hard scrabble, but in my late high school years our finances became pretty stable. In Australian terms we were middle class; nothing special. But compared to the developing world, middle-class Australians led a dream existence. Not everyone, though – even here in the lucky country there is real poverty.

In high school I had a friend whose family was very poor. Visiting her at home, big questions obsessed me: why did some people live well, free from worries about rent, food, a decent house to live in, while others were beset with these worries? I wanted to help right the imbalance.

Personally, I always had Dad in the background. After I left school he often wanted to give me more to live on than I would ask for. He was always over-generous. I had worked in the school holidays when I was at school and university, and I tried to live modestly. The idea of being 'rich' sickened me. But what to do about it?

In my twenties I was apolitical. I had no affinity for politics and was influenced by the Push's anarchist and outsider stances. I did not vote until my thirties. I did not march for Vietnam or for the end of apartheid. I was ignorant of the theft of Aboriginal culture and land. It was only when I came back from Holland, and after Whitlam came to power, that I acknowledged the importance of political life and its ability to make real change. For those disillusioned by politics in this dreary, cynical era, I recommend *Gough and Me*, written by my friend from Video Access days, Christine Sykes, which shows so clearly how a good, principled politician can make a real difference to ordinary destinies. Citizens at the grassroots level also need to push for change. The combination can move a mountain or two.

After the Whitlam years I became an on-and-off activist. When I went to law school there was not much time for that but later, after graduating and teaming up with Anne, I used my university contacts to start a public education project around the High Court's Mabo decision. The idea was to quieten the fear of white people who thought their backyards would be stolen, and replace that fear with accessible information. We produced materials and sent out law students and other volunteers to schools and Rotary and service clubs to discuss the issue. It went well and gave me a taste of what could be done with some organisation, time and a bit of money.

Dad had left everything in his will to Judy and me, with one 'request': to honour small annual payments he made to relatives and friends all over the world. Twenty years later, we are still making these payments, mostly to people we have never met: a rabbi in New York with a sick child (now in his thirties), a third cousin in Tel Aviv, an old friend in Hungary and so on.

Apart from that I had a free hand to put 'socialist' ideas to good effect. For years I had dreamed of having a foundation with a progressive agenda, putting social justice and the creation of equality as the main aim, rather than conventional charity and 'worthy' causes. Easier said than done. What were the real drivers of social change? And what was idealistic nonsense?

In my midlife, my life started to cohere, after meeting Anne and beginning to write, yet there was a missing third leg in acquiring maturity: learning to manage money with less guilt and more responsibility.

Once I knew finally what I had inherited, Anne and I set up a foundation named Becher, after Dad's first business in Sydney, an archetypal clothing factory. (In the family we called it 'Becher' because the first owner was a man called Becher.) The name was a bow to Dad without revealing too much. We wanted the foundation to fly under the radar.

We wanted to go where many other philanthropists did not go. We avoided the more common causes like cancer, hospitals and the mainstream arts, knowing they were ever popular. Our policy, which differed from most other foundations, was to fund social justice programs, for at least three years. Often small organisations get funding for only a single year then have to apply all over again. I had seen from the other side of the fence, when running the Video Access centre, what a time-waster it was having to constantly reapply for grants.

We also made a decision to fund running costs, particularly salaries. Often organisations can get money for 'projects' only, rather than core funding. We usually backed a salaried position for three years to give them a real chance. We also tried to stick with an organisation if we believed in it, even if there was a major crisis. When the struggling Asylum Seeker Centre in Sydney was in trouble, gipped by a dodgy accountant, we stood by them and made up the shortfall.

We had four focus areas that reflected our strong interests: aiding and protecting refugees, funding Indigenous community development, assisting women in the developing world, and supporting projects in rural and regional Australia. A fifth, another bow to Dad, as it was his money after all, was Jewish welfare causes, which he would have liked.

To give a feel for some of the Becher projects overseas: in Laos, disadvantaged rural girls were supported to learn hairdressing while living in a hostel in the capital; in Vietnam, women in a poor rural area were enabled to buy a pig and to house it in the family compound so they could create a small business from the piglets.

In Australia, in the Aboriginal community of Bowraville, we supported a youth project to keep the kids off the streets at night by feeding them and engaging them in creative activities. In another, we helped an Indigenous radio station appealing to the young to get off the ground. Arising out of our time in the Kimberley, having seen the lack of culturally specific mental health services for Indigenous communities, we funded an Indigenous psychologist to work in the famous arts community of Warmun.

In rural and regional Australia, we had a favourite project called 'Halls of Fame'. A community would apply to renovate their local hall, fallen into disuse; it would get money for new windows, new stoves, roof repairs and so on. Funding this project was a 'no-brainer'; these old halls are vital meeting places in a village or town.

We went on a road trip to see some of these refurbished halls. It was lovely to see them come to life, used again for mothers groups, plays, crafts groups, choirs, fundraising, dances, meetings, weddings. We had only one rule – we wouldn't fund aluminium windows for lovely old weatherboard halls!

Sometimes a simple scheme pops up from nowhere. Anne and I were listening to a program on domestic violence, about how many women stay in a violent relationship because they cannot leave their pets. Often the violent partner would threaten to kill the pet. We approached the RSPCA with a scheme for medium-term accommodation for pets so that a woman and kids could leave the house and still keep their animals safe. Once the family had resettled, they could collect their pets. This idea was taken up by the RSPCA with alacrity. They worked with domestic violence services and now a number of women's refuges have facilities for pets.

For the first year or so, Anne and I ran the foundation on our own. Then we found a tiny office in a demountable in Bundanoon, employed an assistant and spent two days a week working on foundation business. Anne and I worked well together. Anne was the CEO and much of the brains behind Becher. I was the Chair, with experience of community work. Later we got more help as the structure and workload started to overwhelm us.

After ten years we decided to close the foundation. We were tired and thought we could still give privately without the organisational structure. The foundation's capital went to the Asylum Seeker Centre, which was being run out of a tiny one-storey terrace in Surry Hills. The space was so small that staff had to share desks. It was ridiculously inadequate given the ever-growing need for its services. They were doing life-saving frontline work. The new building that we, together with a few other donors, bought for them made an extraordinary difference. The number of people using the centre increased ten-fold, as did the services it could offer. So shabby is Australia's treatment of refugees that the Asylum Seeker Centre in Sydney is more and more an essential service to keep people alive while their fate is being decided.

When the building opened, the centre's management wanted to name it after our foundation. So Becher House was named after the first business Dad and his brother bought in Australia, the clothing factory on the Parramatta Road. On a plaque at the front of the building: 'From refugees of former times to the refugees and asylum seekers of today. A bright future for all, free from fear.'

How many of these ideas and schemes bore real fruit and how many foundered? It's hard to know. In this field many factors have to fall into place to achieve success. Often the critical factor is the clarity and drive of the people in charge, who have that extra something, which makes the difference between success and failure. We learnt a lot from running the foundation and hopefully many good things came out of it.

* * *

We had been thinking about escaping the cold winters in the Highlands. After fifteen years of lugging wood to our combustion stove, the romance of foggy, wet, long winters had palled. In the Highlands, the cold weather lasts from April to mid-October. So we went up to Brunswick Heads again to visit my old friend June and started to look around the area.

'Stay on the coast,' June said, 'the breeze is a saviour in summer.' That put paid to our idea of a lovely old weatherboard in Mullumbimby.

One day in Bruns we were inspecting a block of flats that might be worth renovating and sharing with June and her partner, David. The agent saw that Anne and I were not impressed.

'So what would you really like, girls?' she asked.

We had noticed a delightful weatherboard cottage just across the lane, and we pointed to it. 'Something like that.'

'Well, as it happens, it's just come on the market today. I'll give them a ring.'

Half an hour later, we were inside. The house was a mess, dirty dishes piled on the sink, mattresses strewn on the floor. It did not matter. We both fell in love. The house had an instant charm; not only high ceilings and well-proportioned rooms, but the owners had painted in outré, interesting colours; a strong aqua next to baby blue, a musky pink next to yellow. It had personality plus.

'Of course, you'll repaint it,' said June, whose taste was very *House and Garden*; her favourite colour was beige.

'No way,' we said in unison, 'we love the colours. They suit the place.'

The house had a delicious but tiny kitchen, big hall cupboards built meticulously by the carpenter-owner, lovely recycled old timber windows. It was a simple 1917 weatherboard house, bought for a song in rural Queensland and trucked down and renovated over seven years, while the family lived in the mess. I could not understand how they could bear to leave once it was almost finished, but they were off to the next one.

We made an offer within an hour of seeing it, and by the evening it was ours.

The owners stayed on for a few months, finishing off the veranda and other bits that needed doing. Then, after shipping some basics, I spent three months on my own there, working on *Headlong* and haunting the op shops and secondhand places to buy pots and pans, glasses, bedside tables, vases, pictures and more, bringing my treasures home. My best find was a not-bad copy of Picasso's *The Bathers*, which I bought for forty dollars at the junk shop across the road. Picasso's young women with their stylised bathers, their long, long arms and flowing long hair suited the house well. There was even a lighthouse to approximate the Byron Bay lighthouse you could see from our beach. By the time Anne came up to join me, there was a ramshackle but functioning household.

So began sixteen years of annual migration with three dogs, Annie's horse, then two horses, our work paraphernalia and other gear. We migrated for three to five months each year. So in love were we with Bruns that sometimes our loyalties were divided. It was our 'town house', our seaside house, the warm semi-tropical house, and where our friends were younger, more informal, more 'alternative', and the way of living more eclectic.

Another, deeper reason for both of us was that Gyuszi and Heddy had never seen it. It was like a new start, with a new sense of possibility. In Exeter we had spent a sad/happy time integrating some of Mum's beautiful antique furniture into our house, taking care so it would not overwhelm our own style. Still the house became weightier and more 'grown up'. In Bruns, except for an eighteenth-century French table Heddy had used for a bedside table and a rug or two, everything else was thrown together from local finds in a cheerful jumble. The house seemed to accommodate and take to its bosom everything we threw at it.

The physical beauties of the place are quiet yet eternal; this is the place where a broad river meets the sea, the famous cone of the Chincogan mountain in the background. There is a sea wall jutting into the ocean where locals and tourists mingle every evening to see the sunset and glimpse the lighthouse winking from Byron. The caravan parks enjoy the best spots, as they should; the caravan parks with their locals and every-year returnees are intrinsic to seaside Bruns. If they ever get taken over by developers constructing ugly mansions and anonymous flat buildings, it will spell the end to this lovely place. Bruns has been a refuge for eccentrics, aged hippies and people with disabilities who find a haven in backyard flats. But they are being priced out; the soul of Bruns is being eaten away by money and Airbnb.

A few poems came from the different currents in the Bruns air. I wrote one the year Julia Gillard was dethroned by a vengeful Kevin Rudd. She retreated from public life. I often wondered how the woman who made that brilliant, impassioned speech against misogyny was nonetheless daily constrained by the conventions of an outdated and sexist system of parliament.

Spring in Brunswick Heads, 2013
for Julia Gillard

Delicate ears of coastal grevilleas dance,
lemon, gold, cream, every kind of red.
Across the lane, crimson bougainvillea
lunges towards our veranda.

Holiday time. Kids swarm the town.
Life's nasty surprises have not exploded
at their feet yet. Swimming, ice cream,
bikes and boats fill their days.

Last night on the telly,
I saw Julia for the first time
since her Fall. Her eyes
alive and lively again.

Her charm, which fled her
in high office, was back.
The exploding hand grenades
of hatred might have singed

her skin but not scarred her soul.
There's still a young girl in there,
remembering ice creams, bikes and
her dreams of changing the future.

In the morning a lone pelican on the river.
Ungainly, stately, silly, wise.
What greater miracle
than a pelican?

I wish Julia long life
and a pelican each day.

When Anne and I first met we bonded instantly over dogs. We had
the same delight in them, a deep love and respect for their miraculous
natures. My Alsatian, Jed, and her well-named Scruffy became as
close as we were. After they died, there was Jack, then Boy, the pup
we adopted in Broome.

Around 2007, Boy became ill with cancer in Brunswick Heads. He was
only eight. We put him on a program which gave him extra time. His
death about a year later affected Anne especially; he was very much
her dog. She started to write a small book about him, called A Dog's
Life. She wrote it in six weeks. It was one of those books which 'fell
out', newly minted from her mind and from a place of deep emotion.

I think that A Dog's Life is a minor masterpiece. The tone is pitch
perfect and the prose is simple and deeply moving. There are so
many pitfalls in writing about animals but there is no sentimentality
or sweetness in A Dog's Life. It moves between voices: Boy's 'voice' –
his devotion to 'Mistress' and 'Other Mother', his joy in his physical
surroundings and his own doggy troubles – and a form of biography,
mostly seen through Boy's eyes, about what is happening in his
humans' lives. The story starts in the north, when he escapes from
his neglectful owners and finds us, then goes on to what happened
with Broometime, then moves to the effect my parents' deaths had
on Mistress and Other Mother, which brought huge anxiety and
responsibility to Boy himself.

A Dog's Life is a small book but one that says much. It has an adoring
public. Anne decided against giving it to a publisher, thinking it would

fall between too many markets, but brought it out herself with a charming design and illustrations. In reality it's a wonderful book for anyone between the age of eight and eighty.

After a sad pause of mourning for Boy, Sarah came into my life.

That year I was the Chair of the Southern Highlands Community Foundation in Bowral, having sat on the board for a couple of years. I asked one of the other board members whether he might spare a dog – he was a huge dog-lover with ten well cared for dogs. 'Maybe,' he said, 'come and meet Sarah.'

Sarah was being dominated by the favourite, who was even smaller than she was. Never one to jump into laps, she straightaway jumped into mine and said very clearly, 'Take me home!' She was my dog instantly, the love of my life in doggy terms.

Sarah was not one for cuddles and adoration and did not want that from me either. We just understood each other. She was tiny, with long gold hair – hair more than fur – part shiatsu, part Maltese terrier and part chihuahua.

Still, Anne longed for another, bigger dog. When it came to it, we ended up with two big dogs. I saw their photographs in the dog rescue op shop in Bruns and ran home, yelling, 'I've found them! I've found them!' Both dogs were eight years old: Ginger was mostly labrador (with some dingo and ridgeback). Bodhi – a very Northern Rivers name – was part kelpie and part cattle dog. Their owner, Michelle, was going through major illness and hard times, and had to give them up. Later, as she recovered, Shell became part of our lives and a close friend; she was always the dogs' first loving mother.

One of the unqualified delights in life is having a dog. Their take on how to live their lives is so much better than ours. The only big drawback is that they die before us.

Dogs
You outlive them
Over and over
Each dog woven
Into your being

Each death scars the heart

This time it's Ginger,
Big golden girl,
Gentle, stubborn,
Back legs going.

Dogs have no gap, as we do,
between their bodies and themselves.
If bored, they sleep.
Unhappy, they won't eat.

We watch over Ginger,
Weigh the options,
casting for a little bridge
across the chasm of language.

She whimpers, sighs,
struggles to get up.
Her eyes speak pain
yet her inner light is steady.

The gifts she has given us.
The love we give her back.
When she is ready
will she give us a sign?

Rural Australians for Refugees continued to be central to our lives for some years. There is a good book in the history of RAR and I believe that book is in the making.

So just a sketch from me. RAR became a strong advocating voice for refugees. Its strength, in large part, was because it emerged from an unexpected sector – rural and regional Australia – rather than from 'trendy latte sippers' in the inner cities, so we gained some heft with politicians across the board.

When RAR began, the coordination quickly became a very big job, so we funded a part-time position to take some of the load off us. A number of talented and committed people took up the challenge, most memorably Anne and Rob Simpson.

By the time the Labor government came to power in 2007 many of us were facing weariness and burnout. Hoping that policies were changing for the better, a lot of branches faded out. It was a false hope. A handful of RAR groups and dedicated activists in rural areas hung on over the years.

Then in 2013 there was a concerted, successful effort to revive the network, starting up in Victoria. Once again, it is an active body with more branches and more members than the first incarnation of RAR. It was wonderful to see the grassroots model we created spring to life again, yet depressing in another way – so little change despite the efforts of many. But founding and nurturing RAR with Anne and Helen is something of which I, an eternal doubter, am unequivocally proud.

The battle continues. As with all just causes, one persists until the injustice is acknowledged and finally erased. I hope change will eventually happen and compassion and sense will win. That would restore my love and faith in Australia which has taken a battering over the years.

A stroke of fate

It was about eight years since Mum and Dad died. I was finally coming out of grief and confusion. I was researching the new book about the Hungarians. It was not a hugely happy time but I thought we were finally doing OK.

Anne did not think so. She was weary of my short temper, my glooms and my lack of awareness of her own unhappiness. She also thought there might be something wrong with me.

A test in Sydney showed atrial fibrillation. I was quickly sent to hospital where the doctors tried to get my heart back into rhythm. There was no preparation by thinning my blood, which was the usual practice. A doctor told me there was a one-in-a-thousand chance the procedure could result in a stroke. That seemed good odds.

They sent me home to the country the next day. That afternoon, in March 2011, within an hour of getting home, I suffered a serious stroke.

I pay homage to Sarah's intervention. I was tired when we arrived at the farm and went to bed. After waking, I made a phone call about a sofa we were thinking of buying. First the pencil I was using slipped from my hand. Moments later, the phone fell from the other hand. I had no clue what was happening. I just lay there. Then I caught sight of Sarah on the floor next to the bed. She was quivering with urgency. GET UP! FIND ANNE. There was no mistaking her.

I stumbled towards the back door, Sarah at my heels, urging me on. Anne was coming from the garden. I called 'Help me' and collapsed. Words disappeared. I said 'the Secret, the Secret' and another word so random that I have forgotten it, then fell silent.

The ambulance arrived late and the paramedics seemed to have little sense of urgency. They took me to Bowral Hospital, which does not have the precious clot-busting drug. I was in intensive care there for three days.

Spaceship
The room floats on humming air.
The nurse's station suspended
in a greenish light,
beams invisible signals.
Our beds gently circle it,
as if tethered.
Benign murmuring of machines.
Far-away sounds of the street below.

Spaceship ICU.
Bathed in green amniotic fluid,
sandpaper mouth, swelling tongue,
body afloat
in another dimension.
Never have I felt so safe.

From Bowral I was transferred by ambulance to St Vincent's in Sydney. I could not walk or talk. It was a left-brain stroke which affected my entire right side, including the language centres of my brain.

After a week of learning to take a step or two and how to swallow without choking, I was sent over to rehab, where I spent six weeks relearning the most basic skills.

Different Strokes

1.
A stroke of luck.
Someone was there
to help.

Where are my legs?

In Emergency they stroke
my right arm –
a prickly thing.

Not mine.

Where are words?
If they are gone for good
who am I?

2.
In the Stroke Unit they feed
me pap in case I choke.
They prod me for words.
Name, day, month, year.

Wedged between flowers
and euphoria I laugh often,
an unfamiliar gurgling laugh.
I watch light fall on a picture.

In Rehab, mostly stroke patients.
They prod our dangling
strangers' limbs.
'Ten times! Twenty times!'

After four weeks
they take the wheelchair away
and give me a stick.

3.
Winter now. Other hospital
closer to home.
Bare branches, cold air.
Long linoleum corridors
all shiny.
A room of my own!

I stroke weakly through
tepid water in the Rehab pool.
My dead mother swam
a strong smooth stroke.
Will she help me
on this journey back?

4.
On weekend leave
I stroke the dogs.
My right hand can't
feel their fine fur.
But they lean against me
as of old.

Back in hospital I write
this for the therapist:

'Home!!
Dogs – Sasah, Boidie, Gi–gr
See new house – galde
Luche
A day big'

After two and a half months I came home with relief and joy. But our
troubles were only just starting.

Going Home
Home, so familiar.
So strange.
Home hasn't changed.
I have.

Different selves –
one relieved
the other afraid.
Same landscape,
different universe.

How to find
new weapons?

Afterstroke
1.
What is the alphabet?
'a – b – c ...'
Then nothing.

My stroke – own it –
blasted a hole in my brain.
Sounds, words, sentences
disappear like tumbleweed.

Numbers, modifiers,
prepositions
multi-syli-**babble** words –
once friends,
now baleful enemies.
Tiny connections making sense
of the world, and myself,
gone.

Hob-goblins prance and gabble
in the vacant space.

With a stroke of the pen
my writer's life erased.

2.
The pain comes later
It doesn't go away.

That's when, why,
I come undone.

3.
The goblins twist words
into skeins of gibberish.
A gaunt old woman drags
my right leg behind her

Inside a furious child,
red with rage,
fists gouging eyes,
trails after Mummy.
It hurts! Pick me up!

All potential mothers flee
in the face of this monster.

I don't write, save exercises:
Shopping Lists. Days of the Week.
Months of the Year. Post Code.
Vital Phone Numbers.
I recite: 'B-P, P-B. B-P
Shoo-Coo, Coo-Shoo.'
A fountain of self-pity
sprays ceaselessly.

Later, I wrote: 'Now I know what it is that I have lost. I shrink, cry, I panic, grieve, yell. I have lost my compass. How do I live in this familiar, unfamiliar world? The pain sets in. It's akin to phantom limb pain. Not much to be done about it; unlucky they say. More pills, more pain. This is a darkling forest, this, and no-one can follow me in.'

The pain began when I was doing physiotherapy in Bowral as a day patient. It was something equivalent to pins and needles magnified a thousand times, combined with permanent weakness and stiffness. No-one would explain it and no-one dared to tell me that it would stay forever. 'You will get used to it,' the doctors said. I never have.

Annie and I both thought it would be almost over once I got home; a slow but steady recovery. It was nothing like that. The pain – called 'nerve pain' or neuropathic pain – was there 24/7. My terror and dismay erupted.

Anne had no empathy with this alien. She hated the new me, out of control, furious. Sometimes she turned on me.

Rupture
Inasmuch as anyone
knows anyone
I thought I knew you –
my love
partner
true friend.

Not this she-devil
spitting hate.
Murderous contempt
in your turning back.

I can't help
what I've become,
a ruined woman
turned ruinous.
Can't you see that?

Underneath this rubble,
it's still me calling.
Can't you hear that?

But maybe I'm
the spitting devil
furious beyond fury.
I see it in your
frightened
mirroring eyes.

I become useless, reduced to trying to cut up a few vegetables for dinner, even though I can't hold a knife properly. Between sudden rages and with great effort, I can do the basics: getting up, dressing (exhausting); tidying up a little (more exhausting). A few exercises, five minutes walking. After that, I run out of energy for the day.

When day therapy began the community bus came twice a week to take me to outpatients. From 9am to 2pm we had speech, physical therapy, occupational therapy and a sandwich lunch delivered to the outpatients room, where we sat like zombies. Then the community bus took us back to our homes. Not a great intimation of the future.

But after the outpatient program finished, there emerged a wonderful rescue operation from our friends. Lucy, a music teacher, gave me voice exercises and we sang together. She understood that singing was easier than ordinary speech for stroke recovery. Sometimes I cried as we sang old songs. The words came back from nowhere; the music released my grief. Margie, a masseuse and ex PE teacher, took me through physical exercises twice a week. Jen and Maree, retired, talented teachers, devised word exercises and read to me. I asked Jen to read the first chapter of one of my favorite Dickens novels, *Dombey and Son*. The familiar words, replete with his genius, brought tears of joy and gave me hope. My dear friend Helen gave me her endless empathy and love. All had busy lives yet they held out a lifeline not only to me, but also to Anne.

I could not grasp that my brain had changed. It had a big hole in it, the size of a walnut. The medical world said that in the first year I would regain some of my lost faculties as the brain adjusted to the loss. After that progress would be minimal.

And so it was. In the first two months I began to walk again and talk, if badly. I could write a simple sentence, although with two or three mistakes in it. After six weeks I could walk two or three minutes with a stick. After the pain set in, it seemed that progress slowed almost to nothing.

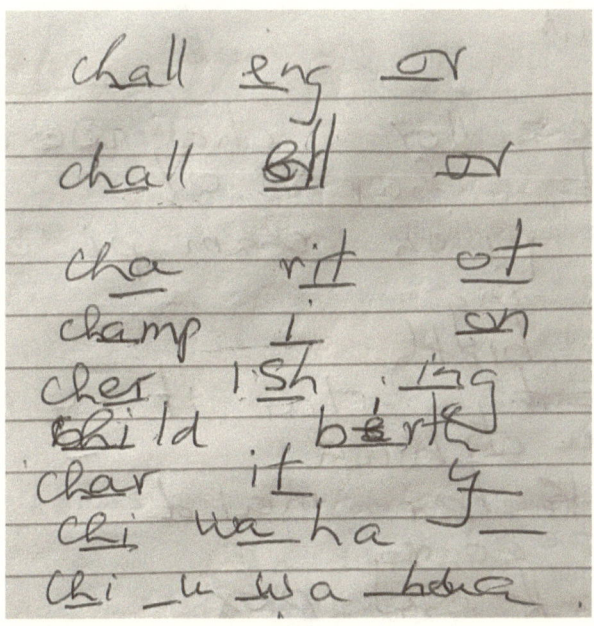

Four months after I came home from hospital we moved from Keil-na-nain, where we had lived for twenty-three years. The decision to sell had been made well before the stroke. We bought, in a rush of blood to the head, a much bigger property: a real farm running 100 head of cattle.

We also decided to build a new house. The work was underway when the stroke hit. I was in hospital recuperating during the build. Anne would rush down to Exeter for a day a week to check progress, then come back to me in Sydney.

A move from a loved home is always a nightmare. Psychologists believe that, after death and divorce, it is next in traumatic impact. In our circumstances, it was close to cataclysmic.

Moving
I want to be a tortoise with
my house on my back.

This house, my beloved carapace,
has grafted itself onto my skin,
mixed with my bloodstream.

Sensible reasons to leave –
uneven ground, steep hills.
Necessary change.

But not now!
I need you, house,
to burrow down,
hide. Heal.

I need your delights
to soothe me.
The morning frosts,
small cobwebs lacing every fencepost

draping each bush in gossamer.
The way the sun settles to sleep
at the front gate each evening.

The first time I saw you
you fitted into my body.

It was the clump of late
winter daffodils that did it.

And the crooked turn in the corridor,
the ugly fireplace, the gun cupboard
to turn into bookshelves.

Winter sweet outside the kitchen window.
Worn cast iron in surprising places.
On the pond, the runic sundial,
slightly askew.

The mad jumble of your daily beauties.

I will leach you from my bones,
scrub you from my skin.
But take pity on me, my beloved home.
Give me back a corner of my heart
so I can bear to leave you.

I could not help much with the work of moving. Anne did almost everything. For the couple of days of the move she put me in a hotel to get me out of the way. The stress level was extremely high. CJ and Jared came from New Zealand to lend muscle, time and psychic support. They saved us; true friends. They witnessed us both at the end of our tether.

One evening during the move, I was feeling useless and discarded, and we quarrelled badly. I was screaming in the garden of the posh hotel, pointing my newly acquired stick at Anne like the wicked witch. She fled. Once I calmed down I was desperate to apologise but could not reach her on the phone. Where was she? Had I driven her too far? Our friend Margie found her at the new house. They were having a calming brandy together when I finally reached her on the phone.

The move to a new, bigger house on substantial acreage opened up a huge crevasse in our relationship. I hated how big it was. I couldn't find the light switches, could not manage the new kitchen, the bath was impossible to negotiate ...

We moved away from each other. Bitterness and anger on both sides became common.

In the first year I did only exercises and speech therapy. I had to sort out the damage to my brain's language centres. In speech therapy terms, I had aphasia – 'a loss of access to language/words' – and, more specifically, dyspraxia – 'difficulty with motor program/organisation, and more complex motor executions, e.g. blends like "spl"; difficulty with multisyllabic words; "sequencing errors" – letters or syllables swap position / around the wrong way'. And so on.

This means, in practice, I confuse opposites: girl for boy, cold for hot. I recognise spelling mistakes but I can't correct them. I confuse prepositions. I write wrong words although in my brain, the correct word is there. Some words won't come at all. Word endings can be arbitrary. The construction of a sentence, once easy, is now strangely hard. I can't speak French or Hungarian anymore, yet I still understand everything. On a bad day, I will start a word with a wrong consonant and get stuck on it. On a very bad day, even spell-check can't make out what I mean. I leave out entire phrases and words. I can't put dates together. I mix up the categories. If I finally remember how to spell a tricky word, the memory does not stick. It's gone within the hour or day. It might return the next, then go again. Days of the week come out wrong, same with months, years. It's like perpetually reaching for the wrong file.

For all these reasons, I write at a fifth of my former speed. My typing is barely understandable. At least I now use spell-check; for the first two years I was too proud and convinced that I would find my old ability again. I believe that without spell-check I would have stopped writing altogether.

I entered the world of dyslexics and others with speech disabilities. I am in awe of the problems they face. And I realise what I have clawed back is precious. But in the first year after the stroke I felt totally defeated. One day, some instinct, and desperation, drove me to my desk and the following came out:

First Poem
An old garden seat,
a new bed of plants
flowering into the New Year.

Old fears, new fears.

Small shoots of thought
sustain me.
Help me, words –
you always have.
                              December 30, 2011

I had no idea that I was going to write a poem, but I had stumbled onto a lifeline. My damaged brain could not contemplate writing a whole page; the effort was too much. But a line, and then another line ... Yes!

The spelling was bad, the word-order awry, words came slowly but the creative impulse was undamaged. I could write a bit of poetry.

* * *

The first couple of years at the farm, Virginia Park, were the worst for both of us, in our different ways. I thought of suicide often. I felt I had no inducement to keep on living. The pain, my estrangement from Anne and my shrinking world all made for a bleak prospect.

Anne was at the end of her tether; she was loving and over-helpful for a long while, then suddenly impatient and angry, cut off. Our relationship fell apart. I began to hate the new house; too big, too long. Its open spaces mocked me. I could not walk the lovely paddocks and lanes. I was too weak. Anne buried herself in the new venture – the cattle, the fencing, schemes for improvement – and disappeared outside.

We lived in our beautiful new property in a kind of existential despair. We could not bear each other's company. Both tried, both failed. Several times, one or the other moved into the guest cottage. Sometimes I went to live there for a couple of weeks, next time Anne would go there, and I was alone in the big house wondering what the hell I was doing there.

We had to part, before we broke apart completely. I decided to go to Sydney to live independently somehow, before I became totally dependent on Anne. We had to break the fraying rope between us.

We lived apart for almost a year. I took Sarah with me to a dog-friendly building. I got myself some domestic help. I managed. The flat I was renting was in Potts Point, in easy reach of a supermarket and a chemist.

Sydney
It's been a long time,
you old harlot.
From my rented flat I see
your big-ticket items –
solid arc of Bridge,
a glinting sliver of Opera House.

Still heart stoppers, old girl.

This corner of The Cross is
the closest I'll get to Europe now.
You were my second home, Sydney,
until I deserted you for a quieter life.

Now I'm back, watching for clues, threads,
pushing my ailing body around your streets.

I take my small companion
onto your piss-riddled pavements
crazed with old tree roots.
She stops at every smell,
sniffs layer upon layer.

I sniff too – air heavy with
shops coffee noise food garbage –
and the heady scent of human stories.

In these back lanes
worn apartment buildings shrug off
druggies and drunks with weary elegance.
They whisper, 'come live amongst us,
we'll weave you close again'.

Sydney you old harlot,
press your brittle bones against
my warming skin.
Make me feel alive again.

Anne came up a couple of days a fortnight and I sometimes went to
the country for a weekend.

Here, There
Here, a small flat
shaded by one generous tree.
A brochure-blue pool.

There, a big house,
garden, stables, paddocks.
Long horizons.

Here, traffic bellows.
Streets heave, sirens shriek.
Trucks racket and spew.

There, magpies, currawongs.
The tin roof pings and pops
as it cools.

Here, a zigzag of tall towers.
Hardy plants battle bitumen.
A tangle of bodies, buildings.

There, earth and sky. Seasons.
Wattle fading, ti-tree coming on.
Two people lost in a flawed paradise.

I feel lonely in that quiet country
yet content in this city's furor.
I track between two places

here, there,
everywhere, nowhere,
                putting up small flares.

The separation was hard. But time in the city broke our downwards spiral. Eventually we decided to try to live together again. Back home in Exeter, the poetry kept coming. It took at least a month to work up a poem. I worked out techniques to overcome my deficits and was kept busy. My old mantra, 'make it as good as you can', returned.

I had no thoughts of publishing these poems, but friends gave me good feedback which helped me to keep on going and made me want to improve. Dale, my stepson's mother, with whom I developed a real friendship over the years, started to do beautiful illustrations for the poems.

I developed a life limited but viable. My writer friends also began to give me feedback and, as always, Anne was my best critic. With her directness, common sense and sharp eye, she was also my last arbiter. Our exchanges about each other's writing never faltered, despite other pillars of our love crumbling around us.

My suicidal thoughts became less. About then, at the three-year mark, we chanced a small cruise to New Zealand – the first time holidaying together in our new reality. I managed the cruise and enjoyed it. Anne enjoyed it, too. It was a sign that our relationship would survive.

Slowly, we climbed out of the pit together.

New age, old age

After seventy we are officially old, according to the Bible. Old age is a curious business; how to deal with a limited future, how to live with the decay of the body and the depredations on the mind. And the inevitable backward glances to the life already lived.

This is the era when deaths multiply and become commonplace. Earlier, 'old' people fell; then a friend or two by misadventure; then the big markers – grandparents, an aunt, mother, father. Finally you become a full adult, and an orphan. Then people begin to disappear. Your personal landscape is denuded.

I first began to notice old lovers disappearing. Peter the wharfie whisked away by a sudden heart attack, Darcy after a long illness, George by his spectacular heart attack on the steps of Fisher Library, Roelof in old age. The drumbeat quickens. The man I married and lived with for ten years, knew for fifty, Anton, is dead.

The lovers have a special intimacy; you knew their bodies, their small private habits. The pictures can't be erased: the smooth olive of Peter's skin; George's constantly running nose, his hanky at the ready; the mole on Darcy's back which he dreaded being scratched during lovemaking. The nights in a suburb of Utrecht when I went to sleep against Anton's back, companionably scratching the scabs of his eczema-affected elbows.

I list these tiny things because they are a mental shorthand of memory – automatic images by which you conjure up a person, the place, the time. When they die, you have these little fragments – scrapbooks or chapbooks of memory. I don't have whole conversations in my head, just a phrase, a tone of voice, a gesture to bring back the dead for an instant.

What do I have of my mother, so huge an influence on my life? I have an enduring picture of her in her nightie a few months before her death, just before she started to deteriorate mentally and physically. It was a pale pink nightie without sleeves (she used to get hot in bed), tied at the shoulders. Her arms still those of a younger woman. She came down the corridor to wish me a good night, saying 'I hope I can sleep better tonight.' Like a little girl wanting assurance. That, and her voice, musical with love as she greeted me at her door, 'Hello mutz,' her favourite endearment. Most of the sixty-seven years I knew her are gone – just flashes of scenes, sayings, a street, a room, a fight. The turn of her head. The way she walked.

And the love. I have been left with so little: photos and a clear flash or two, accepted with gratitude when they come. I await old, old age when they say your younger self returns in vivid detail. It must be nature's consolation for the deprivations of age.

* * *

Indulge me, dear reader, if I mention a few people you have gotten to know, if fleetingly. Loss is a big narrative river when one ages and is not to be ignored or hushed over.

I always stayed in touch with Anton. He started to suffer from Alzheimer's disease a few years ago. As the disease progressed he was wandering at night and was occasionally unmanageable, and needed to be hospitalised. A year before he died I visited him in Perth, where most of his family were living. I tried to see him again but a health crisis with Anne kept me at her side.

I did not expect the tide of emotion and memory after his death. I mourned, not for him so much, as death freed him from bondage to his illness, but for myself, knowing that his tall, loose frame, his 'Anton-ness', would never come my way again unless in memories or dreams.

In the locked ward
I think he knows me.

He has aged beyond his seventy-seven years.
His sentences trail off as if he can't find

the thread he began with.
When lunch comes his eyes light up.

He starts with the sweets first –
(I'd been told about this).

We talk – on and off. Flickering
connections, rents in darkness.

He goes into the toilet, comes
out, fumbling with his belt.

With my arthritic hands
I do it up.

I'm a wife again, forty years
since I stopped being one.

After an hour, I say
'Are you tired?'

He looks up at me, relieved.
'Have a sleep,' I say

and find a nurse
to lead me out.

What a boon is a dream
Last night Anton came back,
not as he is now, in dementia care
but fresh-faced in his late twenties,
laugh-lines just forming around his eyes.

I let out a cry of relief,
rushed to him, clinging to
his back, his arm and
stayed that way
for a long time.

Unlike Darcy or George, the other princes of the Push, both of whom had premature, tragic ends, Roe lived to a good age. I could look back on a long relationship with him, and our infrequent but important interactions.

When he launched Anne's book *Sex and Anarchy* in 1996 he said her portrait of him was painful to read but fair. He himself gave a fair and considered speech on the book. Both of those qualities – fairness and consideration – were integral to Roelof and, in a different way, these are the same qualities that have been the aim in my life. That is one reason we always trusted each other. Another reason was our similar attitudes to money and its uses.

In later life, Roelof became involved with the Aboriginal youth of Glebe, and he came to us, knowing that I had set up a charitable foundation. Annie and I trusted his judgement and put some funding into the project. In his mid-years as a successful gambler, Roelof was extremely generous to friends and, sometimes, causes. He also shared his big Glebe house and set it up as a co-op with a handful of mostly lesbian women who became his loyal friends for life. So when he became hard up in old age, he would turn to me from time to time without any embarrassment. I had money at that stage, he did not. Simple as that. When the roof needed to be repaired or a chairlift was needed to get him up the stairs, I would contribute.

His big eightieth birthday party was held at Glebe. When I arrived he wanted me to sit beside him. He had finally given up on women, after a lifetime of stormy affairs, but he still wanted a woman beside him on a big day like this. I realised then that our long friendship actually ran deep.

About a year before he died, Roelof sent me a piece he had written: Was it OK? I made minor suggestions and he put it on his Facebook page. He wrote of overhearing a group of men in their thirties in the pub, talking about women crying all the time. He was struck by the fact that no-one wondered why women cry:

> At home, I started to draw up a list of all the things that lead humans to shed tears ... In trying to draw up this list I have called on some of the things I cry about, including those I try to suppress.
>
> Tears of simple joy, and those mixed with sadness. Tears of pain. Tears of laughter, tears of release from tension. Tears of compassion,

putting oneself into the position of those in severe trouble. Tears of despair in the knowledge that nothing can be done. Tears of anger against those that can do something but turn a blind eye. Tears of simple sympathy, wishing you could do something to help. Tears which celebrate a solution. Tears on meeting up with someone dear to you and you have not seen for ages.

And there are the tears of failure, many of them. Striving for the top and falling at the last hurdle. Striving in all sorts of ways and not making it. These are the tears of frustration, most evident in the very young and the very old.

… It has taken me many years to understand how most women think and feel. I do not claim to understand fully, but I am sure that if I can get to the point where I can express myself as well as most women do I will be getting closer.

Roe survived numerous health crises, but aged eighty-eight he faced a decision. He had tongue cancer and it was either a major operation or live with constant pain for the rest of his life. He survived the nine-hour operation and was doing sudoku with his daughter Anna the next day.

Soon I heard from Margaret Fink that he was not doing well and losing heart. I went in to see him. As usual, we didn't waste any words.

'I hear from Maggie that you have had enough?'

He couldn't speak but nodded.

'OK,' I said, 'Understood. Fine, but just hang on for another couple of weeks and see what the doctors offer.'

He nodded and we held hands in silence. Then I read him two of my poems, something I would never normally have done. Here is one of them.

Raft
One by one we gather on this haphazard raft.
We touch fingertips, speak in gentle code.
Old friends, glad of each other's warmth.
Long or short?
It's anyone's guess,
this voyage out.

The raft drifts.
We watch the horizon
hoping for a multi-coloured dusk,
dreading violent storms.

The raft holds,
lashed together by old ties.

I don't believe he ever read anything I wrote. This time he smiled, nodded, squeezed my hand. We sat in comfortable silence until he dozed off. I slipped out of the room. He died a few days later.

It was a heavy blow for many people, especially for the ageing members of the Push; he was the last standard-bearer. There was no funeral – he did not want one. Worse, there was no real wake or party. His daughters wanted to acknowledge all parts of his life, including his role as a father and grandfather. For them, the Push was only a small part of him. But the clannish Push had wanted to honour their prince with the best party and wake their ageing bodies could muster.

* * *

It is not only people we mourn as the years pile up, but places, too. Places change, in population, in appearance, in their political atmosphere. During the thirteen years since we last saw Budapest, I knew how much had changed. The ruling party, Fidesz, veered more and more to the right with Viktor Orbán, the poster boy of far-right leaders. I dreaded going there but also felt compelled.

In 2016 I read Susan Faludi's enthralling book *In the Darkroom*, about her estranged father, who returned to Hungary after the fall of Communism. He sent her a bombshell email about his sex change in his late seventies. This was fascinating in itself but the strength of the book came from Faludi's subtle way of linking her Jewish father's search for a true identity to Hungary's constant search for her own 'true' identity. It was a gripping, forensic analysis of modern-day Hungary and where it was going.

I met Susan on her Australian book tour and we struck up a friendship. She felt like a younger sister, our perceptions and reactions to Hungary so eerily alike.

Hungary
Land of horrors, land of my birth: eviscerated
by war, its mountains sheered off to

Romania, great territories eaten
by its neighbours, it brooded its losses.

Twenty years later, wooed by Hitler,
helped by Eichmann, it turned against

its Jews and killed most of them.

Today Budapest is still pock-marked
by bullets from '44, '56.

History is not white-washed here
despite the efforts of governments.

It's embedded in pavements,
hangs in smoky air.

That basement, once a prison
of torture, that flat where a whole

family was taken by the Nazis,
or the secret police, or the Russians.

That brickyard used for concentrating Jews.
That railway station where my father was hounded ...

I've walked Budapest streets,
loving and hating them

more than anywhere else in the world.
Now, as the current government sheds

all niceties, its enemies naked again –
refugees, Gypsies, Jews, homosexuals –
all of them me.

And yet ... I want to be there one more time,
to see the tall windows on wide boulevards,

to sit in its faded cafés, watching
as many fates hang in the balance.

In these streets the struggle
of life is manifest, raw.

This is my addiction – not to horror,
but to the unbearable truths of living.

I see the broad Danube winking
in the summer sun

In 1944, Jews, shackled by
their ankles (to save on bullets)

toppled into the icy river.

I love and hate you,
land of my birth

So we fly into Budapest with some foreboding. From the beginning it is different. Most of the old relatives are dead. Two good friends have left the country: one to live in Belgium; the other, ironically, as she is Jewish, to live in Berlin. Tony Abbott has only just left the country after a mutual admiration love-fest with Orbán.

In six days you can glean much, especially from taxi drivers. Asked about the government, one driver says, sullenly, 'My company doesn't like us to talk about politics.' Shades of the Communist era!

So I shut up. Then, deciding to take a risk, he unburdens himself a little about the miseries of life under this regime. The only good thing he says is that Budapest is getting ahead; a lot of European Union finance and the city swarming with tourists.

Another taxi driver, a pleasant young man, maybe thirty, surprises me by asking me about myself. I tell him I left when I was five, after World War II. His sense of history doesn't go that far back. He was born after the fall of Communism. His political consciousness was formed by the rise of Fidesz and their last ten years in power. For him, I am a curious relic of the distant past. Not my parents – me! That gives me a shock.

What am I doing, still engaging with a country that has moved past me in a direction I am deeply unhappy about?

Interestingly, he is open about his hatred for Orbán – the corruption, the nepotism, the wealth of the ruling elite. 'He must go, he will fall!' But as to how or when, he grows vague. It becomes clear that his political education is limited to what he has gleaned from American news channels and a couple of websites.

We meet with a young couple: she the daughter of our friend Réka; he Portuguese. They have lived and worked in London and Paris, children of the EU.

'I feel no real ties here,' she says. 'We've cut off from what's happening here – we will leave as soon as we can.'

We meet them at the new, stylish National Dance Theatre. 'Where is the money coming for all this?' I ask.

They raise their eyebrows in unison: 'From the EU, of course, which Orbán hates and denigrates every day.'

Our friend Kati is back 'home' from Berlin for work. She says that Orbán doesn't need to be a dictator. He has hollowed out the key institutions and media. He can do what he wants.

'What about the Left?' I ask. She is full of scorn. 'The only Left radio station still bleats the tired old ideas – out of touch with reality. Totally ineffectual.'

I visit a Jewish relative, retired and eking out life on a pension, living in a flat that hasn't changed since the 1990s. She says she survives because she turned off the TV and radio years ago. Otherwise her life would be unbearable.

I think about how often important things in public life in Hungary are merely window-dressing. From our elegant hotel on the Pest side of the river we see the imposing Royal Castle on its hill and remember that it has never had a king in it. A little further on is the largest parliament building in Europe, built in a country which has little democratic tradition. I think back to Admiral Horthy, the Regent of Hungary between the wars; the Admiral who never had a fleet in this land-locked country. So much sham.

The only joy I find in Budapest is in meeting Gaby, Rózsi's daughter and Robi's beloved stepdaughter. Both had died, Rózsi just the year before we come back to the city. Gaby has managed to be in Hungary at the same time as we are, and she is emptying their house for sale. I never expected to see their house again, the site of countless meals lovingly cooked by Rózsi and of the meaty Hungarian jokes told by Robi at which my mother always laughed uproariously.

In their small house on the outskirts of Budapest, everything is hardly touched, as if they still live here: the five blue china horses in the living room, the bright green fish tank in the corner, the brush set in the hall, the familiar pots and pans in Rózsi's small kitchen, the kitsch kangaroo plate hanging in the dining 'hall' from their visit to Australia.

I feel an unexpected joy to be with them one last time. It is as if they have forgiven me for not having been there at their deaths. It is a complicated, sad joy, sharing Gaby's grief as we go through their belongings. I come away with one blue china horse with its chipped ear and a painting they had kept for me. A great privilege had been granted me.

As we leave, in my last hour on Hungarian soil, I experience something that brings up the visceral fear that has always lain beneath my relationship with Hungary. A young airport employee takes charge of my wheelchair. He is loud, rough, rude and treats me like baggage. I'm in the hands of some sort of maniac. But when we reach the security area I realise he is not alone. The whole staff scream abuse at each other. An elderly Indian lady, also in a wheelchair, is pushed into a corner, left trembling and confused. I am shaken to my core. The brutish behaviour of petty officials; I recognise this ugly seam from Hungary's history. I never want to see the place again.

I have always felt so lucky and relieved when I come back to Australia, but I've never thought Australia a bastion of truth and goodness. Here, too, there are disturbing trends and some of the freedoms which Hungarians have lost are in peril. Some recent examples: new prison terms for journalists and advocates under the Espionage Act; raids on the ABC and News Corp; stronger restrictions on freedom of information; the whittling away of ordinary people's freedoms under the guise of anti-terror laws; a harder and harder line on refugees' rights.

The Morrison government has been very good at normalising a right-wing agenda, so that most Australians now accept what should alarm them. If we don't fight this authoritarian trend we might eventually be in danger of becoming a burgeoning fascist-style state, like Hungary is now.

* * *

I continue to make some new women friends but the shared history of the friends made early in life is especially precious. They knew your parents, knew your first boyfriend, together we discovered a great book or record. They form the arc of your life.

Female friendships have been the mainstay of my life, but to my bemusement I can't really write about them – not here anyway. They are a book in themselves. But more likely they might never appear in a book of mine at all. These relationships are too rich; I can't capture the myriad ways my women friends have nourished me. Some friendships have been problematic, or simply died without pain, or of boredom. Some break up in trauma but sometimes can be reborn.

I've mended a few bridges over the last few years. My deep and important friendship with schoolfriend Masha is back, although not in the same way as in long-ago life. We talk occasionally on the phone but now with ease. As always, we talk books and in a way that I never talk books with anyone else. This is a deep affection akin to family.

After Anton's death, I rang my friend Bobbie from uni days; we had hardly seen each other in thirty years. She knew Anton and I when we were all in our twenties. Again, the ease of shared experience, especially our 'giddy youth', outweighed everything else. The fondness was back in an instant.

My close friend Noelle, once the young girlfriend of George Molnar, is back in my life, I am happy to say, after a long silence in which we went in very different directions. Such gathering-in is one of the consolations of age. Old clothes that warm and comfort you.

Friendships can have the intensity of love affairs and the work to save them can be just as intense. A good friendship is patterned with brilliant hues. The mutual growth of intellect, the subtle exchange of emotions, support, loving criticism, loyalty. My women friends are multifaceted people, their minds flexible and expansive.

I would love to say the same of men. I have known brilliant men, kind men, loyal men. But very few are as *richly* human (and humane) as women. The men who are the equal of women are mostly homosexual, and a number of those are my closest friends. Our treasured couple, CJ and Jared; Adrian, the barrister I once worked with, now living in England – we share an unbreakable tie, even though he has been known to vote Conservative at times!

Clearly men are struggling with their changing roles. Giving up power and unbridled domination is no easy task. It might even be impossible. But sometimes I meet a young man of twenty or thirty who is a subtle and compassionate human being. That gives me some hope.

When a close woman friend dies – so far only two have – it is a different grief, like a layer of skin peeled off my body. I feel cold, impoverished.

Meryl was the first to leave. Our friendship lasted sixty years since we met at ten at Artarmon Opportunity School. I still see her at age ten, a lone figure, perched on her Globite school case, immersed in Scott and Austen. At high school we used to vie for the top place in English. We did not live in each other's pockets but remained close all our lives. What made my grief worse was that she asked to see me on her deathbed. I did not get the message because in a fit of pique with technology, I had turned my mobile off for three weeks. I will regret that mistake for ever.

For Meryl Constance

At school I met a friend for life,
a singular creature,
lithe and beautiful
in body, agile of mind,
reserved in spirit,
private in habit.
Sometimes judgemental,
secretly kind.

Above all, tenacious, loyal.
A woman of courage, choosing to live
differently – each day tough, carving
a new path from the unforgiving rock of habit.

Courageous too, in doing battle with
a betraying body, over and over again.

The last battle over, my friend is gone.

'Hello friend' was how she always
greeted me.

She is first amongst us,
although the winnowing-time
is coming closer.

With her death
I'm like a tree with a limb missing,
or like a soldier with a true friend
                                        fallen in action.

I was luckier to be with another very old friend in her last days, June,
who I met at uni at seventeen, when she was a firebrand Trot. She
mellowed into a loyal Laborite. June and I shared a lot of our lives
from uni days to our seventies. She knew my parents well. We shared
our love lives, secrets, politics and our mutual loves of crockery and
china, house decorating, music. Her family – her twin Jan and niece
Liberty – became my family.

As things worsened for June, we flew up to the north coast to spend
a little time with her. Strange to say but it was a joy to be with each
other. We talked only a little; she was very weak. The best time was
when I would lie beside her on her double bed and simply hold her
hand. We would smile at each other. People coming into the room

smiled and laughed at us. We dozed a little together. We savoured these moments, our hands lightly transmitting love for each other.

In the last few days she had to go back to hospital.

'I know this is not what you wanted,' I said.

She shrugged her shoulders in resignation.

'At least,' I said, trying to make her laugh a little, 'it's better than dying on a rubbish heap in India.'

Her face lit up. 'Too right! We are so lucky, Susan. We have had good lives.'

Two days later, she was gone.

Epilogue

When I began this book I had just turned seventy-four; now I am approaching seventy-eight. Much has happened in the last eleven years that is too close to write about. I also don't want to weary you. I am a little weary myself.

At fifty, when the first intimations of death came to me in that little basement flat in Amsterdam, I had no idea how rocky the road to ageing would be, how many boulders would come up as the body starts to age, well before the mind can cope with the idea of decay.

New disciplines need to be nurtured, new joys to be found to replace those that have faded or been lost. No easy, slow, hardly noticeable decline; no rocking chairs, no companionable yarns by the fire with old friends. Not that I expected any such. But nor did I expect to have to dig so deep to find new, essential skills to survive until death finally takes me.

At first it seems a nasty final irony, to have got this far with no rest or reward. But then *will* takes over; this won't defeat you. Even here, at this stage, joy can be found and mined. Maybe the hardest joy.

I have found one road to joy is quite simple. The pleasures of childhood are rediscovered and put into play again, as my global view narrows to a smaller scale. You return to your first walk in a garden, to your first strains of music, the first flower you ever studied at close range, the first sunset that thrilled you. You lose a lot yet gain much. You are starting to learn a language of a new age.

Virginia Park was meant to be our home for at least ten years. Anne so loved the land, the space and her cattle that I could not lobby to leave. But after five years, there was a breakthrough. She began to think that maybe Virginia Park was too big and too much work. To my great relief she decided to put the farm on the market, partly because we were wanting more time in Brunswick Heads. The other major reason was that she knew I had never settled happily into the big property.

Some time before, we had bought two acres in the middle of our village, thinking we might eventually 'retire' there. This was to be a smaller, less ambitious house, a smaller garden, though with room for the donkey and the Shetland pony. Later we acquired two more acres at the back, room for two retired horses.

It has been four years since we moved here. I love the place a little more each day. I can set my ageing roots down. I am in a place where I can find sanctuary again. I feel the same good fortune that I did every day at Keil-na-nain. I hope to die here among the pictures that mean so much, among the animals I love, the glories of the garden, and with the person I love most.

After the stroke, as you know, I did not write for a year, then some poems started to form and I became increasingly intrigued and in love with my new discipline. I had almost forgotten the period about twenty-five years ago when I had written quite a bit of poetry. Writing poems seemed like a new experience, a whole new direction that the gods had given me.

It was only after reading some thirty poems I had written over three years that I suddenly saw there was a narrative peeping through, and with a few more linking poems I might have the makings of a book. Possibly, I could be a writer in the world again.

I sent the manuscript to the publisher of *Headlong*, Terri-ann White, then at UWA Publishing. I knew that our friendship would not influence her judgement or integrity. She liked the book. Five years after my stroke, something happened that I thought would never happen again: I was published, and with my first book of poetry. The first launch was held in Brunswick Heads in the old picture house, newly reopened as a burlesque venue. The hall was full of lively, responsive people. It reverberated with joy.

The book, which I named *Rupture*, was commended in the prestigious Anne Elder Award for a first book of poetry. It was picked as one of the four best poetry books of the year in the *Australian Book Review*. It seemed to resonate with many readers. Even though only the first section speaks about stroke, people found some comfort and meaning in it. It has been used in stroke awareness exhibitions, my damaged stroke voice reading over x-rays of stroke-damaged brains.

DIFFERENT STROKES

1.

A STROKE OF LUCK.
SOMEONE WAS THERE TO HELP.

WHERE ARE MY LEGS?

IN EMERGENCY THEY STROKE
MY RIGHT ARM -
A PRICKLY THING.

NOT MINE.

WHERE ARE WORDS?
IF THEY ARE GONE FOR GOOD
WHO AM I?

2.

IN THE STROKE UNIT THEY FEED
ME PAP IN CASE I CHOKE.
THEY PROD ME FOR WORDS.
NAME. DAY. MONTH. YEAR.

WEDGED BETWEEN FLOWERS
AND EUPHORIA I LAUGH OFTEN.
AN UNFAMILIAR GURGLING LAUGH.
I WATCH LIGHT FALL ON A PICTURE

IN REHAB. MOSTLY STROKE PATIENTS.
THEY PROD OUR DANGLING
STRANGERS' LIMBS.
'TEN TIMES! TWENTY TIMES!'

AFTER FOUR WEEKS
THEY TAKE THE WHEELCHAIR AWAY
AND GIVE ME A STICK.

3.
WINTER NOW, OTHER HOSPITAL
            CLOSER TO HOME.
     BARE BRANCHES, COLD AIR.
LONG LINOLEUM CORRIDORS
                ALL SHINY.
      A ROOM OF MY OWN!

   I STROKE WEAKLY THROUGH
  TEPID WATER IN THE REHAB POOL.
MY DEAD MOTHER SWAM
  A STRONG SMOOTH STROKE.
              WILL SHE HELP ME
     ON THIS JOURNEY BACK?

                    4.
     ON WEEKEND LEAVE
         I STROKE THE DOGS.
MY RIGHT HAND CAN'T
          FEEL THEIR FINE FUR.
  BUT THEY LEAN AGAINST ME
              AS OF OLD.

    BACK IN HOSPITAL I WRITE
       THIS FOR THE THERAPIST:

      'HOME!!
  DOGS - SASAH, BOIDIE, GI - GR
    SEE NEW HOUSE - GALDE
                   LUCHE
              A DAY BIG'

          - SUSAN VARGA

FROM RUPTURE POEMS (2012-2015) BY SUSAN VARGA

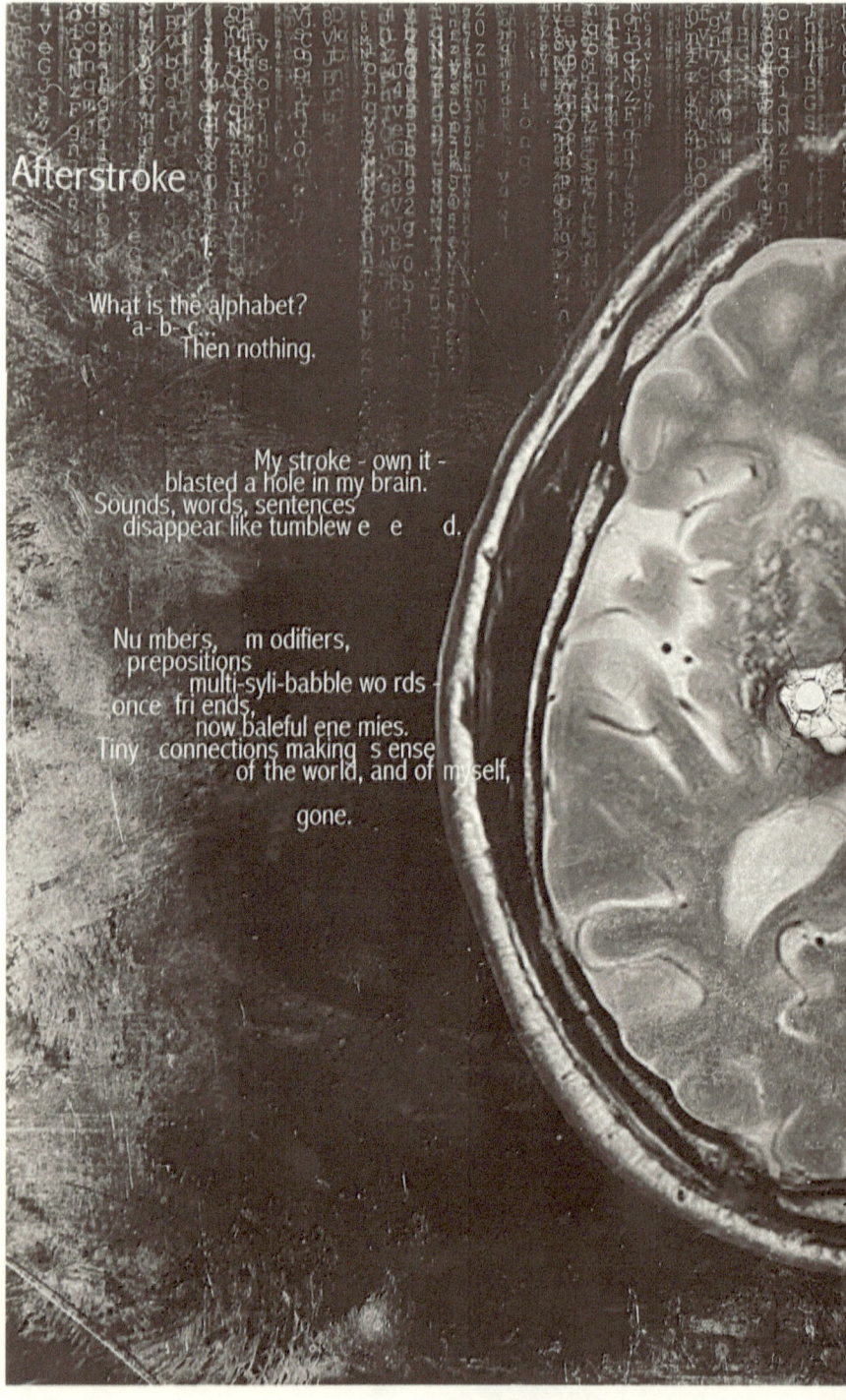

Afterstroke

I.

What is the alphabet?
a- b- c...
Then nothing.

My stroke - own it -
blasted a hole in my brain.
Sounds, words, sentences
disappear like tumblew e   e   d.

Nu mbers,   m odifiers,
prepositions
multi-syli-babble wo rds -
once fri ends,
now baleful ene mies.
Tiny connections making s ense
of the world, and of myself,

gone.

Hob-goblins prance and gabble
in the vacant   space.

With the stroke of the   pen
my writers life   erase d.

2.

The pain comes   late
It doesn't go away.

That's when, why,
I come un done.

- Susan Varga

from RUPTURE poems (2012-2015) by Susan Varga

When I came out of hospital, a nurse said to Anne, 'Put her in a nice armchair, dear.' Well, bugger that!

I have two achievements in this new age. Most days I have learnt to live with chronic pain and the bone-awful weariness it brings. In this I join with many thousands of people much more uncomplaining than I am. Some days I backslide into self-pity and defeatism but I have made my compromised life viable again. Without the help of Anne, I'm not sure it would have been possible. To her everything is owed. Without her much less would have been achieved, far less enjoyed.

And I have kept writing. The paradox is that it is the hardest thing I have ever done. But without it I suspect I would not be here.

Very likely this is my last book. If you read my words with even half the deep pleasure and profit that I have had with good books throughout my life, then I have done my job. To spend the last thirty years writing has given my life deeper meaning. The hard joy I take

in writing is in communicating not only the stresses and difficulties of life, but also the nuggets of joy, beauty and truth we excavate along the way.

My next goal will be to learn how to shut up and savour (and suffer) life until the great silence begins. This new era is frail and without timeframe. What will each day bring? Maybe a day of irritation and frustration; maybe a flower or a poem or a snatch of music will grace it. A new puppy to put to bed. A good line or sentence created or read. A meal enjoyed together. A small caress before sleep.

Acknowledgements

Once one finds a shape for a book, many choices are made and other paths are therefore closed. So there are many people who have made my life richer but who are not mentioned (or barely) in *Hard Joy*. To include them here would make for a long and self-indulgent list and would be bound to be incomplete as well.

But I do want to acknowledge my 'other' family: Anne's mother, Barbara, and her father, Don, neither alive now, both kind, loving people. Carrying on their tradition are my sister and brother in law, Jenny and Ian Morphy; thank you for your support and affection through all our trials and joys. Also, in my now sparse family, my thanks to my sister, Judy Langton, and cousin, Eva Hillinger, for their interest and affection.

Sincere thanks to all the people who have helped me put this book on the page, through typing much of the text and correcting many errors and often giving me good advice on the way. Firstly, Ben Mawston, who did the lion's share of the work with empathy and patience. Also to Lucy Bainger, Jane Howard, Jordanne Stewart, Valerie Hardy and Jan Gibson. Thank you all.

My fellow writers and friends Emma Ashmere and Lesley Lebkowicz have provided comments and suggestions as I tried out drafts of various chapters on them. Both have been generous and astute. I haven't burdened Andrea Goldsmith with this book but she has given me encouragement and good advice at the last stage.

My heartfelt thanks to Terri-ann White of Upswell. I am proud to be published by an outstanding new press which has the creation of good literature as its prime reason for being. This is my third book to be published by Terri-ann. I am grateful for such a loyal, fruitful partnership between publisher and author – difficult to find in these crossroads times for book publishing. Thanks to Kelly Somers for her punctilious, thoughtful editing.

Anne Coombs, my partner (and now spouse!), is my best and most hard-headed reader and editor. As always, my enduring love and thanks to her.

Sources

Heddy and Me, Penguin, 1994. Reprinted (with photos) in 2000 by Bruce Sims Books.

Happy Families, Hodder Headline (Sceptre), 1999.

Broometime, co-authored with Anne Coombs, Sceptre, 2001.

Headlong, UWA Publishing, 2009.

Rupture, UWA Publishing, 2016.

Some poems in *Hard Joy* have been previously published in periodicals and journals:

The six poems of the 'Jean' series were published in *Southerly*, volume 58, no. 3, Spring 1998.

Six poems in the 'Sylvia' series were published in *Ulitarra*, no. 13, 1998.

Three 'Sylvia' poems appeared in *Scarp*, no. 31, October 1997.

'Sydney' appeared in *Griffith Review*, no. 44, 2016.

A version of my last visit to Hungary was published in an essay, 'Shadow life', in *Griffith Review*, no. 69, 2020.

'The Ocean' from *People's Poems* edited by Jennifer Compton.

Other works cited (in order of mention in the text):

Joan Didion essay in *The Writer on Her Work*, edited by Janet Sternburg. W.W. Norton, 2000.

Sue Stuart-Smith, *The Well Gardened Mind*, William Collins, 2020.

W Hart-Smith, *Poems of Discovery*, Angus & Robertson, 1959.

Anne Coombs, *Sex and Anarchy: The Life and Death of the Sydney Push*, Penguin Books, 1996, pp. 29, 204, 262, 307.

Susan Varga, 'Twice the man', *Sydney Morning Herald*, 9 August 2003.

Patrick Modiano, Nobel Lecture, 2014, available at https://www.nobelprize.org/prizes/literature/2014/modiano/25238-nobel-lecture-2014/.

John Hughes, *The Dogs*, Upswell Publishing, 2021.

Lyn Gain, *Witch Girl and the Push*, Valentine Press, 2013.

Helen Garner, 'The invisible arrow: how does one stop writing?', *Griffith Review*, no. 68, 2020, available at https://www.griffithreview.com/articles/the-invisible-arrow/.

Maria Tumarkin, *Axiomatic*, Brow Books, 2018.

Bernhard Schlink, *Olga*, Hachette Australia, 2020.

T.S. Eliot, 'The Dry Salvages', 1941.

Christine Sykes, *Gough and Me: My Journey from Cabramatta to China and Beyond*, Ventura Press, 2021.

Susan Faludi, *In the Darkroom*, HarperCollins, 2016.

Photographs

All photographs in the possession of the author

innovative, inter-professional, reflective learning resource for current and future health professionals.
Depth of Field | UWA Faculty of Health & Medical Science | School of Allied Health

Acknowledgements

About Upswell

Upswell Publishing was established in 2021 by Terri-ann White as a not-for-profit press. A perceived gap in the market for distinctive literary works in fiction, poetry and narrative non-fiction was the motivation. In her years as a bookseller, writer and then publisher, Terri-ann has maintained a watch on literary books and the way they insinuate themselves into a cultural space and are then located within our literary and cultural inheritance. She is interested in making books to last: books with the potential to still be noticed, and noted, after decades and thus be ripe to influence new literary histories.

About this typeface

Book designer Becky Chilcott chose Foundry Origin not only as a strong, carefully considered, and dependable typeface, but also to honour her late friend and mentor, type designer Freda Sack, who oversaw the project. Designed by Freda's long-standing colleague, Stuart de Rozario, much like Upswell Publishing, Foundry Origin was created out of the desire to say something new.

www.ingramcontent.com/pod-product-compliance
Lightning Source LLC
Chambersburg PA
CBHW020837020726
47497CB00005B/1141